I opened a can of kitty tuna and put it in a dish I took out of the cupboard.

The cat attacked the dish before it even reached the floor. I rinsed the can and watched the cat eat for a few minutes, then explored the kitchen.

A door with a glass pane in the top half led to the outside. It had a kitty door in the bottom panel. I could envision Chubby going out and raiding neighborhood cat dishes. Another, solid door formed a corner with the first door and was closed. I guessed it went to a basement space of some type.

I returned to the cat's mat and picked up a pink ceramic dish with WATER written on its side. All that tuna had to have made him thirsty. My own cat Cher refused to drink water out of a dish. She had to have fresh water in a cup she could dip her paw in, or have a sink faucet turned on to just the right flow so she could lick it.

I filled up the water dish. As I set it down, I thought I heard another thump. I stood up and listened. The house was silent. I moved to the closed door and opened it on a pitch-black space. A quick grope of the wall to the right of the door revealed the light switch. I know I flipped the switch, but that's the last thing I remember.

THE
WIDOWMAKER

A Harley Spring Mystery

❧

Arlene Sachitano

ARLENE SACHITANO

ZUMAYA ENIGMA   AUSTIN TX

2010

THE WIDOWMAKER

© 2010 by Arlene Sachitano

ISBN 978-1-934841-56-3

Cover art and design © April Martinez

"Zumaya Enigma" and the raven colophon are trademarks of Zumaya Publications LLC, Austin TX. Look for us online at http://www.zumayapublications.com/enigma.php

Library of Congress Cataloging-in-Publication Data

Sachitano, Arlene, 1951-
  The widowmaker : a Harley Spring mystery / Arlene Sachitano.
    p. cm. — (Harley Spring mystery ; bk. 2)
  ISBN 978-1-934841-56-3 (trade paper : alk. paper) — ISBN 978-1-934841-57-0 (electronic)
  1. Murder—Investigation—Fiction. 2. Electronic industries—Fiction. I. Title.
PS3619.A277W53 2010
813'.6—dc22
                              2010013903

In memory of Myca Morgan.

We always thought we'd be
the last Hags standing.

ACKNOWLEDGMENTS

This book would not be possible without the help and support of many people. I'd like to thank everyone who answered questions, listened to excerpts and gave opinions, and generally supported my efforts. In particular, I'd like to thank the following people: Jim Park who explained how management retreats do or don't work; Dr. Doug Lyle, for his willingness to answer forensic questions; Scott Ryon and Ed May, retired law enforcement officers and active Ducks Unlimited members, who are always willing to answer questions, no matter how crazy; Katy King and Luann Vaughn, my supportive critique partners; Kathryn, Kathy, Susan, and Donnie from the Harriet Vane chapter of Sisters in Crime, for sharing their knowledge and support. Brenda and Bob, in-laws who believe; Susu and Suby for their unending support and daily grilling about how many pages I've written; Sister-in-law and brother-in-law Beth and Hank Bohne, medical people who are always willing to let me know if my killing methods stand up to medical scrutiny and to offer alternatives if they don't; my family Jack, Karen and Malakai, Annie, Alex and Amelia, David, Ken, Nikki and Kellen and especially my sister Donna who taught me to write during a cross country trip in the back of the family station wagon. Without the support, of all these people, I couldn't write.

Lastly I'd like to thank Liz and Tina at Zumaya Publications who, with their guidance and support, have made all of this possible.

CHAPTER 1

"EXCUSE ME, SIR?"

The small man in a dark business suit ignored me and grabbed the door to the air shower that led into the clean room. I grabbed him by the arm and spun him around.

"You can't go in there. Can I help you with something?"

"I think you have been already too much help," he said in Japanese-accented English. He pulled his arm free and began to open the door again.

"Look, Buddy. I don't know who you are, but you can't go in my clean room. I don't even know how you got this far," I grabbed at his arm again, and he swatted at my hand.

Before I could react, his feet were swept out from under him and he was dropped to the floor. Allan Sayers, our materials manager, had a knee in the little man's back and had pulled his hands behind him.

"Harley, call security," he barked at me.

"Are you sure we need to?" I asked. "He seems confused, not dangerous. Let's see who he is and what he wants."

"He hit you," he said. "Besides, he doesn't have a security badge — that makes him an intruder."

I reluctantly called security and then helped Allan pull the man to his feet.

"Who are you?" I asked.

"My name is Mr. Komatsu. I am here to kill Mr. Romeo Martinez," he said.

The color drained from Allan's face.

"What'd I tell you? Where's security?" He looked around for signs of the guard.

"Wait a minute," I told him. I looked at Mr. Komatsu. "Why do you want to kill Romeo?"

"He dishonored my daughter. Her life is over. For that he must die."

The security guard showed up carrying his walkie-talkie and flashlight. I looked at Allan. At Sil-Trac, a computer chip manufacturer located in the pastoral community of Hillsboro, just west of Portland, Oregon, the guards are mainly observers. I've not seen one that was this side of sixty-five yet.

"Why don't we call Mr. Iguchi?" I suggested.

Senior managers rotated to our Oregon plant on a regular basis. Tadanori Iguchi was the latest, and the highest-level Japanese manager onsite. From previous experience, I knew the Japanese community in Portland preferred to solve their own problems if given the opportunity.

Mr. Iguchi arrived, and after a brief discussion in Japanese, he and Mr. Komatsu headed for the corporate suites. Allan and I went back to our desks, grabbed our backpacks and headed for a waiting bus.

"What kept you two?" Dave Swain, a trim, six-foot ex-marine who's also a production manager, asked as we climbed the three steps onto the bus. He moved over and made a place for me next to him.

"I'm not sure what was really happening, but a Mr. Komatsu was about to murder Romeo. We stopped him, though."

"Glad it was nothing serious," Dave said with a laugh.

I stood up and looked for our human resources manager.

"Karen's not on the bus yet," I said. "Maybe she'll have some info on what happened."

The deluxe bus we were on was filled with managers and senior lead people. Our esteemed management had decided that a few days in the country doing an Outward Bound-style program was just the thing we needed to cement us together as a team. So far, it was working. To a person, we agreed the idea was stupid and we wanted to be anywhere but here. There was a discussion going on in the back of the bus about how best to protest and still remain employed.

"If we aren't leaving, can we go back in and work for a while?" Jose Flores, the heavyset manager of the DRAM area, asked no one in particular.

"Maybe Karen knows," I said as she approached the bus.

Karen Hatcher could have stepped out of an L.L. Bean catalog. Her plaid flannel shirt was deep red and green with a silver stripe that perfectly matched her neatly combed gray hair. Her small feet were in new-looking brown suede hiking boots. As she walked from the front entrance, not a hair moved out of place despite the warm early-summer breeze that ruffled the leaves on the young trees planted by the flagpoles in front of the plant. A new tree was planted each time a building was built on our campus. The trees would eventually dwarf the flagpoles, but no one seemed to think that far ahead in these industrial-landscaping schemes.

Karen was in the unenviable position of having to implement today's little adventure. She boarded the bus, followed by Mr. Iguchi.

Mr. Iguchi stood at the front of the bus and fiddled with the microphone that was attached to the dashboard.

"Greetings, everyperson," he began, and then launched into an enthusiastic, if stilted, welcome to us in what we all, Japanese and American alike, referred to as Jinglish. He expressed his appreciation to all of us for being so willing to participate in this activity. I'm not sure what planet he lived on, but only the presence of words like *mandatory* and *insubordination* in Karen's memo had made us all show up.

No mention was made of the vignette that had taken place just before we left the factory. After another round of thanks and a few bows, Mr. Iguchi retreated to the maroon late-model Lincoln Town Car he and the other senior managers would take to the location of our forest adventure.

When we got underway, I walked to the front of the bus and sat down beside Karen.

"Harley," she greeted me with a warm smile, "are you ready for this?"

"I'm not sure ready is how I would describe it. I do have all the items on the list you sent us, if that's what you mean."

"I don't think it's going to be as bad as everyone thinks. These people come highly recommended. I even called their list of referrals. No one reported anything worse than a few cases of poison oak. Amy at MiCorp says they went, and it really did help team-work. She said it even helped their senior management team."

"I don't believe it," Dave said. He managed the area next to mine. He had joined us while Karen was talking. "Stressing peo-ple out by making them face fears they aren't ready to deal with isn't good no matter what anyone says. Besides, do you think our competitors are going to give you the straight scoop? The victims of the humiliations probably agree not to talk about it. And what about follow-up? What if a person can't be torn apart and put back together in four days? Who cares about that?"

"Could you try to have a more positive attitude?" Karen asked. "At least until we get there and see for ourselves what they want you to do." I could tell by the white around the edges of her lips our reluctance was beginning to wear on her.

"You guys don't have to worry about a thing." A new voice joined our discussion. Allan leaned out into the aisle from his seat two rows back. "I was an Eagle Scout and did a whole summer of Outward Bound between my junior and senior years of college. It's a piece of cake. I'll take care of everything."

"How is that going to help me if I have to jump across an open space ten feet in the air?" I asked.

"All the exercises have a way out if you can just be clever enough to think of it," Allan said.

"Says who?"

"They have to do that," he said. "There always has to be an escape hatch."

"Maybe in your video games, but I read the pamphlet Karen has and it talks about 'conquering fears.' It says nothing about al-ternate routes or escape hatches," I said.

"Think what you want, but I know I can handle it. All of it." Allan leaned back and put his iPod buds in his ears and closed his eyes, ending the discussion.

Allan was our purchasing manager. His job was to make sure parts and materials were ordered and arrived in a timely fashion. It gave him a great deal of power over all of us. Without raw ma-terials, we were dead. I could only remember once in the ten years I've been at Sil-Trac that his team had caused a production delay. He was about six foot three, two hundred-thirty pounds and was aggressive with our suppliers. His face had a flushed look most of the time, like his skin was about to burst.

But he and his team got the job done.

His second-in-command Jeanette Malone was in the seat behind him reading a book. She was a plain woman, and the perfect foil for Allan. Her calm unflappability was just the right balance for his grandstanding bravado. He would light fires, and she would make sure they didn't rage out of control or burn the wrong people. The third person in their group was seated next to her. Tim Park was a recent college graduate who had interned at Sil-Trac his last two years of college. He worshipped Allan and was in awe of Jeanette. The three of them were just different enough to work well together. Jumping through hoops and walking across hot coals were part of their daily job description. This trip would seem like a vacation to them.

I hate camping and anything associated with it. It's not that I have a gripe with Mother Nature — it was my ex-husband Sam. He insisted we be in a state of readiness — for what, I never knew. The last year we were together, he insisted his young son Noah and I go on camping trips I can only describe as forced marches. He would drive us to some nameless place in eastern Oregon, and we would have to hike for two and a half days with only what we could carry in our pockets for supplies. When I found myself at the army surplus store buying cargo pants and stuffing the pockets with freeze-dried spaghetti and multi-use tools, I called a halt to the charade. Our marriage ended shortly thereafter. I never found out if he was the "international operative" he claimed to be or the paranoid psycho I came to believe he was. In the end, it didn't matter — I couldn't live with either one.

The one good thing that came from my marriage was my stepson Noah. I'm his legal guardian, although Sam still pulls the strings. Sam is forcing Noah to attend a military school near San Francisco, but when he isn't at school, he lives with me.

"So, Karen," I said in my most charming tone of voice.

"Harley, you know I can't tell you anything."

"Doesn't that only apply if it's a Sil-Trac employee? I've never seen that man before, have you?"

"You're right, he's not an employee. But I still can't tell you anything."

"What did they arrest him for? Isn't that a public record?" I fished.

"They didn't arrest him. Or at least, they weren't planning on it. They just detained him so he could calm down enough to hear and understand US law."

I went back to my seat next to Dave at the back of the bus.

"I have a bad feeling about this, Harley," he said when I sat down. "They could do some real damage to some of these people. Can you see Jeanette climbing anything? She has to be three hundred pounds if she's an ounce."

"Just because she's large doesn't mean she's in bad shape," I said. I'm not what you could call obese, but I'm no featherweight.

"Have you ever watched her climb the stairs at work?"

"She always takes the elevator like everyone else," I said.

"My point exactly."

I wasn't looking forward to the next three days, but I also didn't think it would be the end of civilization as we know it, either. I pulled the latest Sharan Newman paperback from my backpack and immersed myself in medieval France for the rest of the trip.

CHAPTER 2

I WOKE WITH A START. The bus had stopped. I picked up the paperback that had fallen onto my chest when I dozed off. Something was wrong. I looked out the window.

There were Douglas fir trees on all sides. They were tall and thick; the trunks were so crowded the branches started far above our heads, creating a canopy that blocked the sky. The ground was a bed of fir needles. No lodge was in sight. For some reason, I had imagined we would have indoor accommodations, or at least a tent.

"Everyone gather your carryon stuff and come outside," Karen announced. "The driver is opening the luggage bay. We walk in from here."

You could have heard a pin drop when she finished speaking, except of course for the fact we were in the middle of the woods. After a moment of the shocked silence, everyone began speaking at once.

"They expect us to carry our own luggage?" "How far do we have to go?" "Do they have bellboys?" This last was from a Barbie-like creature in pink skintight jeans who managed the secretarial pool. I grabbed my backpack and got out.

The quiet of the woods was finally broken by the increasing sound of a motorized vehicle approaching. A red two-passenger all-terrain vehicle came into sight. A muscular, tanned blonde man jumped off.

"Ms. Jeanette Malone?" he said and looked at our group.

Jeanette stepped forward. He put his hand on her elbow and guided her toward the vehicle.

"What the hell is going on?" Scott asked. He was a slender man in his early thirties who managed a group similar to mine.

Jeanette looked back with a sheepish smile and held up an inhaler.

"Asthma," she said. She turned back and settled her padded hips into the passenger seat of the ATV and they were gone.

"That's not fair," an unidentified voice said from the back of the group.

"So, just how far is it to the camp?" I asked Karen when she joined Dave and I.

"About two and a half miles."

"They obviously told you not to share this part with us," I said. She nodded. "Is there anything else you've held back? Are they going to make us fast, or dig pit latrines or anything?"

"You know I couldn't tell you if they were, but no, they're not doing those two particular things," she said.

This was beginning to feel decidedly Sam-like. I shouldered my pack and started up the trail.

"This is exactly what I was afraid of," Dave said as he caught up to me. "They don't know if everyone is fit enough to make this kind of hike."

"They obviously did some homework. They sent an ATV for Jeanette, after all."

"Yeah, but that's because we've all seen Jeanette use her inhaler at work. Someone might have asthma that doesn't kick up at work."

"You-all need me to carry anything?" Allan said as he jogged to catch up to us. He had a large belt bag, and that was all. "I can carry your backpack, Harley."

"No, thanks, Allan," I said. "I have it."

"This is gonna be fun," he went on. "I can hardly wait to see what we get to do."

He had to be the only one. This was beginning to feel decidedly "Sam-like."

I shouldered my pack and started up the trail. If I'd realized we were going to be hiking right off the bat, I would have tied my bushy hair back with a bandana before we'd gotten off the bus. I was no longer in the physical condition I'd been in during my

"Sam" days, but my five-and-a-half-foot frame still tended more toward muscle than fat, so I knew I could easily make the hike, even with a rather heavy load on my back.

I was wearing canvas cargo pants, an olive-green T-shirt and a well-worn pair of Danner hiking boots. I'd never admit it to Sam, but I was glad I'd saved them when he left.

After forty-five minutes of our trudging along a narrow, fir duff-padded trail, the trees became smaller and more spaced out, as if they had been cleared in the past. The Douglas firs gave way to cedars and pines. The trail rose steeply to the top of a grassy ridge. When I reached the top and looked down, it took my breath away.

The lodge sat in the middle of a bowl formed by the ridge we were on and the surrounding hills. It was magnificent. The main house was made of giant hand-hewn timbers. Woodcarvings surrounded the massive double doors. Stained glass panels of fish and bears and other wildlife topped the ground-floor windows. A river rock chimney dominated the south end of the structure.

A single row of identical log buildings, complete with chimneys, angled away to the left between the main lodge and the hill. Those must be the guest cabins. Maybe this wouldn't be so bad after all.

CHAPTER 3

A YOUNG WOMAN WITH A blazing red mane of hair passed out room keys and informed us that our presence would be required in ten minutes in the main hall. I stowed my bag and found that my roommates included Jeanette and Karen but, thankfully, not Barbie.

We learned our red-haired hostess was named Ashleigh. She was waiting at the big doors to the lodge when we arrived and directed us to a large, open-beamed room to our right. Platters of food covered a roughhewn sideboard. Piles of roast beef and turkey were surrounded by rows of carrot and celery sticks. Red and yellow cherry tomatoes filled hand-thrown pottery bowls. Woven twig baskets held a variety of home-baked breads. This was getting better by the minute.

After our feast had been consumed, we were directed to meet in the great room across the lobby.

"This might turn out okay," Dave whispered in my ear as we walked. "As long as they keep the food coming."

"I think they're just trying to keep us off-kilter. You know, shock us with the hike then kill us with kindness in the form of food. I'm guessing that was the softening up for the main event."

"Hello, everyperson," Mr. Iguchi began in his familiar tone, once we were all seated. "Thanks very much to come here today." He went on to ask for our cooperation and then introduced our guide, a muscular, blue-eyed Adonis named Steven.

Steven explained there would be two phases to our adventure. An organizational part would cast us in predetermined roles and

11

be conducted indoors. The activity portion would take place outside on a challenge course set up for this purpose. Two teams would start on opposite sides of the loop, passing each other midway through the challenge.

As the indoor portion unfolded, the group was divided into three groups. Senior managers and administrative managers comprised two "management" groups. I was in the larger third group—we were the so-called "worker" group. The members of the worker group would be "hired" by the two management groups to complete the outdoor course. I think the plan was to divide us into two approximately equal groups. It didn't end up that way.

Karen or someone from her department must have provided some input on the groupings. Random selection would not have resulted in one group including all the aggressive people and the other all the passive (and somewhat ineffective) managers.

The two management groups were to select a team each from the remaining victims. The worker groups would then perform the "work" of doing whatever the outdoor course had in store for us. Theoretically, the best-managed team would work better together and therefore complete the course first.

That was the plan. What happened was nothing like that.

While the management teams were learning about the motivation system that was available to them and devising the rules for fair selection of teams, the worker group was busy. We took one look at the division of managers and decided to unionize. In the end, everyone worked for the passive group, with half of us subcontracting out to the aggressive managers. Allan let them know in no uncertain terms that any abuse of our team would result in a time-consuming strike.

"Assholes," he said. "They think they can make us win by force, but they have another think coming." His red face was getting redder. He had just completed a heated exchange with Brit Langly, the head of the DRAM Products group. "He had the nerve to pull me aside and tell me if our team didn't win, I would feel it in my next raise. He's forgotten who he's talking to," Allan went on. "He can just watch his schedule slip if he wants to play that game."

"Calm down," I told him, and held his arm, preventing him from going back to the management group. "This is only an exercise, and Karen isn't going to let them get away with anything. She has to review all evaluations, you know that. Let's just get through the next two days and then things can return to normal."

Yeah, I thought. *Normal. Where strange men come into the workplace and threaten to kill your workers.*

With the groups divided, we broke up.

"It doesn't matter if the teams are uneven. The smaller team will have one person do each task twice," Steven explained. "If anyone wants to walk the course with me, meet here in ten minutes. If not, we'll meet back here after dinner to discuss the course and how we will proceed."

I was first in line to get a look at the course.

"I've done this kind of thing before," Allan reminded us. "I don't need to walk the course. It'll be more fun if it's fresh. I'm going back to the cabin to check my equipment."

What equipment? I wondered. We were limited to a water bottle and watch.

Jeanette also started toward the cabin area.

"Are you skipping the walkthrough?" I asked her.

"My allergies are really kicking up," she said, and swiped at her already-red nose with a tissue. I wondered how she was going to make it tomorrow.

A small group of us followed Steven up a short trail to the rim of the bowl formed by the hills that surrounded the lodge. We entered the woods almost immediately. The pine trees perfumed the air with their distinctive scent. A loud crack broke the silence. I flinched. Sam's marches tended to be in rocky, high desert country. I wasn't used to being surrounded by trees.

"What was that?" I asked.

"It was probably a widowmaker," Steven offered without slowing down. "Or maybe someone is at the shooting range."

I didn't know what to be more afraid of.

"What's a widowmaker?" I had to ask.

"During the winter, branches get damaged by the ice and snow. When the dead pieces dry, they sometimes break off and fall to the ground. You can probably figure out the rest. "

"Where's the shooting range?" Scott asked.

"It's behind the main lodge through the trees," Steven answered. "You don't have to worry. We'll be up on the rim when we're back that way."

I wasn't sure why that was supposed to make us feel better. All the guns I'd ever seen could be pointed up.

We reached the first stop on the route. A large net made of rope was stretched across the trail. The openings were varied in size, with most of the largest at the bottom and most of the smallest on top. The rule was that everyone has to pass through the web, but only one person can go through each hole. Clearly, you needed to plan who went through which hole before anyone started.

Our next stop was a wall. Again, it was more of a planning function than a physical challenge. Maybe Allan was right. There was a way out if you planned carefully.

The course continued in this fashion until we got to the water activity. While Steven wasn't willing to give away the punch line when we got to that portion, the presence of a single small boat suggested some kind of cooperative effort would be required. Of course, there was always the possibility we were supposed to have all-out combat and whoever was left standing got the boat. I wouldn't have bet much money on that option, though.

We doubled back and circled the water to continue on. In the end, the overall course was a large figure eight with the lake in the middle. Between the slope of the hills and the trees, there were only a few spots along the upper trail where you could see the lower trail. If a team were reasonably quiet, it could conceal its progress from the competition, adding to the team's psychological advantage.

CHAPTER 4

IT TOOK US AN HOUR and a half just to walk the 600-acre course. Steve told us we could return to our cabins to unpack and rest until dinner. The one I shared with Karen and Jeanette was the last in the row. The cabin I walked into after the hike did not resemble the one I'd dropped my pack in several hours earlier.

The beds were no longer in a straight line parallel to the door. Jeanette reclined on hers. A small fountain now dribbled water onto a bowl of small smooth rocks on a table next to her head. Semitransparent batik scarves were draped over the industrial window blinds. The scent of lavender permeated the air. I located the source. A large vase of fresh lavender sat on the floor by the bathroom door.

"What happened?" I asked.

Jeanette sat up.

"Hi, Harley. Do you like it?" She waved her hand to indicate the surroundings. "I knew I would be spending time in the cabin. You know, with my asthma. So, I brought the scarves to soften the light and my music to soften the ambiance. Then, when I asked Ashleigh to come help me move the beds into a better alignment, she brought the fountain and the lavender. Doesn't it smell divine?"

"It's amazing," I said. "I guess I shouldn't be surprised. You can get shortage parts out of customs and to our plant in less than a day. This is probably child's play."

She straightened her shoulders and blushed at the compliment.

I walked to my bed. It now sat at an angle to the wall and had two pillows. One of Jeanette's scarves was fastened by its middle to the ceiling above each bed. The ends trailed down on either side of the pillows, forming a tent-canopy and providing us each with a little sleeping privacy. I was impressed. This was clearly a woman who knew how to lounge.

Dinner was another sumptuous spread—barbecued meats were the featured item. Steve, Ashleigh and their brother Mark wore matching denim cowboy shirts.

After dinner, the group met in the large room near the massive fireplace. Karen led a series of teamwork exercises with names like "Icebreaker" and "Lost in the Woods." Which didn't bode well for the upcoming day's events.

It seemed to me we were way past this kind of activity. As a team, we sat through meetings at work that made grown men cry. We all knew who was running around on his wife with a production operator, and who was gay and not out to their family yet. Revealing three sanitized facts and trying to guess who they referred to was pointless. It did fill up the evening, though.

Karen, Jeanette and I returned to our cabin. Jeanette pulled a clock radio out of her pack.

"I hope my music won't bother anyone. I started listening to music when I go to bed when I moved back in with my parents. They were noisy sleepers at the end. Now, I've gotten so used to it…" She trailed off.

Jeanette had been forced by circumstance to move home and care for her terminally ill father when her mother was unable to handle things on her own and her other children pulled a no-show. Her father, I had heard, died more than a year ago. Her mother passed on this past February. Jeanette said her mom was so devoted to her dad she just seemed to give up on life after he died.

Allan had reported all this when Jeanette was off, settling the estate. He was furious. Her absent siblings showed up when Mom died and demanded their share. According to Allan, she didn't even put up a fight. She just quietly bought out their share of the house and let them have all the rest. I'm not sure I'd have been so gracious, given the years she'd put in caring for her dad. Allan said she argued she didn't need money, or anything else, complicating her life.

"Fine with me," I said. "I'm used to my stepson playing music at all hours of the day and night."

Karen indicated she was fine with it, too.

We settled into the feather beds covered by down comforters and Jeanette's scarves. I had expected to spend a quiet night and awake rested. After what couldn't have been more than an hour, I heard a long, slow squeak. I looked toward the door, and just made out the silhouette of a person slipping out the door then pulling it shut. The metallic click of the latch sounded loud in the quiet stillness of the room. I could hear the rhythmic breathing of one of my roommates, but with Jeanette's drapes over the heads of our beds, I couldn't see who was missing. We weren't in prison, so there was probably no rule about leaving the cabin at close to midnight, but it was odd, if you ask me.

For lack of a better plan, I decided to get up myself and go to the bathroom. The angle of the beds also prevented me from seeing who was missing as I crossed the room.

When I opened the bathroom door for the return trip, my remaining roommate groaned. I looked at both beds, but whoever had left had done the pillow trick, because there seemed to be a body in both beds. I could have spoken out loud and waited to see which lump moved, but I couldn't think of what my next move after that would be. In the end, I crawled back into my bed to ponder the possibilities.

I woke again when Jeanette's clock radio blared Beethoven's Fifth at 5:30. An arm reached out from her draped bed and silenced it. Karen's legs swung over the side of her bed.

"Good morning," she said in my direction. "Are you ready to start this adventure?"

"I guess this means we can't just go back to sleep and pretend we didn't hear the alarm." I said and slowly sat up. "You can have the bathroom first," I added.

I grabbed the hand-knit afghan Jeanette had added to the foot of my bed when we'd arrived and wrapped it around my shoulders. I walked past her bed to the door. She appeared to be sound asleep. I opened the door on a beautiful dawn. The sun was shining on the dew-covered grass outside the cabin. A gentle breeze blew, causing the trees to whisper quietly among themselves. I took a deep breath. The scent of the pines mixed with the smell of the English lavender planted in the flowerbed in front of our cabin. If I weren't sure that every moment of our experience was being orchestrated, it would have been pleasant — impressive, even. As it was, I couldn't help feeling like all our senses were being manipulated.

As I stood there, breathing, Steven walked up, blond sun-streaked hair riffling in the breeze. He held a large basket with several ceramic carafes inside it.

"Good morning, Harley," he said. "Would you ladies care for some coffee or tea?"

"Sure," I said. "Tea would be great." I checked my appearance in the mirror of my mind. My hair was sticking out at odd angles, and my forehead was greasy. I was wearing a cast-off T-shirt from Noah's brief heavy metal phase, plaid flannel pajama pants, and the afghan on my shoulders.

If Steven noticed, he was gracious enough not to show it. He handed me the carafe of tea and a small basket with packets of honey, sugar and nondairy creamer, balancing the larger basket on one tanned, well-muscled forearm. He renewed his grip on the handles of the basket, flashed me a megawatt smile and was off to the next cabin.

"He's quite the hunk," Jeanette said from her bed. "Too bad he's not our type," she added.

"Speak for yourself," I said.

"Can you see him holding your hand while you barf your guts up, or cleaning up dog poop off the carpet?"

"Is that your measure of a man?" I asked. No wonder she was single.

"That's not the only thing, but it certainly is one thing. I don't want some useless pretty boy."

I thought of Sam. "A pretty boy could be fun, for a while anyway."

"Next," said Karen as she walked out of the bathroom toweling her short hair.

"Go ahead," Jeanette said, and took the tea and basket. "I'm going to have some tea first."

We all dressed in our own version of appropriate attire for the adventure. Karen had on teal green climbing pants made out of lightweight rip-stop nylon, topped off by a pink Capilene long underwear shirt and a flowered camp shirt. Jeanette, on the other hand, had on a pale-yellow cotton knit sweater set over a washed denim wraparound skirt. I was relatively ordinary in Levi's, a white T-shirt and the latest version of the Sil-Trac zip front sweatshirt.

People were quiet at breakfast. I scanned the group to see if anyone looked like they had been up all night with one of my roommates. I couldn't tell, but then, neither Karen nor Jeanette looked particularly tired, either.

We met outside the lodge to begin the adventure. The basic setup was much like we had imagined. Each team was taken to opposite ends of the layout, their respective management team in tow. If things worked out right, we wouldn't see the other group until the lake. The management group was equipped with walkie-talkies and could be called for advice twice per team after our initial pep talk. They were allowed to check progress and offer encouragement if they chose to.

Allan and Jeanette were in my group. We were threatened by our management team one last time and then began the climb up the trail to our first activity. Allan led the way and set a brisk pace. I brought up the rear with a red-faced Jeanette. She dabbed at her nose with a yellow handkerchief. When Jeanette and I crested the first rise, we saw a fork in the trail. Loud voices came from the left branch.

"That sounds like Allan," Jeanette said.

We followed the trail to the left another twenty feet. The clearing in front of us held the spider web.

"What's the problem?" I asked.

Two groups of people started talking at once.

"We've had a little misunderstanding," Dave said when the noise subsided.

"Misunderstanding?" Allan protested. "These people are idiots. That's no misunderstanding. I'm reading that loud and clear."

I looked back at Dave.

"A few people started on their own before we read the instructions," he explained. "As you can see, the net has large holes and small holes. Each time a person goes through a hole, Steven puts a strip of tape across the opening, meaning we can't let anyone else use that hole. As you can see, Barbie, Mitzie and Erin are on the other side of the net."

"Yeah, and notice how it is the three biggest holes that are taped shut," Allan said through clenched teeth.

"There are just enough holes for the number of people on the team," Dave continued. "You probably noticed that the big holes are lower and the little holes are up higher."

"That means three of us bigger people are going to have to figure a way to squeeze through the small holes which are, oh, by the way, *at the top*," Allan sputtered. "I could wring Barbie's scrawny neck." He scowled at the three women, who were huddled together looking miserable on the other side of the obstacle.

Jeanette moved to the net. "Let's just get on with it," she said and grabbed a horizontal rope above her head.

I was curious to see how this would go.

She put her feet on the nearest lower rope and began to climb. She went up one row and stopped. Her face turned red, and she began to wheeze. She hung by one hand and dabbed at her nose with the yellow handkerchief. The net shook, and Jeanette swayed.

"I think you better come back down," I said. She continued coughing. "Allan," I said and looked at him, "do something. Get her down before she falls and breaks her neck."

Steven climbed the net before I had finished speaking. He grabbed Jeanette's free hand and put it on the rope, and then he swung his foot across so he essentially pinned her to the net, preventing her from falling. He stayed like that until she had finished coughing and then helped her back to the ground.

"Sorry, guys," Jeanette said sheepishly when she had finished wheezing. "I was just trying to get it over with." She pulled an inhaler out of her pocket and pumped it into her mouth.

"I'm going to call Karen and excuse Jeanette from this," Steven said and started talking in a low voice into his radio. He waited for a moment and then spoke again. When he finished, he turned to Jeanette. "Karen says you're excused from the physical activities. I told her you probably would need to lie down for a while. She says go ahead and go back to the cabins and then, if you feel up to it, you can rejoin us after lunch. Do you need help getting down the hill?"

"Oh, no," Jeanette said. "Don't worry about me. My life is like this. I'll just sit here and watch a moment while my inhaler kicks in. When I can breathe again, I'll just walk back down the hill and lie down until lunch. Really, it's okay. It's always been this way. I'm used to it." She took another drag on her inhaler.

I took her place on the net.

"I'm with Jeanette," I said. "We can't undo what's been done, so let's just get on with it." I climbed two rows up and twisted my body through one of the smaller openings. Allan climbed on next and went to the top where the smallest holes were.

"Are you sure you can fit that far up?" I asked.

He didn't answer, but when Dave had to go up and help pull him out of the hole he was stuck in, it became moot. After two tries, he was able to get through somewhere in the middle.

While he and Dave were aloft, I got the rest of the group to line up by width. If everyone went through a hole that was one spot smaller than planned, we could make it. I didn't envy the smallest people, who had to go to the top of the net. It took what must have been twice the time it should have, but we all got through.

"It's been fun, kids," Jeanette said, and got up from the stump she had been sitting on. Her color had returned to normal. "I'm going to go back to the cabin now," she said, and started back down the trail. "Somebody come wake me up when it's food time." She then went out of sight, skirt swishing as she walked.

We went on to the next exercise. The trail opened on to a wooded glen. The green grass was ankle deep. We were given three segments of two-by-six to be used in crossing the glen. The whole group had to cross and no one was allowed to step on the grass. This meant we all had to huddle up on two of the boards and continuously lay the third board in front of us, picking up the first once we were all safely on the second and third to repeat the process. We were making good progress, holding on to each other and passing the board efficiently forward each cycle, when trouble struck.

Dave was in the front anchor position, with Allan in back picking up the board and passing it forward. On one pass, Dave went to throw the board out in front of the line when a large sliver caught in the web of his right thumb and buried itself.

"Ouch!" he hollered, and stepped off the board. He held his wounded thumb aloft with his good left hand. Blood dripped down his arm.

Allan jumped off and pulled a small first aid kit out of his pocket. He tore open a pack of antiseptic and dabbed at the sliver in Dave's thumb.

"Ouch!" Dave repeated, and danced out of Allan's reach.

Steven came across the glen and looked at Dave's thumb. "You're going to need to see the nurse back at the lodge," he announced.

"Don't you have some kind of field dressing?" Allan asked.

Steven looked at him. "It's a sliver, okay? Dave's going to live, but you've all stepped off the boards, so you're back at the starting line again." He looked at his watch and pushed a button. This was a timed event, and he had just restarted the clock.

"Hey, that's not fair," Allan protested.

I grabbed his arm and dragged him in the direction of the start line.

"Life's not fair, big guy, and the clock is running,"

"I don't care if all the women here *are* drooling all over that guy — he's an asshole," Allan said and turned back to the task at hand.

We had just gotten back across the glen when Dave rejoined us. He had a Band-Aid over the spot the splinter had been in.

"My growing fear is that the blond gods that run this place don't know what they're doing. I had to wonder what Steven would have done if I'd sliced an artery or something. You know, he didn't have any supplies up here. And that Nazi in a nurse's uniform back at camp isn't much better. If Allan hadn't had his bootleg first aid kit I would have had nothing. It could have been bad if I'd done something worse to myself."

"You're right, it could have been worse." I said. "We'll just have to be careful. Besides, it's only one more day."

Dave and I brought up the rear as our group headed out of the glen and back into the woods. Allan was at the front, setting his usual brisk pace. We arrived at the edge of the lake a good ten minutes ahead of the other group. Our "management team" was waiting for us.

Allan's face was red from exertion when we came out of the woods and into the small clearing. The veins in his neck bulged, and I could see a convulsive twitch in his jaw when he saw Brit Langley. The two men didn't exchange words. They didn't need to.

"Breathe, Allan," I said. "You won't be able to save me if you pass out."

The management team followed a path that appeared to lead around the lake. When they were out of sight, Allan opened the now-familiar envelope containing our instructions. He read them and sat down on the grassy slope leading to the lake's edge.

"Damn," he said. "We have to wait for group A."

It turned out the instructions said we had to ferry each member of our group across the lake to the opposite shore, one at a time, and then return the small boat to its original location. The equipment we were give included a pulley, an anchor pin and about half the rope required for the task. Group A was to be given a pulley, anchor and an amount of rope equal to ours. If we pooled our resources, we could accomplish the task easily. There were still more timed activities after the lake.

We decided Allan would be the first one to cross the lake — since we had beaten the other group to the glen, we had earned the right to have that. He would set the first anchor and pulley, string the rope, row across the lake carrying the ends of the rope, set the second anchor and pulley, tie the rope, and then use the system to send the boat back. While the second person from our group crossed, Allan would run on up the course to see what our next activity was. He would come back and let us know what lay ahead.

Dave would be our last person to cross. The last person had to help maneuver the boat back into position and dismantle the pulley system. His Marine Corps experience made him the most suitable candidate for this job.

Allan tied the two rope pieces together and threaded them into the pulley. The sun was beating down on us. Allan took his shirt off. The hard muscles of his broad back gleamed with sweat as he climbed into the boat and rowed across the lake.

CHAPTER 5

ALLAN GOT OUT OF THE BOAT on the far shore and started it back across the water. Dave and I pulled the rope to bring the boat back while Allan disappeared up the trail. When the boat reached shore, I got in. The rowing was made easier by my teammates' pulling on the rope.

Allan had not returned from the next exercise location. I knew from my walkthrough it was only about 500 yards up the trail, so I was surprised he hadn't returned. Steven hadn't said the exercises had to be taken in order, but I had assumed we followed the progression along the figure eight.

I landed the boat without mishap and set it on its return course.

"Where's Allan?" Dave yelled across the lake.

"I don't know," I yelled back. "I'm going to go look."

I hiked up the trail to the next activity area. The "Instructions Here" sign was still hanging on a tree trunk, but the Group B envelope was missing. The clearing seemed unnaturally still. I had started for the tree when I spotted Allan. He lay collapsed not ten feet from the tree trunk. I ran to him and knelt by his bulky form.

"Are you okay?" I said, stupidly echoing the prescribed words from my first aid class. It was clear he wasn't okay—he lay on his side, his face down in the dirt. I pushed on his shoulder and rolled him onto his back. I could see blood seeping from a depression in the side of his head; a trickle of blood-laced foam oozed from the corner of his mouth. The bloody B Group envelope was still clutched tightly in his hands.

I put my face close to his. His chest moved convulsively.

"Help," I screamed. I wasn't sure if anyone could hear me. I prepared Allan for CPR. His chest rose and fell in barely perceptible motion, but I wanted to be ready. "Allan, don't do this to me now."

"Harley," a voice shrieked. "What have you done to Allan?" Barbie stood at the end of the trail.

"Go get help, quick," I yelled at her. "Tell Dave Allan has had an accident, and I need him here right now, and then find Steven or Ashleigh and tell them to call nine-one-one." I knew one of our hosts had to be nearby. To her credit, Barbie ran back down the trail and did as I asked.

"Hang on, Allan," I whispered near his good ear.

While we waited for help, I looked around the area. To Allan's left was a large broken tree branch the size of a small telephone pole. One of the notorious "widowmakers," I assumed.

An eternity later, Dave arrived with Steven hot on his heals. He knelt beside Allan and looked at him helplessly. Steven pushed him out of the way and lifted Allan's left eyelid.

"Hey, what are you doing?" Dave asked.

"I'm trying to evaluate your friend," he said, his hands never stopping. "I'm a doctor," he added as an afterthought.

I couldn't even think about that little revelation.

"Is he okay?" I asked stupidly.

Steven looked back at me. His expression was grave.

"Your friend is in very serious trouble. I radioed for the Life-Flight helicopter, but it will take them at least twenty minutes to get here."

"Can you do anything for him?" I asked, tears starting to trickle down my cheeks.

His look softened. "I can't really say until we can get an x-ray of his head."

I could tell he was lying. Dave put his arm around my shoulders and guided me over to a log, where we both sat down. His eyes were wet with tears.

We were still sitting on the log when we heard the throb of helicopter rotors. Ashleigh had arrived and taken control of the scene. When the chopper was in sight, she had everyone except Steven clear out of the area. We watched mutely from a distance as they loaded Allan, took off and disappeared over the horizon.

CHAPTER 6

THE DEPARTURE OF ALLAN'S HELICOPTER signaled the end of our adventure in the woods. We were ordered to our cabins and instructed to stay there until dinner was announced. Jeanette was lying on her bunk reading a book about material planning. A small fire was burning in the fireplace.

"You're back early, aren't you?" she asked.

She was horrified by my account of Allan's accident.

"Can we go back to town now?" she asked. "Someone needs to be with Allan."

"Apparently not. We were sent to our rooms and told to stay here until we're called for. The company wants to investigate. It's horrible, but I guess it's a Worker's Comp accident, since we *are* being paid while we're up here." I went to the bathroom and washed my face, effectively ending our conversation. When I came out, Jeanette was sobbing softly into her pillow. I lay down on my bed and fell into a restless sleep.

My sleep only lasted a scant thirty minutes. An older man in a denim workshirt came for me.

"You the gal that found the guy?" he asked. "They want to question you." Without waiting for my answer, he turned and headed back toward the main lodge. I grabbed my shoes from beside the door and put them on as I left.

* * *

"Did someone want to talk to me?" I asked as I came into the main lodge.

Steven separated from a group of men in uniforms.

"The sheriff's deputy wants to question you," he said. He put his hand on my back and guided me over.

"Who called them?" I asked.

"I did. They have to investigate any time someone is..." He paused. "Any time someone is seriously hurt," he finished.

I stopped. "He *is* going to make it, isn't he?"

I looked into his clear blue eyes. He looked troubled.

"I can't lie to you. It's not good. He has a very serious depressed skull fracture. He was not very responsive, and he had a flight ahead of him before they could even do a CAT scan. Still, people have survived worse."

"You're not holding out much hope, though, are you?"

"In this kind of situation, it's not as much about whether he'll survive as what shape he'll be in when he recovers. He's young and strong enough to survive the trauma, but I seriously doubt he'll ever be the man you had breakfast with this morning. If you know any prayers, this would be a good time to say them."

With that, he nodded to the sheriff's deputy and left.

The deputy took me into a small, book-lined office off the great room.

"You're the one who found the victim?" he asked.

"I found Allan, if that's what you mean," I said.

He indicated a chair opposite a large pine desk. He sat behind the desk.

"I'm Deputy Henry Reed," he said. "Please, sit.

"I don't mean to sound insensitive about your friend," he continued after I'd done so. "But considering the seriousness of his injuries, I need to cover all possibilities. The Holts have operated this retreat for three generations. I'd hate to see anything happen to them."

"Happen to *them*?" I said, and jumped up. "It's Allan that's in the hospital clinging to life. The Holts seem just fine to me."

"Sit down, miss. I didn't mean to ruffle your feathers. It's just that any suggestion of negligence could ruin the lodge."

"Negligence?"

"That company of yours is flying in a group of investigators this afternoon. I know they have their own butts to cover, but I aim to make sure they don't cover 'em at the expense of Dan Holt and his kids."

"They have to investigate," I said. "Since Allan was on work time, they probably have to report it as a Worker's Comp accident. That doesn't mean they're trying to pin anything on anyone. We have to investigate if someone gets a bad paper cut. Besides, it looked to me like it was just a horrible accident."

"What exactly did you see?" he asked, and pulled a notebook out of his pocket.

I explained what had happened. He interrupted with a few questions about who was where at different times, how long I was alone with Allan before Barbie came across the lake (good question, I thought), where the people from Group A were while I was with Allan (again, a question for which I had no answer). He eventually had to conclude I didn't know much. I hadn't expected to find Allan injured, so I hadn't taken notice of the details leading up to my discovery of him under the tree. It seemed clear to me that one of the infamous widowmakers had done its fabled deed.

Deputy Reed didn't seem so sure.

When he ran out of questions, he instructed me to return to my cabin and stay there until further notice and I left.

Jeanette was sleeping in her bed when I got back to the cabin; Karen had gone up to wait for the company investigators at the lodge. It took three minutes of listening to Jeanette snoring for me to ditch the deputy's plan.

The fire Jeanette had made was almost out. I poked at the sticks she had used as fuel. I threw a bigger piece of wood onto the embers from the canvas stand next to the fireplace. A scrap of yellow caught my eye. It might have been a page from a legal pad—it was hard to tell. I poked at it, but only succeeded in pushing it deeper into the ash.

I shut the fire screen, wiped my hands on my jeans and slipped out the rear door. The forest shaded the back side of the cabin. Ferns crowded the damp narrow path that ran from one cabin to the next along the rear. I could hear a stream that must parallel the path.

I counted the cabins until I came to the one Dave shared with Jose and Allan. I tapped softly on the window. Dave pulled back the curtain. A moment later the door opened.

"Harley, what are you doing here?" he asked. "We're supposed to be in lockdown."

"Karen is at the main lodge and Jeanette's snoring was getting on my nerves. I've got to get out of here for a while. You want to come?"

He hesitated a moment.

"Yeah, sure," he said. He drew back inside then came out a moment later and shut the door. "I told Jose I was going to sit outside for a while. He's hitting the shower so he won't come looking for a while."

We continued along the trail. When we passed the last cabin, our path turned away from the cabins and crossed the brook I'd heard. A short segment of trail rose steeply, and when we reached the top, I could see we were on the main trail that circled the rim. I led us to the right.

"Harley, don't even think what you're thinking," Dave warned.

"We won't touch anything," I said and headed toward the lake.

It took about fifteen minutes to walk around it. Other than being marked with a few more footprints, the edge of the lake looked about like it had the first time we saw it. We continued up the trail to the meadow where Allan had been injured.

"I can't believe no one is up here," Dave said.

I walked over to the spot where Allan had fallen helpless in the dirt.

"Something doesn't seem right," I said. "Look at where Allan was." I pointed to where the dirt was smooth and the weeds flattened. "He was here. See where the dirt is black? That's the blood from his head," I turned a quarter-turn to my left. "And here's the widowmaker." I pointed at the large tree limb that had fallen from high above. "It seems kind of far away, and there's no blood between here and there." I walked to the widowmaker and rolled it over with my toe. "I don't see any blood on the limb, either."

"That might not mean anything," Dave said. "It probably rolled away after it hit him."

"You're probably right."

We returned to the lake and continued around the back half of the figure-eight trail. We didn't run into anyone. Most of the hike we didn't talk. It felt good to walk.

Dave went back into his cabin, and I continued on to mine. I hesitated for a moment and considered going back inside, but I still felt restless. I decided to go back to the main lodge and see if there was any news on Allan.

The trail continued along the creek, past the backs of the remaining cabins, past two other slightly larger buildings and on behind the lodge. The foliage was heavy and dark. I heard voices as I passed the first of the two outbuildings. I slowed, and then inched along the trail until I saw two people between the buildings. I stepped off the trail into the thick woods where my presence would be concealed yet I would be free to look. The rush of the brook concealed any noise my footsteps made.

I peered around the mossy trunk of a large maple tree. The couple were kissing and groping each other like high school students behind the bleachers at a football game. They came up for air and separated briefly. I had to bite my hand to avoid making a noise. Karen pressed against Steven's lean body. I guessed that answered the question of who had left our cabin last night.

It didn't answer what the fifty-something and married Karen was doing with our thirty-something host Dr. Steven, but I decided it was none of my business. I stayed in the woods and picked my way toward the lodge until I was safely past the trysting couple. When I was clear of the outbuildings, I stepped back onto the trail and went on to the lodge.

Nobody seemed to care that I had left my cabin. According to Ashleigh, there was no change in Allan's condition. Mr. Iguchi and Brit Langly were huddled with the other senior managers. Brit was gesturing, and Mr. Iguchi was listening, no expression on his face. To its credit, Sil-Trac was not into spin-doctoring. They were more into taking responsibility and paying whatever money it took to keep things "dignified."

There was a buffet set up with coffee and small snacks. I loitered near the food a few minutes and overheard the man who had summoned me to the questioning arranging for a wagon to come pick us up and take us back to our bus at the main road. We would be driven out an access road from the gun club.

Jeanette was awake when I returned to the cabin. Her eyes were swollen.

"Where's Karen?" she asked.

"Last time I saw her, she was talking to Steven," I said.

"I want her to get us out of here. Someone needs to be with Allan. You know he doesn't have any close family. We're all he has." Her eyes filled with tears. "I'm going to find her."

The door to the cabin opened, and Karen walked in.

"Are you okay, Jeanette?" she asked. She looked at Jeanette's swollen red eyes. "I'm sorry, I know you're not okay. I meant your asthma. Is your asthma okay?"

Jeanette looked at her. "I'm fine," she said stiffly. She turned and went into the bathroom.

"Is something wrong with her?" Karen asked.

"You mean besides her best friend hanging by a thread in the hospital?" I asked.

"I did come to check on her earlier, but Steven called me about Allan before I talked to her."

"It may not be fair to bring it up now, but I think you know no one wanted to come on this trip. Unfortunately, since you had to implement the adventure, people are going to blame you for the consequences."

The energy drained out of her. She sat down on her bed. Her face was pale, and for the first time I could see the spider web of wrinkles around her eyes.

"This wasn't supposed to happen," she said.

"Once we get home and people are in their own environment, they'll be able to see this more clearly for the tragic accident it is," I said.

It didn't look like she was buying my attempt to make her feel better, so I shut up and began taking Jeanette's scarves down and folding the soft material into neat squares on her bed. An hour later, two green vans emblazoned with "Flying H" shuttled us out to the main road in two groups. We loaded our bags onto the big bus, and when everyone was assembled, we were driven back to town.

CHAPTER 7

IT WAS LATE AFTERNOON when we got back. I went straight to my car and drove home to my house in the northeast section of Portland. I live in what is known locally as a Portland Bungalow. That means it has two bedrooms and is more than forty-five years old. It also has ten-foot ceilings and beveled glass windows. The garage is separate from the house.

About twenty years ago, my neighborhood had been all but overrun by gangs and drug dealers. The older neighbors held their ground, and people like me bought reclaimed houses and were renovating them. We still lock our doors, but we're no longer serenaded by the sound of gunfire when we go to bed at night.

Mrs. Johnson, my housekeeper, is the one indulgence I allowed myself when Sam and I divorced. She and her husband live two blocks away. I pay her to come twice a week to grocery shop and do basic cleaning. Since her husband retired two years ago, she comes more often, whenever he gets on her nerves. They both like to cook, and since I like to eat, it's a compatible relationship.

When I pulled into the driveway, I could see Mrs. Johnson in the kitchen window. Frank Green was also in the kitchen. Frank is a detective on the Portland police force. We'd met last spring when one of my workers was killed. Frank and I are not what you'd call friends. Our relationship is based on my fifteen-year-old stepson Noah thinking the sun rises and sets over Frank Green.

Noah is badly in need of a father figure—calling Sam an absentee father is generous. In Sam's paranoid world, he thinks direct contact with Noah puts his son's life in jeopardy. Knowing he has a father who follows and controls his every move, yet refuses to spend time with him, is worse for Noah than having no father is. Having a stepmother who wasn't able to stay married to his dad didn't help, either. I'm not wild that Noah has attached himself to someone in a profession that puts him in the line of fire, but Noah is so needy I don't have the heart to tell him he can't see Frank.

My stepson is home from military school in the summer. I've managed to convince Sam that spending the summer attending military camps is not healthy for him. When I told Noah I was attending an out-of-town seminar, he jumped at the chance to have Detective Green stay with him.

"Hey, Noah, look who's home," Green said when I walked up the steps and into the kitchen. "Aren't you home early? We weren't expecting you until tomorrow."

Noah came into the kitchen. He and Green were dressed in gym clothes.

"What are you doing here?" He glared at me.

"Last time I checked, I still lived here," I said. They both looked at me expectantly. "There was an accident. One of the men I work with got hurt—badly. They decided that, under the circumstances, it would be better if we went home."

"We can still go to the gym and the movie," Green said. "Harley looks like she could use a little time to herself."

"You boys go on and leave Harley to me," Mrs. Johnson said. "She needs a hot bath and a good cup of tea." She went into the bathroom. I heard the sound of water running.

Green gave Noah the keys to his car and told him to go start it.

"You have your cup of tea," Green said. "But when I bring Noah home, I want to hear all about this accident."

"There's nothing to tell. A guy I work with got bashed in the head when a big limb fell from a tree. He hasn't regained consciousness yet. They say it's not looking good. There's nothing more to tell."

"What do the local police say?"

"The sheriff seems worried that it may impact the bookings at his buddy's dude ranch."

He didn't move toward the door. "What aren't you telling me?"

"Nothing, It was an accident, like I said." He waited. "Okay, so I was the one to find the guy. That was a coincidence."

"I don't believe in coincidence. In my line of work, I can't afford to."

"This was just an accident. End of story. We're all just praying Allan wakes up." I turned and went to find the bath Mrs. Johnson had waiting for me.

The bath did help relax my tense muscles, but with Noah still gone with Green, I was restless. I tried reading, but couldn't concentrate. In the end, I put on clean jeans and T-shirt, grabbed my keys and drove to the Oregon Health Sciences University. I'd overheard Steven telling Deputy Reed that Allan had been taken there. Portland has two hospitals that are perpetually vying for top trauma hospital status, so I had a fifty-fifty chance of being at the correct one.

A receptionist in the emergency room directed me to the waiting room of the critical care area. Jeanette and Karen were already there, sitting on worn chairs, silent.

"Any news?" I asked.

"They have him stabilized," Karen said. "Steven said they would probably keep him in a light coma until the swelling in his brain goes down. He said something about them removing a piece of his skull temporarily to make more room for it until then, too."

"Well, at least he's still hanging on," I said. I never know what to say in situations like this. Not that I had any experience with friends or loved ones having large pieces of tree fall on their head. Or whatever had happened.

An hour or more had passed when Steven came into the waiting room. He looked different in green hospital scrubs. He was still extremely good-looking, but he was definitely in his element here.

Karen went over to a coffee carafe that sat on a small table at the back of the waiting room and poured a cup. She put in two spoons of sugar, stirred and brought it to him.

"So far so good," he said after a few sips. "As I suspected, he's strong, and a fighter to boot. The first twenty-four to forty-eight hours are critical, so we'll know more tomorrow and the day after. He's getting the best possible care here."

35

"Thank you for helping him," I said. "I am a little curious, though."

"Let me guess," he said. "You want to know why a surgeon is working at a dude ranch in Tillamook."

"Something like that," I said. *That and what your relationship with Karen is,* I thought but didn't say.

"My father and grandfather have operated the forest retreat for decades. Gramps hosted the jet-setters before they had jets. My dad is the one who courted the Outward Bound crowd. The latest version is the management training course."

"And you're breaking the mold by becoming a doctor?" I ventured.

"I'm the spare," he said. "My older brother runs the business with my dad, and Ashleigh and Mark pitch in when they can. Philip is vacationing in France with his wife for the next two weeks. I was just helping out in his absence. Besides, my grandmother on my mom's side was a pediatrician, so it's not completely out of left field." He finished his coffee and stood up. "I need to go check on a couple of my own patients while I'm here, but I wanted to let you know that they'll let you each go in to see Allan for five minutes. Only one per hour, though. It'll ease up after these first two days." He paused and didn't have to say *If he lives that long.*

With that he dropped his Styrofoam cup in the wastebasket and walked out.

Since each of us would only get to see Allan once in the next three hours, we agreed on a schedule. Karen would go first, I would go next and Jeanette would follow. Jeanette announced she was going to find food and left. I looked at a well-thumbed copy of *Time* magazine.

I was dozing in my chair when my turn finally came. Jeanette had returned and was quietly crocheting something large and pink. An afghan maybe. One of Allan's nurses came and got me.

"It's important for his friends to visit," she explained. She said they never really knew how much a coma patient was aware of, so I should talk to him, and encourage him to fight.

Allan didn't show any sign that he knew I was there. His head was wrapped in a large white bandage with a tube coming out of it. I tried to focus on his hand. It lay on the bed beside him and had a tube coming out of its back, but looked more normal than his swollen face did.

I did my best to talk to him, but it's hard when someone you care about is barely clinging to life in front of you. My five minutes passed too soon, and I left using a stairway that didn't take me back past the waiting room. I didn't want to talk to anyone. When I got home, Noah was still out. I left him a note and then collapsed onto my bed and into a dreamless sleep, fully dressed.

∼ ᥱ∽

The next week was a blur of trips between work, the hospital and home. Allan was still in a coma, but the doctors said that was normal given the severity of his injury. The swelling in his brain was improving each day, and they were discussing the timing for closing his skull. Our visitations had been increased to ten minutes, and we were able to have two people at a time if we promised to keep things calm. I stopped by on my way to work each day and again during my lunchtime if things were going well in the cleanroom. Jeanette and Tim took turns during the day, and both went in the evening. Karen went less often, when her meeting schedule allowed.

No one could tell us yet what Allan's chances were for a full recovery, but we grew more encouraged with each passing day.

CHAPTER 8

A WISPY CLOUD WAS STUCK to the surface of the Willamette River when I drove across the Fremont Bridge and headed west at daybreak a week after Allan's accident. It seemed automatic now to cut through downtown Portland and head up the hill to the hospital.

Allan's nurses were by now familiar with his regular visitors.

"Hello," the night nurse, a large redheaded woman, called out. "Mr. Sayers had a good night," she said. "In fact, the doctor has lightened up his medication. We might expect him to start waking up some time soon."

"That's good news. Right?"

"Yes, it's very good. I wanted you to be prepared if he opens his eyes or moans or something. It's normal, but would you press his call button if that happens? Once he starts coming out of it, we'll try to stimulate him a little and see if we can help him find his way back."

My step was quicker as I approached Allan's room. His doctor had spoken to Karen and me last night. He'd wanted to reinforce the fact that Allan would not be his old self when he woke up. They wouldn't know the extent of his loss of function until he did wake up, but the doctor wanted us to be clear that Allan wouldn't be returning to his present job any time soon.

Even with the doctor's gloomy prognosis, it had to be good he was waking up.

The room was a riot of color, with vases filled with purple iris and Shasta daisies and pink and yellow snapdragons vying for space with Mylar balloons encouraging Allan to "Get Well." I took each vase and emptied the water, then refilled it with fresh. Mrs. J said the flowers would last longer if I did that. I talked to him while I did it. I told him about my new lead operator and about how well the new probe card he'd gotten us was working. Nothing earth-shattering. Just the normal, everyday stuff we would have been talking about if we had been having coffee at Sil-Trac.

When I was finished with the flowers, I sat in the chair by his bed and held his hand. In spite of the night nurse's predictions, Allan lay motionless, and after a half-hour of one-sided conversation, I squeezed his limp hand, said goodbye and assured him I'd be back later. I walked to the end of the hall and down four flights of stairs to the parking lot, mentally counting it as my cardio for the day.

Several roads crossed the hill the hospital sat on. You could easily drop into downtown Portland or go the opposite direction and head west toward Sil-Trac. I chose the back road that took me to a neighborhood Starbucks. My firm belief in the power of chocolate was all the justification I needed for the chocolate croissant I indulged in. I read a newspaper I found lying on my table as I sipped my hazelnut latte. When I'd finished both, I pointed my car west and headed for Sil-Trac.

A large number of electronics companies in the Portland area are located within a mile of Highway 26, known locally as the Sunset Corridor. The gray skies fit my mood—it looked like it was going to rain before the day was out. In Portland, you can't really count on sunny days until after the Fourth of July, and even then it's not guaranteed. We still had a few weeks to go.

The security guard didn't call out his usual "Hi-de-ho" when I came through the first set of glass doors at the employee entrance. I stopped. He was sitting in his chair. His headset was on the desk in front of him. His eyes were rimmed in red.

"Harold," I said, "are you okay?"

He didn't answer. He looked at me and took a deep breath.

"I just took a call from the hospital." He paused. "Allan's dead."

"That's not true," I protested. "I was just there. He was fine."

Tears ran down my face. Harold picked up his headset and talked briefly to someone. Dave came to the entrance and put his arms around me.

"Dave, he can't be gone. I just saw him. He was fine. Well, not fine, but he was alive. The nurse said he was going to wake up. Any time. She told me to call her if he woke while I was with him."

I'm sorry, Harley. The doctor called for Karen, but she's not in yet. Harold gave him to me."

"I can't believe it. You call them back, right now. Tell them they made a mistake. The nurse said he was about to wake up. Maybe they just moved him or something."

"I talked to the doctor, Harley. They don't know what happened. He said he might have had a heart attack or massive stroke or something. They won't know until they do an autopsy. He said those things happen sometimes in a case like Allan's."

"But I was just there," I said again.

Dave guided me back to my desk in the maze of management cubicles and went to the vending machines. He set a Diet Coke in front of me.

"I'll go get our people started," he said. "You just sit here for a while."

I don't know how long I sat, staring at nothing. I just couldn't absorb the fact that Allan was dead. I'd just seen him. I wiped my face with a Kleenex and got up to go see if Karen had arrived yet.

"Excuse me," a soft voice said from the hallway outside my cube. A young Japanese woman stood, hands clasped and head down. "Can I talk to you, Miss Spring?" she asked.

I didn't want to talk to anyone, but it was my job, so I invited her in.

I sat back down and pointed to the guest chair near my desk. "How can I help you?"

"I am Mitsuko—Mitsuko Komatsu. You know Romeo?" she said and looked at me.

Romeo Gonzales worked in my photolithography group. That meant he spent his day looking at very small images that were magnified a few hundred times through the viewfinder of an expensive camera, aligning the pattern layers that make up the integrated circuits we manufacture. The typical microprocessor we sold might have as many as forty patterning layers before it was finished. It kept Romeo and his coworkers constantly hustling to catch up to the schedule.

"I need to marry him." She looked at me eagerly.

"What is it you want me to do about this?" I asked.

Production workers have a tendency to expect their managers (or in this case, any manager) to solve every problem in their life, not just their work related issues. As a group, we are well-trained in the art of staying uninvolved. At least, the good managers are. Sometimes, though, you need the distraction. This was one of those times. I didn't plan to get involved, but I was curious. "More important, does Romeo know about this?"

She didn't look like a stalker, but then, no one ever did.

"Yes, he wants to get married, too."

"I guess I'm confused. You want to marry him. He wants to marry you. What's the problem?"

"Can we do that?" she asked.

"How old are you?"

"I am twenty," she said.

"Then there's no problem. You go to the courthouse, pay a few dollars for a license, maybe take a blood test and then pay a judge or a priest to marry you a few days later." I hoped I remembered the sequence right. I had one data point of personal experience, and the ever-controlling Sam had made all the arrangements that time.

"What about my father?" She looked at me round-eyed.

"What about him?" I asked, and then the pieces fell into place. The man Allan had decked before our trip must have been her father.

"My father has planned my marriage since I was a young girl. His business partner has a son. They arranged it many years ago. We will inherit the business, and it will stay in our families forever."

"I take it you don't want to marry the son?"

A look of revulsion took over her face. "He is ..." She was obviously searching her knowledge of English to find the right word. "A geek."

With that indictment, she slumped back in her chair. Worse things could be said about a potential husband. He could be a control freak who had delusions about being a super-spy.

"Your father can't stop you from marrying whomever you want to. He may not like it, and he may disinherit you for it, but he can't stop you. And despite his visit a few days ago, he can't come in here at will. The guards will make sure he can't get in again. We can get Karen to talk to them about it. We can even get the guard to walk you to and from your car, if they need to."

Mitsuko wrapped her arms across her lower abdomen and winced.

Karen, walking up to the door of my cubicle, interrupted before either of us could say anything else. She was wearing a gray wool suit in a shade slightly darker than her hair. She had on a string of Barbara Bush pearls. She looked at Mitsuko, who got up immediately and stepped outside my cube, allowing Karen to come in.

"I'm afraid I have some bad news," she started. "It's about Allan."

"Harold told me he passed away." I said. "I can't believe it. I was there this morning and he seemed fine." A loud sob came from outside my cube. Karen leaned out into the hall.

"I don't know who that was, but they must have overheard."

"I was just talking to Mitsuko Komatsu. She was a little upset. I think she works for Jose. I'd be surprised if she knew Allan. Jeanette usually has all the contact with the production people. Did you talk to the doctor? Did Allan wake up before it happened?"

I knew the answer, but I had to ask.

"No, he didn't. The doctor said they don't know what happened. One minute he was doing better and they were expecting him to wake up and the next he was dead. It's so sad. He apparently doesn't have any family, either. Mr. Iguchi asked me to put together a memorial service for him. I'll see who he listed as his next of kin in his file and check with whoever it is."

Karen sat down in my guest chair and fussed with an imaginary spot on the pocket of her jacket. I waited.

"This trip was supposed to bring us all closer together," she said.

"We've been through this, Karen. People are in shock right now, and it will probably get worse when they hear about Allan. There's nothing you can do about that. Why don't you arrange a memorial service that anyone who wants to can attend and then just try to stay out of the way and let people grieve?" I stood up. "Has anyone told Jeanette yet?"

She shook her head.

"Why don't you let me tell her?" I said. "I'll go get Dave, and he can help me."

"All right," she said and got up to go. I had a brief flash of her, and Stephen groping each other at the lodge. "Let me know how it goes."

Jeanette was composed, all things considered. She assured us she would be okay and said she would send letters to our vendors and let them know what had happened.

Dave and I were on our way to the cafeteria an hour later when Karen came up from behind.

"Harley, can I talk to you alone?"

"Is it about Allan?"

She nodded.

"Dave can hear anything you have to say. I'm going to tell him anyway." Personnel people like to pretend no one ever talks to each other or gossips about anyone. Every now and then, I like to remind Karen about the real world. She glared at Dave, but led us both into a small conference room.

"I looked at Allan's file…" She paused.

"And?" I prompted.

"Well, I told you I was going to look to see who his next of kin is. On his application, he had listed his attorney. I went ahead and looked at his insurance form, assuming it would be the same. Did you know he listed you as his beneficiary?"

CHAPTER 9

THE REMAINDER OF MY DAY was spent in meetings. I hoped we
hadn't decided anything important, because I'd been a million
miles away. Judging by the blank stares on many of the faces in
the meeting room, I wasn't alone.

After our last meeting, Dave and I walked silently out to our
cars and left for home. The rain that had threatened that morning
had come and gone while I was inside the factory. My car was still
wet with raindrops, but the sky was clearing and the sun flashed
between the fast-moving clouds. With the increasing traffic load
on Sunset Highway, it usually took me twice as long to drive
home as it did to go to work in the morning. I listened to audio-
books on my way home. If I didn't, the slow pace of traffic would
have driven me insane years ago.

Today's selection was a self-help book on taking control of
your life. When I pulled into my driveway, I still wasn't sure if Dr.
Stan was telling me to accept that I would always be about twenty
pounds heavier than the weight charts wanted me to be. The flip
side was to accept that I would never be able to eat anything again
but celery. The author suggested that we all know the answer in
our hearts. My heart was at war, and tonight the "let's be fat" side
was winning.

I went into the house and changed into a pair of snug jeans in
the hopes it would help discourage my urge to salve the pain of
Allan's death with more chocolate. When I came out of my bedroom, I found a generous slice of ginger cake on a blue ceramic
plate wrapped in cellophane on the kitchen counter. A note from

Mrs. Johnson indicated it was to be my afterwork snack. A note from Noah was stuck to the cabinet above the cake. "Gone to shoot hoops with Chris," it said. There was no indication of when he'd left or when he would return.

Peace and quiet are rare in my life. I decided to take advantage. I took my cake, grabbed a glass of nonfat milk and had just settled into my overstuffed leather chair in the living room when the doorbell rang. Before I could get up, Frank Green walked in the front door.

"Don't get up on my account," he said. "Any more cake in the kitchen?"

I bit my tongue and reminded myself how much Noah liked this man.

"No," I answered in what I thought was a cheerful tone.

He stopped.

"What? You want me to wait till you come to the door now that you're home again?" he asked. "I just thought you wouldn't want to get up."

"It's fine," I said.

"Something's wrong," he said. "Why don't you tell me about it?"

"Look, I don't mean to be rude, but we aren't suddenly best friends just because you're spending time with Noah."

"Well, excuse me if I'm overstepping my boundaries," he said.

He looked forlorn, but I knew it was an image he cultivated. In his job as a homicide detective on the Portland police force, he had found that if he dressed in worn polyester pants and loud shirts with mismatched ties, people were less threatened and tended to talk more. He had all the downtrodden expressions to go with his outdated wardrobe and could turn in an Academy Award-winning performance when required. According to him, contrary to popular belief, he solved most of his cases by spending countless hours talking to witnesses.

"Don't give me that look," I said. "I'm not one of your witnesses."

He dropped the look. He had gone to the kitchen and gotten a fork while we were talking.

"Mind if I have a bite," he asked and took a fork-full of cake.

"Would it matter if I did?" I said and moved the cake closer to him. "If you're here to see Noah, he's at Chris's playing basketball."

"Actually, I'm here to see you. I heard your friend died. I wanted to see how you're doing."

"Well, now you've seen. I'm fine. I'm drowning my sorrow in cake."

"I knew you needed me to save you from yourself," he said and took another bite of my cake. "I also wanted to tell you it's looking like your friend may have had a little help."

"What do you mean help?" I leaned forward in my chair.

"The doctor's asked the ME to have a look at your friend. He said the hospital did a bunch of tests on your friend, and his heart was strong and healthy. They scanned his head post-mortem, and it looks fine. No clots, no bleeds, nothing but the injury they knew about, and that was healing. He said it's like the guy's heart just stopped beating. For no reason."

I set the plate of cake on the end table next to my chair.

"Don't get excited, but the doctor says he has serious doubts the injury to your friend's head was caused by a widowmaker, either. He said he's seen a good many broken heads in his time, and he thinks a much smaller-diameter object caused this one. His bet is it will turn out someone hit him with a bat or bar or something similar. He said it's unlikely something that small could fall from the tree with enough velocity to create that kind of wound."

"So, what are you saying?"

"I'm *saying* maybe someone hit him in the head. I'm also saying that, if that's true, then maybe his heart didn't just stop beating on its own."

"Murder?" I said. "No one would want Allan dead. Sure, he was opinionated, but he was harmless. I can't believe someone would want him dead."

"It's usually your loved ones that want you dead," he said in a matter-of-fact way. "In the end, it will probably turn out to be an ex-wife with a beef about child support or an adult child who wanted to speed up the inheritance process or something like that."

"You think his ex-wife, if he even had one, would come up to the woods? Or even know about the trip to the woods?"

"I'm not saying anything yet. I'm just saying stranger-to-stranger crimes are rare."

"Karen looked in Allan's personnel file today. He doesn't have any family. He listed his attorney as next of kin."

"The company must have an insurance policy on him. Did she say who his beneficiary is?"

I picked up my cake plate, stuffed a big bite in my mouth and chewed slowly. I was saved from having to share my newly learned status by Noah's arrival.

"What's for dinner?" he asked me and then immediately turned all his attention to Frank. "Did you find out anything?"

"Find out anything about what?" I asked, and looked at Frank.

"As a matter of fact, I did." He hesitated. "Maybe we should talk about this later."

"Oh, no, you don't. There aren't going to be secrets that Harley isn't in on," I said. "I've got to explain whatever it is to Sam when he finds out about it, and you both know he *will* find out about it."

"Fine," Green said. A slow twitch played across his jaw. Noah's eyes got big but he kept his mouth shut. "Noah asked me to look into who his mother is. I got a copy of his birth certificate, and ran the woman through our system. Noah, the woman listed as your mother is a sixty-five-year-old Mexican woman with a record of petty crimes dating back to the early nineteen-fifties. For what it's worth, I doubt she's really your mother."

"How dare you?" I asked through clenched teeth. I turned to Noah. "And you. What do I have to do to get it through your head that your dad can yank you out of here and put you back in that school or some paramilitary camp or who knows where else and there isn't a damn thing I can do about it? You know he's paranoid. It doesn't have to make sense to us. Sam lives in his own reality. Secrets are his stock-in-trade. If he finds out you have Frank trying to help you dig up information about your background, he could take you away and I'd never see you again."

Noah stood up. "I see. It's all about you. You'd never see me again. Maybe that wouldn't be so bad."

Frank looked at him. "You watch your mouth, son."

Noah stormed down the hall and into his room. He shut the door just short of a slam.

"Harley, the kid has a right to know who his mom is," Frank said to me in a soft voice.

"The kid does not have a *right* to know anything. It's unfair that he had to get a paranoid jerk for father, but that's what happened. Sam has complete control of Noah's future until he is at least eighteen, and there's nothing Noah can do about it. I am his legal guardian, but only because Sam lets me be. Noah can do all the digging into his past he wants when he's an adult and no longer under Sam's control. I don't understand what's so hard to understand, for you or Noah."

Green leaned forward with his elbows on his knees. He rubbed his hands over his short brown hair. Finally, he straightened up.

"Can I talk to Noah? Try to make him understand? I don't agree with keeping the kid in the dark, but you're right. Having him yanked out of here and sent who knows where isn't going to help him. I think I can get through to him."

"Words can't express how much I resent your interference," I said. "But Noah isn't going to listen to me right now. If he'll listen to you, fine, as long as he stops digging."

CHAPTER 10

SEVERAL DAYS PASSED, and my life should have eased back into its normal rhythms. I think it would have if Allan's lawyer hadn't called me.

Our conversation was short and to the point. Not only did Allan leave me his company insurance, he'd left me his everything. The attorney would send a copy of the will by messenger for me to read. He set an appointment for the following week for us to go over the details.

Along with the will was a sealed letter addressed to me. I recognized Allan's handwriting. I held the envelope for a moment and then smelled it, but it smelled like paper—not a trace of Allan's Old Spice cologne. I got up and looked to make sure no one was in the aisle outside my cubicle then sat down again. Finally I picked up the small brass replica sword that served as my letter opener and slit the long edge of the envelope.

"Dear Harley," the letter read. "This probably is coming as a surprise to you. If you are reading this, I am dead. I hope you are a gray-haired old lady right now and I slipped away quietly in my bed after a vigorous game of shuffleboard with the boys.

"You probably don't remember the conversation that led to my decision to leave you my estate (such as it is). We were in the cafeteria at Sil-Trac. Karen had given us our beneficiary forms to fill out when the company changed insurance carriers. You said you were leaving your insurance to your stepson Noah in the hopes that he would have choices you never had. It made me think. As an only child, I was given everything. I was able to make choices.

Harley, my parents are dead, and I have no close relatives. The fact that you are reading this letter means I didn't find anyone else to share my life with. Please take whatever I have left and enjoy it. The only thing I ask is, if I still have a cat, take care of it.

"Don't be sad for me. I've enjoyed my life so far and plan to keep on enjoying it for a long time to come."

It was signed "Your friend, Allan."

A tear fell onto the paper.

"Oh, Allan," I said out loud. I squeezed my eyes shut. Strong arms enfolded me. I could smell Dave's blend of laundry soap and cologne. He drew me to my feet and hugged me, patting my back like you would a child's. I cried.

"I know," he whispered. "We all miss him."

I broke free of his embrace.

"It's worse than that," I blubbered.

I handed him the letter. He sat down in my chair as he read.

"Wow," he said, and handed it back.

He might have said more, but my phone rang. It was Karen.

"Harley, I need to see you in the lobby conference room right away. I'll explain when you get here." She hung up.

I stared at the silent receiver.

"Karen wants to see me right away out front."

"You want me to tag along?" Dave asked. The choice of the front conference room indicated an outside visitor was involved, usually a salesperson. The conference room allowed us to do interviews and vendor cold calls without having to bring the visitor through the security procedure. I glanced at my schedule. I didn't have any notes indicating anyone was coming in.

"No, thanks, it's probably just Paul." Paul Eberhart was a salesman who refused to believe that Jeanette really did pass out the new product brochures he gave her. He insisted on speaking to each of us supervisors on a regular basis, and I was due for a turn. If it weren't for the fact that he gave Jeanette a really good price on an expensive style of wafer tweezers my people liked, I would refuse to see him.

Paul was definitely the last person I wanted to talk to today, but I knew from past experience that once he was here he wouldn't leave until someone saw him. If I didn't go, he'd start paging all the supervisors in turn. It was best to just get it over with.

I took the stairs to the ground floor.

The lobby has dark carpeting and walls. Samples of our chips are cleverly suspended from wire in glass display cases. The cases are lit from below, giving the space a museum-like quality. In reality, much like a museum, the cases are wired to the security system. If anyone tried to remove one of the chips, the National Guard would arrive in a matter of moments. Or so they told us.

The voices coming from the open door of the conference room were familiar. As I approached, Detective Harper came out and stepped toward me. Her lime-green linen suit looked freshly pressed. The left lapel of her jacket sported a small branch of flowers embroidered in white silk, suggesting she'd bought it someplace considerably more expensive than JC Penney. Her low-heeled pumps were dyed to match. Her abundance of fine black braids was pulled back into a neat bun at the nape of her neck. She was not smiling.

Detective Green followed her.

"Give us a minute?" he said, and waited for her approval. She nodded once and went back into the room.

Green was not dressed in his usual ill-fitting polyester pants and outdated shirt. He was wearing a charcoal gray wool suit that might have been custom tailored. His maroon tie matched the width of his lapels and his socks were patterned and dark gray. He looked forty pounds thinner. He stared at me; his gray eyes fixed on my red-rimmed green ones.

"We've got about two minutes," he said. "Start talking, and don't leave anything out."

I was unable to form words for a moment.

"What are you talking about?" I finally said. "And what is she doing here?"

"She's here to arrest you, unless you've got a really good story. Why don't you start with your relationship with the victim?"

"I told you already, at my house." I looked at him, and sat down in one of the chrome-and-foam contraptions that pass for chairs in the lobby.

"You told me you work with the guy. Harley, people you work with leave you their coffee cups or their paper clips. They don't leave you their whole estate. Come on, talk to me."

My shock at the idea of being arrested was quickly displaced by anger.

"How dare you accuse me of lying? I told you everything." I stood up, brushed past him and went into the conference room. "Detective Harper," I said. "I understand you want to talk to me."

"Sit down," she ordered. "I would like to ask you a few questions. You're not under arrest. However, I think you should know it is your right to have an attorney present when you are questioned."

"I don't need an attorney," I said. "I haven't done anything."

To her credit, Detective Harper didn't roll her eyes to the ceiling. You could feel the restraint radiating from her.

I realized I was still clutching the copy of Allan's letter. I thrust the tear-dampened page at her. Green came into the room and closed the door. When Harper finished reading, she passed the letter to him.

"All this tells us is that you didn't know about Allan's plan when he wrote this letter..." Green glanced at the top of the letter. "...three years ago."

"Talk to his attorney, he'll tell you. I just found out about this. He'll confirm it." I could hear my voice rising. Green took me by the arm and aimed me at a chair

"Sit down." He thrust me into the chair. If someone told me to sit one more time, I was going to grow a tail and bark. "We'll talk to his attorney, but that only proves you didn't know about that letter. It doesn't prove Allan hadn't told you about his intentions sometime after he wrote the letter."

"I didn't know," I insisted. Even I could hear how lame I sounded. I sat back in the chair. "Now what? Do you read me my rights? Maybe I should call my attorney. What?"

"You are *not* under arrest," Detective Harper repeated. "We're still gathering information."

"Are you questioning anyone else?" I asked.

"I'm afraid that's none of your business."

She made me recite my finding of Allan in the woods three more times. I had nothing new to add. Nothing else had happened.

"Now tell me about the morning he died," she said.

"What are you talking about?" My face felt hot.

"You were the last person to see the victim before he died."

"Allan was fine when I left."

"Unfortunately, no one saw you leave," Green said.

"I went down the stairs. I always went down the stairs."

"Did you see anyone on the stairs?" Harper asked.

I shook my head.

"So, no one knows when you left and no one else came after you."

"I'm confused," I said. "Have they figured out how Allan died?" I looked from Green to Harper and back again.

"Yeah, they figured it out," Green said.

"Someone put potassium chloride in his IV. It stopped his heart." Harper snapped her fingers. "Just like that."

"They figure it happened about six-forty—his monitor started going off then. By the time they got to his room he was gone," Green added.

"I left around six-thirty. I went to the Starbucks in Hillsdale."

"Did anyone see you?" Green asked.

"Lots of people. There was a line out the door."

He pulled a small spiral notebook out of his coat pocket and made a note. "I'll check it out."

"I think we're through for now," Harper said as she rose and looked at Green.

"I'll meet you back at the shop," he said. Harper didn't say anything, but I could tell she didn't approve of his decision. She picked up her purse and notebook and left.

"Harley, this is serious," he said when she was gone. "So far, you were with this guy when he was found with his head bashed in, you were the last one to visit before his IV was injected with a lethal dose of potassium and you inherit his estate, which is not small. To a cop, that looks like motive and opportunity."

"How can you say that? I know I keep saying we aren't friends, but surely you know that I'd never take someone's life. I couldn't," I finished lamely.

"I'm hurt. I've slept over at your house, and you don't even think we're friends?" His attempt at humor didn't help. That he'd stayed at my place earlier in the year was not by my choice and I'd spent the time since then trying to forget.

"I don't even know what I've inherited. Karen says he had company insurance, but beyond that I don't know anything. He could have a bunch of debts that would use up the insurance money." I looked at Green, as if he could say something, anything, to make it all go away.

"For the record, I don't think you killed anyone. Judging by where you live, you probably don't overspend your annual salary. So, we can rule out greed." He looked at me and stopped. Even he could see these weren't the words of comfort I needed. "Maybe now *would* be a good time to call your lawyer," he said. "Can I walk you back to your office? Maybe buy you a cup of coffee?"

"Thanks, but I think you've helped enough."

He put the small notepad he'd been holding back into his coat pocket. He fiddled with his pen cap and finally put it in the same pocket. I knew I'd hurt his feelings, but I didn't care. This wasn't about him.

He started to leave then turned back.

"I'm not the enemy here. I don't think you did this, but so far I'm the only one in your camp. Harper and I are going to continue our investigation. It would help us a lot if you would cooperate. Tell us what you know."

I stared at him as he walked away. Tell him what? What did they think I knew?

As for calling my lawyer, he hadn't even been able to keep my wiener dog out of the slammer when Sonny bit a stranger. Two neighbor children who were desperate for a dog had kidnapped him. They thought all dogs were friendly. Sonny taught them what it was like to own a spoiled, ill-tempered pet. He had then bitten a man when they took him out for a walk and he tried to escape and come home. I thought the dog had a good case for mitigating circumstances. The county didn't see it that way, despite my lawyer's arguments. They said broken skin meant quarantine, no exceptions.

Given that, I didn't hold out much hope for my own case.

CHAPTER 11

THE BUILDING ALARM SOUNDED just before I reached my cubicle. Being an evacuation veteran, I went on to my desk and got my car keys, purse and coat. Jose was in the cubicle across the aisle doing the same thing minus the purse.

"Any word on what's happening?" I asked him.

"Yeah, I heard Jim say a workman kicked a hydrogen line loose in the mezzanine. I guess they were putting new labels on all the gas lines. He panicked and pulled the alarm. The line spewed for probably five or ten minutes before anyone got the main valve shut off."

"I wouldn't want to be in the facilities department when Mr. Iguchi goes looking for whoever let workers up in the mezzanine without an escort." I said. Jose and I joined an assortment of people at the staircase, some in white cleanroom bunnysuits, and some in business suits, flowing down and out the doors and on to our assigned gathering points around the parking lots.

The process of fabricating memory chips or integrated circuits, the main product of Sil-Trac, involves the use of a number of poisonous, flammable and/or explosive gasses and several equally dangerous acids and solvents. To accommodate these materials, and the required filter and drainage systems to support them, each of the three stories of manufacturing space in our building has an equally large floor above it. These mezzanine levels are a network of pipes, tanks and filter units of various sorts. Unauthorized access is strictly forbidden, and even workmen are not supposed to be allowed in without an escort from our facilities department. The company escort is intended to be someone who knows how to reconnect gas lines or restart filters or generally undo anything the untrained contract worker might do accidentally while trying to carry out a more mundane task like labeling.

Unfortunately, the facilities workers found this task boring, and sometimes sneaked away for a cigarette break. They did not comprehend the expense involved in an evacuation.

The clean rooms are kept clean by large air-processing systems that circulate the air downward and then suck it through giant HEPA filters. The air pressure is kept positive, which means there is more pressure inside the room than in the surrounding hallways and entrance chambers; so, if a door is opened, particles will flow outward and nothing will come in.

All this assumes the door will not be open for an extended period of time. In the case of an evacuation, all systems could be cut off and all doors opened. Today's crisis involved hydrogen, a colorless gas that was extremely explosive. All power would be cut off to avoid an errant spark blowing up the building. Although there probably wasn't a high enough concentration to do that today, you could never be sure.

With all the air-processing systems off, our clean rooms would be full of particles of dust or lint. Even though they would be too small for us to see, we still had to assume they were there. For the next three shifts, we would have to suspend production and spend precious time wiping everything in the room with alcohol. Then we would have to test the air until we could demonstrate it was back to an acceptable level of cleanliness.

Sil-Trac's state-of-the-art memory chips can take as much as four months of continuous twenty-four-hour-a-day, seven-day-a-week processing to fabricate. A single particle at the wrong time can ruin a chip. Now, every chip in the clean room was at risk. With luck, we wouldn't lose too much time, but even the three shifts were going to kill us. The ship schedule for my department already needed this month to have thirty-four days.

My group was in the appointed waiting area at the north end of the parking lot. Romeo had taken roll call and assured me all our members were accounted for.

"Now that we're counted, you can go to your cars or over to the Blue Whale until they let us back in. I'll call over and have Skip announce when we're back in," I told them.

58

The Blue Whale was a pub across the street from Sil-Trac, established as soon as the company had broken ground for the factory. Since Sil-Trac was otherwise in the middle of farmland, the Whale was the only food-and-drink establishment within a mile. This status allowed it to serve second-rate food at inflated prices and still have a full house at meal times.

Skip was the Whale's head bartender. He saw himself as something of a gourmet chef, spending his spare time creating new sandwich combinations out of prefabricated chicken patties and chemically embalmed veggies. With its broken-down pool tables and torn-up dartboards, the Whale still gave people the illusion of being away from work. No one in their right mind would go there as a destination of choice, but it was what we had, and most of my group headed across the street.

Skip had folding chairs in the back room to accommodate the crowd on just such occasions. I could see him through the window, setting them up. He had probably started when the alarm went off. Sil-Trac evacuated an average of two to three times a year, so the Whale had perfected the drill over the years.

My car wasn't far from our meeting point, so I decided to wait there and avoid the crush at the Whale. Skip dutifully sorted people into groups by smoking preference, but when you got that many people in that size space, the smoke drifted.

I was just opening the driver's-side door when Romeo came up to my car.

"Can I talk to you a minute?" he asked.

"Sure," I said. "Just let me put my things in the car here." I put my purse and planner in the back seat and pulled out my coat, which I threw over my shoulders. "How can I help you?"

"I know Mitsuko talked to you," he started. "I guess I want to ask about the same thing."

"Mitsuko probably told you what I said. She's over eighteen years old, so I don't think her dad can stop you from marrying her. If you wait however many months it takes for her to turn twenty-one, she'll be completely free of any parental control."

He stared at the ground. "We don't have a few months."

"I see," I said, finally getting the picture. "I don't know what else to tell you. You've obviously made some major choices without Dad being involved. I think it's a little late to start worrying about him now."

"It's hard to figure out," Romeo said, finally looking up at me. "Family and tradition is everything to Mitsuko. But I don't want her baby born without a name. It deserves a father. And then there's my family. My parents grew up working in the fields. They're saving all their money so I can graduate from the university. I'm the first one in my family to even graduate high school. They'll be crushed if I don't start this fall."

"Seems like you and Mitsuko should have thought of that before you decided to throw caution to the wind."

His dark eyes bored into mine. "Of course, you would see it that way."

He turned his back on me and walked slowly over to the Blue Whale. With all the education kids receive in school and the easy access everyone has to multiple forms of birth control, I continue to be amazed by the number of unplanned pregnancies that occur. We have several "surprise" babies each year at Sil-Trac.

And it's not just the young people. We've had more than one change-of-life baby born to women who decide to sow their oats after their husbands of twenty-plus years have left them for younger women. The Sil-Trac health nurse puts out literature and even offers personal counseling but it doesn't seem to change anything.

I still couldn't agree with Mr. Komatsu's desire to kill Romeo, but I was beginning to understand it.

CHAPTER 12

WE WERE ALLOWED BACK in the building just in time for the shift change. Day shift went home, and the night shift people were left with the task of starting the cleanup and recovery. Fortunately, we only lost a small lot of wafers that got left in an acid-etch process one of my newer workers had been doing manually — my more experienced workers stabilized whatever they were working on before they left the clean room during evacuations. They were more afraid of the aftermath of the evacuation than they were of any real danger of the building blowing up or catching on fire. People who work with dangerous materials on a daily basis are like that.

Noah was eating dinner with his friend Chris, so I stayed for a few extra hours and helped with the cleanup. I thought for a fleeting moment about going home and soaking in a hot tub with a good book. Reality set in as I remembered Allan's letter and his request that I take care of whatever cat he had. I didn't have a key to the house yet, but with luck, it would be an outdoor cat. I seemed to remember him saying something about his cat not getting along with his neighbor's, which implied it was an outdoor pet.

Allan's house was in southwest Portland, in a community called Multnomah Village. The houses were older, but were on larger lots than similar homes in my neighborhood. The area was hilly and wooded. Allan's house was at the end of an unpaved street. I had been there once or twice when we were working on projects or budgets and once for a summer barbecue. His back yard was shaded, and had that damp feel you get when you're deep in the woods. It had smelled of pine trees and earth. The scent in my yard varies between boiled cabbage and fabric softener sheets, depending on what my neighbors on either side of me are doing.

I liked Allan's yard.

I pulled into the driveway. His car wasn't there—I made a mental note to look for it in the Sil-Trac parking lot. One more new responsibility I'd acquired. The cat wasn't in sight. I walked up the three steps of the front porch to get a better look. There was a small ceramic frog in the windowbox to the left of the front door. I recognized it from a display I'd seen at the garden store. I picked it up and turned it over. With a deft twist, it separated into two halves, one of which held a shiny brass key.

"Thank you, Allan," I said.

The key opened the door with only a little jiggling of the lock—it had probably never been used. I left the door ajar and went inside. I called for the cat. I heard a thump, as if a heavy object had hit the floor, followed by a large orange blob flying down the staircase in front of me. The cat immediately started crying for food.

I went around the staircase to the kitchen at the back of the house. A can opener was on the counter. I opened cupboards until I found several cans of kitty food and a bag of dry kibble. The cat's dishes were on a placemat printed with kitty images in pale blues and green that matched the color of the kitchen curtains.

There were still crumbs of dry cat food in the dish. I couldn't believe this obviously healthy eater had left food untouched. Yet there it was. I put some fresh kibble in the bowl. The orange blob sniffed at it and began circling my legs meowing. Obviously, he or she was not starving.

I opened a can of kitty tuna and put it in a dish I took out of the cupboard. The cat attacked the dish before it even reached the floor. I rinsed the can and watched the cat eat for a few minutes, then explored the kitchen.

A door with a glass pane in the top half led to the outside. It had a kitty door in the bottom panel. I could envision Chubby going out and raiding neighborhood cat dishes. Another, solid door formed a corner with the first door and was closed. I guessed it went to a basement space of some type.

I returned to the cat's mat and picked up a pink ceramic dish with "water" written on its side. All that tuna had to have made him thirsty. My own cat Cher refused to drink water out of a dish. She had to have fresh water in a cup she could dip her paw in, or have a sink faucet turned on to just the right flow so she could lick it.

I filled up the water dish. As I set it down, I thought I heard another thump. I stood up and listened. The house was silent. I moved to the closed door and opened it on a pitch-black space. A quick grope of the wall to the right of the door revealed the light switch. I know I flipped the switch, but that's the last thing I remember.

Chapter 13

A SHARP PAIN IN MY LEFT wrist brought me back to consciousness. I was lying at the foot of a steep flight of stairs. The dim light bulb at the top revealed I was in a basement, but I could have identified it with my eyes shut by the damp musty smell it had in common with all older basements. It had the usual array of discarded or seldom-used items.

Allan had two bicycles—one mountain and one road. He had an odd number of snow skis, one with a broken tip and two singles that didn't seem to match any others. There was a rack with clothes on hangers under a clear plastic cover; what looked like a powder-blue leisure suit was lodged near the midpoint of the rack. Assorted cardboard storage boxes were stacked against the wall. A washer and dryer took up one corner.

I turned back to the stairs and used the handrail to stand up. My head throbbed, and a quick inventory of my body parts revealed an ugly blue knot forming on the side of my right ankle. The door was shut. I crawled to the top of the stairs and tried it anyway. It wouldn't budge. I could hear the faint ringing of my cell phone from the confines of my purse, which was on the counter where I had set it when I fed the cat. I glanced at my watch. It was probably Noah. He was good about checking in and letting me know where he was and what he was doing. It was one of the few glimmers of maturity that shone through the anger and attitude that had so far marred his early teen years.

I descended the steps, slowly this time. A circuit of the basement revealed two small windows sealed by metal bars. A wooden door was padlocked shut with a metal hasp in addition to the lock in the doorknob. There was a trapdoor above the laundry corner that might be a laundry chute. It was shut from above. It was doubtful I could fit myself through it even if I could figure out how to reach it.

Careful inspection revealed a chest freezer under the stairs. I opened the lid and pawed through the packages. Frozen meat, veges, two loaves of bread and a box of Popsicles. At least I wouldn't starve to death immediately.

I put on a ratty coat Allan must have worn when he worked outside. There was a large grass stain on one arm. It smelled like gasoline. I took a grape Popsicle from the freezer and sat down to ponder my situation. Noah would call Detective Green when I didn't show up. He would start looking for me eventually. But would he ever think to look at Allan's?

Further rummaging turned up a discarded boom box with a broken CD changer, and an airhorn like people use on sailboats or at sporting events. I tried to figure out where the windows were with respect to the other houses. If I was right, the window to the right of the stairs was on the side of Allan's house that was closest to a neighbor. I rearranged the stack of boxes so I could climb to the window. A broken ski pole proved small enough to fit between the metal bars and strong enough to break the window glass. Next, I blasted the air horn in what I thought sounded like the international distress call—I can never remember if it's two sets of long blasts with one set of short in the middle or the opposite. I propped the boom box on a box close to the window and plugged it in. I selected a rock station and cranked the volume as loud as it would go.

My hope was that the neighbors were nosy enough to know Allan had died—or at least wasn't at home. The noise eventually should cause them to call the police. I only hoped it was sooner rather than later.

An hour passed. It didn't seem possible that the Allan I knew played loud music at night to the point the neighbors were used to it. There was always the possibility the neighboring house was vacant, but I hadn't noticed a for-sale sign when I arrived.

Allan had a small workbench buried under a pile of tangled wire and small metal boxes of the sort electricians use to shield switches. A project he would never finish. I found a wooden-handled claw hammer and a Phillips screwdriver. Maybe I could get the hinges off the door and open it.

The steep narrow stairs I would have to balance on complicated my plan. I had just positioned myself on the top stair when I heard a muffled pounding. A moment later I heard a voice call, "Harley?"

"Noah, I'm locked in the basement," I yelled.

"Stand back," he replied, and I went down a couple of stairs. The door opened with a boom—he had kicked it open. I came up the stairs and out into the kitchen. Without thinking, I grabbed him and hugged him. He hugged me back.

"You look a sight," said a voice behind him.

"Neva Dean, what are you doing here?" I asked the short white-haired woman standing in the kitchen. Neva Dean Willett was the neighbor of the employee of mine who had been murdered earlier in the year. We'd met and become friends, of sorts. Neva Dean was a self-professed "Angelologist." She sees the angels that watch over people and seems to think she receives communications from them. She says she gained this skill when her first child died as an infant. I have no reason to doubt her.

"The angels were all a-twitter tonight, and then I saw one of your group who was particularly distressed," she explained. "I called your home just to make sure you were all right. Noah told me you were missing. Since you weren't supposed to be anywhere, we put our heads together and figured out you might have come here."

"I know you're kinda upset about getting this guy's stuff," Noah said. "I just thought you mighta come here to see what he left you."

Noah never ceased to amaze me. Just about the time I was convinced what he wants most is to see me drop off the face of the planet, he does something sweet, like rescue me.

"How did you two get here?" I knew Neva Dean didn't drive anymore.

"We took a cab," she explained. "My son gives me prepaid taxi coupons so I don't have to ride the bus if I go someplace in the evening."

"How did you know how to break a door down, young man?" I asked. "Is that what you're learning in military school?"

"Hello—television," he replied.

"Well, I'm glad you're observant. I need to turn off the radio downstairs, and then if you two will help me catch the cat and put him in a box or something, we can be on our way."

I didn't ask why Noah had chosen this time to not call his buddy Detective Green, but I was glad he hadn't. I couldn't prove I'd been pushed down the stairs and locked in, and until I could I didn't want Green nosing around, scaring off whoever had done it.

"I'm going to take a quick look upstairs," I said.

I used the white-painted bannister to help take pressure off my ankle as I climbed to the second floor. The light on the landing showed two open doors with beds in view, a tiled bathroom and a fourth room with the door pulled shut. I went to that room, opened the door and turned on the light.

It must have once been Allan's office. It had also been the target of my attacker. Files were scattered all over the floor. Drawers hung open, and the wastebasket had been dumped on top of the files. Two matched small upholstered chairs were tipped over, their cushions on the floor. Someone had made real sure they found whatever they were looking for.

"Harley, we have the cat. Are you coming?" Noah hollered up the stairs.

"Be right there." I would come back tomorrow and investigate more—I wasn't ready for Noah to see the mess and tell Green about it. I made a mental note to call a locksmith tomorrow to change the locks.

On the desk, a picture calendar with twelve months'-worth of Siamese cat pictures caught my eye. I picked it up and took it with me without looking at it.

We drove Neva Dean back to her apartment in southeast Portland. I walked her to the door, leaving Noah in the back seat with the yowling cat.

"Honey, you be careful," she said. "Your angels are settling down, but they're not acting like the trouble is over. Why don't you invite that police fella over and tell him what happened tonight?"

"I appreciate your concern, but I'm not sure anything really did happen. All I know is, I ended up at the bottom of the stairs with a sprained ankle and the door locked. The last thing I remember is reaching for the light switch. Maybe I just fell down the stairs, and the door shut behind me. I've locked myself out of the house like that before—you know, the button on the knob is twisted to the lock position, and the wind blows the door shut." I didn't believe my story and besides I'd been locked in with a key, but I wasn't ready to involve Green in this. Who knew how he'd twist this around, and I was already suspect number one.

"You just be careful, young lady," she scolded. "Mark my words, this isn't over yet."

CHAPTER 14

NOAH AND I DROVE home with our new cat. I tried out my "fell down the stairs" story on Noah. He wasn't impressed. Fortunately, he didn't see angels or any other thing that might allow him to voice his doubts.

The attic of my house has been finished off into a large multipurpose room. We have a futon for overnight guests and several worktables designed for various types of projects. My sewing basket was beside the futon. I had Noah take the new cat up there. Cher rules the main floor of our house, abetted by Sonny. I decided a gradual introduction would be best.

A long soak in a lavender-scented tub diminished the aches and pains I'd acquired during my inadvertent trip to Allan's basement. Noah was in his room with the music cranked up, so it seemed like a good time to look over Allan's calendar. I propped my bad ankle up on the navy blue ottoman that matched the two easy chairs in my living room. I started with January.

Allan faithfully noted his semiannual tooth cleaning, his oil changes for his car and when the guy came to spray his fruit trees. In March, he had apparently had friends from out of town visit for a few days. There was a flurry of activity involving house cleaners and various fix-it type people. I made a mental note to see if I could find out who Ken and Susan were, and where they lived. It wasn't much, but I was grasping.

Nothing else noteworthy happened until the week before our outing. Allan had taken the cat for his vaccinations and then to the kitty hotel. I read on. Two days after Allan died, the calendar read, "Pick up Cyrus at Purr Tender Lodge,"

"Noah," I yelled. He didn't answer, but I was already halfway to his room. "Noah," I yelled again, this time turning the volume down on his stereo boom box as I said it.

"What's wrong?"

"We've got the wrong cat. I was reading Allan's calendar. It says 'Pick up Cyrus at the kitty hotel.' He obviously didn't make that date, and I don't know who else would have. Go catch who-ever that cat is and let's take him back before someone misses him."

He ran upstairs, and I called the number in the phone book for Purr Tender Lodge, but no one answered. I would have to look for a card in Allan's office. There was probably an after-hours number people could use to check up on their pets.

Noah captured the big orange cat in a box and put it in the back seat of the car. I still had the key I'd found on my first trip. Noah grilled me on the ride to Allan's about how I could have the wrong cat. I didn't have a good explanation. He was right. It was careless of me to assume Allan's cat was the only one who would know how to use the kitty door to get in and out. I just thought cats marked their territory or something.

Allan's house looked cozy when we pulled into the driveway. The porch light cast a yellow glow on the boxwood shrubs on either side of the sidewalk. I could almost see Allan coming to the door as we climbed the steps onto the porch.

"Harley," Noah asked. "Did you turn on the porch light when we left earlier?"

"No. Why?"

"I don't mean to be creepy, but I don't think it was on when we left. It was just starting to get dark, and I remember it was kinda hard to see the steps."

"Well, maybe it's on a timer or something," I said and un-locked the front door.

"He'd have to have a pretty good system to run the lights that are hardwired in," he said.

"What are you trying to say?"

"It's just kind of weird being in some dead guy's house at night. Specially since someone pushed you down the stairs a while ago."

"Do you want to wait in the car?"

"No," he said in that tone of voice like I'd just insulted him. "I just think maybe we should tell Green about today."

"We can't tell him, because right now, he's the enemy. Because Allan gave us this house and some insurance money, it makes me their number-one suspect in his murder."

"Yeah, but Green doesn't think you did it, does he?"

"No, but he's an officer of the law. Anything he sees or hears can be used against me in court."

"He wouldn't do that," Noah said.

"Yeah, well, I'm not so sure he'd have a choice. Let's let the cat out in the back yard, and then I'm going up to Allan's office to look for a phone number for the pet hotel."

Noah stayed close to me. I was still thinking of how I was going to get him back downstairs when I cracked the door to Allan's trashed office open, blocking Noah's view with my body. My fingers turned to ice on the doorknob. I stopped.

"Harley, what's wrong?" he asked.

"Not a thing," I said and opened the door wide, exposing Allan's now-tidy office.

The entire mess had been cleaned up. The file drawers were in place; the chairs were upright with their cushions in place. It was as if my previous visit had been a bad dream. I tried to keep my face neutral as I crossed to the desk. I couldn't feel my feet.

I sat in the green leather chair that was now pulled up to the center of the desk. I pulled open the file drawer to the left of the chair and located a file with the name Cyrus on it. Allan had been a fanatic about his cats. Cyrus's pedigree was next to a written physical description of him when he was a kitten. He was apparently an Abyssinian. In addition, there were 12-by-12-inch sheets that looked like they went into a photo album. Each page had a year in stick-on letters along the top and a series of cat pictures mounted with construction paper matting in various colors. I presumed these would go into an album when Cyrus passed on. I was thankful Noah had come into my life so I didn't have to resort to making pet scrapbooks to fill the family void.

A quick scan of Allan's Rolodex produced a card for the Purr Tender Lodge, complete with night number. I took a quick look at the remaining files but nothing seemed interesting. I would have to find a way to look at his work files, too. Maybe it would turn up an employee who'd gotten a bad review, or a vendor who'd been dropped.

An additional search produced a tattered address book, held together with two large rubber bands. I would look for Ken and Susan in it later. I agreed with Noah—things were creepy here.

We were in the car, backing out of the driveway, when I noticed the door to Allan's mailbox wasn't quite closed. I stopped and had Noah retrieve the small pile of mail inside. I also made a mental note to try to find out if a neighbor had taken in the mail while Allan was up in the woods. Whatever arrangement had been made, it had obviously ended when Allan was expected back.

A quick survey of the mail revealed a power bill, an envelope full of coupons, a renewal notice from *Time* magazine and a plain white envelope addressed in blue ink. The return name was K. Higgins. I ripped it open. A check fluttered into my lap. The brief note it had been wrapped in read, "Sorry, this is all I could scrape together this month."

I looked at the check. It was made out for three hundred dollars. The signature was for Ken Higgins. I definitely had to find out who Ken was and why he was sending Allan money.

CHAPTER 15

THE NEXT MORNING at Sil-Trac was ugly. Our sales rep in California discovered one of our customers had booked orders with both our competitor, MiCorp, and us. Whoever delivered first got the three million in orders. The other company got a big cancellation.

We were now five days behind thanks to our evacuation. We were working at full capacity, and our plan for adding manufacturing space wouldn't be carried out for another six months. That left us with the uncomfortable task of juggling orders in process. The only way we could expedite one was to delay someone else. Any way you looked at it, we were going to have an unhappy customer.

The scheduling meeting broke up just after noon. I went by Allan's area in the hopes his crew would be out to lunch and I could paw through his files with abandon. Jeanette was sitting at her desk, a telephone headset firmly attached to her head. She was picking at a piece of whole grain bread on her desk with one hand and writing notes with the other, all the while listening and making the occasional *uh-huh* in response to her caller. The call ended with her saying "Okay, will do," and punching a button.

"Harley, how can I help you?" she asked.

I didn't know what to say for a minute. I decided on the truth.

"I was hoping to have a peek at Allan's files."

"I can tell you everything you need to know about your accounts," she said. "I could save you some time."

"I'm not really sure what I'm looking for."

Jeanette looked at me, waiting for me to say more. She was probably hoping for a more compelling reason to let a manufacturing supervisor dig through purchasing records.

"Allan and I were talking about developing a new source for clean room paper," I said. I could tell she didn't believe me. She and I both knew I would have had that conversation with her, not Allan, but she had no grounds to challenge my authority.

"The keys to the files are in his top drawer, in the paperclip box," she said.

I thanked her, retrieved the key and opened the files. She watched me as I began looking through them, one by one. It quickly became clear the ones in the cabinets were created and maintained by Jeanette. Allan's distinctive signature was here and there when approvals were needed, but Jeanette's neat handwriting recorded the everyday transactions on a log sheet at the front of each file.

Every vendor we bought parts from had a file. The folders weren't thick, as most transactions took place via computer. They contained signed contracts, packing slips from problem deliveries and other similar paperwork. Nothing in them indicated why someone would want to bash Allan in the head. I went through each one anyway.

When I got to Z-Drive, Inc., I found another small group of files in red folders, neatly alphabetized. They seemed to contain the same type of information the others had.

"What are these?" I asked Jeanette.

She looked up from her work.

"The red ones? We do government contracts, so we're required to use women- and minority-owned vendors for ten percent of the work. I have to track their business to make sure we maintain the minimum required."

"Is it easy to find minority vendors?"

"It depends on what kind of business they are," she said. "Sometimes, we pay obscene amounts for goods and services just to satisfy the government. Luckily, it's a small percent of our overall spending—the ten-percent requirement is only applied to total government contracts. It's a drop in the bucket compared to our overall business."

"It doesn't seem like a fair way to solve the problem," I said.

"Yeah, but what are you going to do? The white American males in business have plenty of advantages, if you ask me. Think about it, Harley. Even in our company, how many female supervisors do you see? Where are your peers?"

"Yeah, I know, but the male supervisors aren't losing money because of my job."

"Take it up with your congressman," she said. "Do you need anything else?"

"No, thanks, Jeanette."

The files had yielded nothing. I put the keys back in the paperclip box. Next to the file key was one marked "spare/desk" on the white paper disc it was attached to. I pocketed the key and shut the drawer. I didn't plan on rifling Allan's desk under Jeanette's watchful eye. That could be done later, after hours.

When I returned to my desk, I called the Purr Tender Lodge and arranged Cyrus to stay another week. I wanted Cher to have a chance to recover from the orange cat before she had to face another interloper.

The rest of the afternoon was spent working with my lead operators trying out different schemes on paper to see if using overtime could buy us anything. Our manufacturing labs were already running round-the-clock shifts. With so much of our process being machine-dependent, it didn't always help to throw more labor into an area. The people just fought over equipment and stepped on each other, literally. We did figure out a few places where tests and inspection slowed us down, and David, my new lead technician, was pretty sure he could rig up a second test station from borrowed parts. It wasn't much, but at this point, anything was better than nothing.

My desk was a mess when I returned to it, but I had bigger problems. Someone had killed Allan, and despite what I'd told Noah, someone had pushed me down the cellar stairs at Allan's house. I decided to pay Allan's lawyer a visit. If there was someone who thought they were going to inherit when Allan died, he might know. I called him. His secretary didn't want to let me talk to him, but my having honed my persuasive skills badgering vendors to deliver shortage parts and coaxing stuck parts out of unwilling customs officers, she was really no competition. He agreed to see me in an hour.

I went across the street to the Blue Whale. With its red-flocked wallpaper and smoky interior, it has a Texas whorehouse feel to it. The place had to be raking in money, but you couldn't tell it from the heavily scratched bar and cracked plastic seat covers in the booths. I'd asked Skip who the owner was and why he didn't keep the place up better, but he said if he told me he'd have to kill me. I wasn't amused.

"Hi, Skip," I said as he brought me a Diet Coke without being asked. He wore white jeans and a white T-shirt. During the lunch hour, he covered his balding blond head with a white chef's hat. His thin sinewy body made it hard to judge his age. I used to think late twenties; now I was leaning more towards late thirties.

"That was awful what happened to Allan, huh?" he said.

"Yeah, it was really sad. Did you and him talk much when he came here?"

"Sure, we talked. Mostly just tennis, though."

"Tennis," I said, trying unsuccessfully to keep my voice neutral.

"Yeah, he really helped me with my game. We used to play on Wednesdays over to the rec center, when he didn't have to work late."

I was stunned into silence. I wasn't sure if I was more shocked that Allan played tennis without me knowing about it, or that Skip played tennis at all. I wondered how much else I didn't know about the man I had seen nearly every day for the last five years.

"Do you know anyone who might have wanted him dead?" I asked when I had regained the capacity of speech.

"Nah," Skip replied. "Everyone liked the guy, near as I can tell. He wasn't like you production supes—he didn't write nasty reviews that pissed people off like you do."

"Thanks a lot, Skip,"

"You know what I mean, Harley."

"I guess." I finished my soda and got up. "Keep an ear to the ground and if you hear anything let me know, okay?"

"Sure thing, boss."

CHAPTER 16

I LEFT THE WHALE and drove into Portland. Allan's lawyer had a small office on the edge of downtown. It had been a house once. His secretary sat in what had been the living room. The adjacent sitting area was furnished with antique furniture—the kind with a lot of carved wood and very little padding. Not the kind of place you wanted to sit for very long. Mr. Thomas Bates, Esq., did not keep me waiting.

"Miss Spring," he said, and stretched his hand out to shake mine. "Come in and tell me how I can help you." He indicated I should precede him into his office, a former bedroom.

I had intended to ask him if there was anyone else he knew of who might have thought they should have inherited. I did end up asking him that, but not before I'd spilled my guts about being pushed down the stairs.

"Have you told the police?" he asked.

"I didn't really feel like I had anything to tell. I didn't see anyone, and the stairs are steep enough that I could have simply fallen."

"But you don't think so?" he asked.

"Well, if I overbalanced or tripped or anything like that, I sure don't remember it."

"Were you knocked out?"

"Yeah, that's the problem. I don't think I was out long, but one minute I was reaching for the light switch and the next I was on the floor at the bottom of the stairs."

"You're right, it's not much for the police to work with. I still think you should let them know, though. So, you were hoping there was someone who might be angry about you being named the heir, and willing to kill you for it?"

It did sound foolish now that he said it.

"I guess I'm grasping at straws."

"Unfortunately, there was no one else close to Allan." He paused, and chewed on the corner of his lip.

"What? Did you think of someone?"

"Not exactly," he said. "It's probably nothing, but Allan called and asked me some questions about how you establish paternity when you aren't married and aren't sure you're the only candidate. It was a week or so ago. I assumed one of his workers had gotten into a situation. He used to call me with questions like that every now and then. It's probably nothing."

"I didn't think he'd been seeing anyone lately," I said. Of course, I hadn't known he played tennis with Skip, either.

"He hasn't mentioned anyone to me since that schoolteacher he was seeing ran off with her principal," he said, and lapsed into silence.

The teacher had been the last female he'd talked to me about, too. If he was talking about paternity, though, there was clearly *someone* in the picture.

"Since I assumed it was one of his workers, I also assumed it was an as-yet unborn child, but he didn't say that. He could have had a child—or at least wondered if he did—any time in the past. Knowing Allan, if there was any real possibility, he would have made provisions for the child." Thomas said.

"Any idea how I'd go about finding out if he has a child out there?"

"If he wasn't listed on the birth certificate as the father, it would be impossible. Almost anyone could surface and claim to be his child, and if he's cremated there will be no way to do a DNA test to establish paternity. As we both know, he has no close relatives to reference."

"What's your gut feeling about it?"

"As a lawyer, I deal in facts, not feelings. Unless someone walks in with a DNA test they took before Allan died, you're home free. Even then, they may or may not be able to attack the will."

80

"That's not the point. If he has a child out there, I'll give it the estate, whether it has a legal claim or not. Allan would want his child taken care of."

"I didn't mean to imply you were trying to protect your position. I just think you should know your rights. And frankly, I don't think he was asking for himself. I think he would have told me if that were the case." He stood up. Our discussion was clearly over. "If I can help you with anything else, please feel free to call me." He handed me a business card.

I left without any more idea of who might have pushed me down the stairs. I made another mental note to try to find out who Ken and Susan were. If Allan had bothered to clean up the house before they came to visit, then maybe they were good enough friends to know about the phantom child.

Heavy traffic on the Banfield freeway occupied my attention until I got to my neighborhood. Then, the information I'd learned came rushing back. Besides being a closet tennis player, Allan potentially had a child. It seemed like the kind of thing you would know about someone. We spent hours every week in meetings and more hours over coffee and diet colas, digesting the impossible schedules we had to make happen. He knew about Sam and Noah. There had to be more to the story. The trouble was, I couldn't see a place to start digging. I needed some peace and quiet to mull it over.

Noah was in the driveway throwing a basketball through the rusty hoop attached to the front of the garage.

"Hi," I said and smiled.

He held the ball and looked at me without speaking.

"What?" I said.

"Don't get wound up, but I invited Green to dinner tonight. There was nothing on your calendar, and Mrs. Johnson said she would cook his favorite stew."

Green was the last person I wanted to see. "Any particular reason?" I asked, trying to keep my voice neutral.

Noah set the ball down and came to stand in front of me.

"He needs to know that someone tried to kill you at that dead guy's house," he said, his look daring me to argue. "I didn't tell him about it, but you need to."

For once, I appreciated his overactive sense of loyalty. He may not agree with me most of the time, but he respected my request not to tell Green.

"When is he coming?" I asked.

"He said he thought he could get here by seven."

At least that would give me an hour or so to figure out what I was willing to say.

Mrs. Johnson was at the sink when I came in. She was wearing a pink dress in a small floral print, and a pale yellow cardigan. A diet cola in an iced glass was sitting on the table. A plate with three snickerdoodles was next to it. She turned and pulled out a chair.

"Take a load off," she said.

I sat and waited for her to continue.

"Don't get mad at the boy," she started. "He's not trying to be defiant."

"Even though I expressly told him I did not want to talk to Green?"

"He's scared. His body may be big, but he's still a child in many ways. That business last spring scared him. How many children in America have seen a murder victim by the time they're fifteen?"

"Probably more than you think, but I get your point. I did keep him safe, though. He was in no danger that whole time."

"But he didn't know that. And neither did you, I'd say. Plus, no matter how difficult he seems, he loves you and doesn't want anything to happen to you."

"I know, but Green is the last person I want to see right now. As long as I'm a suspect, I'm taking a risk talking to him. Noah believes Green can do no wrong, but he might not have a choice no matter what he thinks about us personally."

"Green wouldn't turn on you," Mrs. Johnson said. "He's a good man. He'll do what's right. You can count on it."

"Oh, great, not you, too. The Frank Green fan club chalks up another member."

"You could do worse as far as friends go, missy."

I couldn't take any more. My whole family was turning on me. I left Mrs. Johnson to her cooking and changed into my shorts and Minnie Mouse T-shirt. I had just enough time to put in a half-hour upstairs on the exercise bike and then get cleaned up for dinner. I had a feeling I was going to need all the endorphins my workout could generate to get through the meal.

Mrs. Johnson waited until I was out of the shower before she left.

"The table is set, the stew is on the stove, and the rolls are in the oven. There's ginger cake on the counter, and mugs are chilling in the freezer. You be honest with the detective, Harley. Someone killed your friend, and we both know it wasn't you. That means a killer is still out there." She turned and left before I could reply.

It was not likely I was going to forget Allan's killer, even without my friends and family reminding me.

Allan was old enough that if he'd had a child when he was in college he or she could possibly be reaching adulthood by now. The problem was, I would think the child, or at least the child's parent, would want to have paternity established before they killed him for the money. It didn't add up. Surely, people didn't kill their absentee parent before they've even introduced themselves.

CHAPTER 17

GREEN'S CAR PULLED INTO the driveway before I could figure anything out. I watched him get out; he was carrying a brown paper bag in one hand. His mother had trained him well—it's always better to come bearing gifts, especially when you're going where you're not always welcome. He had obviously changed clothes. I wasn't sure why, but I was relieved that the Goodwill look he normally sported really was a conscious plan and not a lack of taste. Tonight, he was wearing khaki Dockers and a Ralph Lauren polo shirt in a shade of pale blue that highlighted his gray eyes. I had to admit he looked okay.

He climbed the steps to the back door. I opened it and waved him in. He handed me the paper bag. It felt cold.

"I thought maybe you could use some chocolate," he said.

I looked in the bag. Stacked inside were two cartons of Godiva chocolate ice cream. He had pulled out the big guns.

Out in the driveway, I could see Noah pulling the hose over to Green's car. Green had obviously hired him to wash it, giving us time to talk.

Green looked at me for a moment. "Let's not play this charade all evening," he began. "Noah has some agenda, or he wouldn't have arranged this dinner. He would have been asking to go to a ball game or something. What does he want?"

I wasn't ready to plunge into the topic at hand this directly, but he was right—I didn't have the energy to play games, either.

"He's spooked by what happened to Allan."

"Harley, we both know Noah. Just having someone die is not enough to spook that kid. What else has happened?"

"You mean, besides you suspecting me?"

"He doesn't believe that, and you know better, too."

"Do I?" I asked. "Okay, I'm going to assume that you care about Noah, but I'm not sure I should talk to you as long as I'm the only suspect in Allan's death."

"You know I can't tell you the status of an ongoing investigation. There might be other suspects."

"Might be?"

"It's possible."

Noah was rubbing foamy soap on the car with a fuzzy mitt I'd never seen before. "Okay. I went to Allan's house and ended up locked in the basement."

"Go on."

"That's it. I was locked in, and Noah and Neva Dean came looking for me. They let me out, and we went home."

"Back up," he said. "How did you get into the basement?"

This wasn't going as smoothly as I had hoped. "That's the part I'm not real clear on. Allan's basement is down a steep set of stairs. I think I fell down the stairs. I was knocked out, briefly and when I went back up, the door had locked behind me."

"Jesus, no wonder the kid's worried." He looked straight into my eyes. "Do you really think you just fell down the stairs, and the door locked itself behind you?"

I'm all for evasion, but lying while someone is looking in your eyes is not in my repertoire.

"No, I don't." I said. "I just don't have a good alternative right now. I was reaching for the light switch one minute, and the next thing I knew I was waking up at the bottom of the stairs."

"Any idea who would do it?" Asking the victim must be a police technique. Kind of how shrinks expect you to solve your own problems. If I knew who had pushed me down the stairs, and why, what would I need a detective for?

"I spoke to Allan's lawyer today, just to see if there was anyone else he knew of who should have or could have inherited. He says there's really no one." I didn't think he needed to hear the speculation about a child just yet.

"Someone had a beef with him. People don't kill people without a reason. Most of the time, anyway."

"I went through his calendar and his mail. Some guy named Ken sent him a check. It looked like he was paying off a loan. I thought maybe I could go back and look through his desk and files and see if there's a note written up for the loan."

"Why don't you give me the name, and *I* can check this Ken out?"

I got up and got the check. Green copied the information, including the bank the check had been drawn on.

"Anything else?" he asked.

"I can't think of anything," I said, knowing this wasn't strictly true.

"I don't think it's a good idea for you to go back to his house alone."

"That could get a little awkward, since I own the house now. I'm going to need to keep it up until I figure out what to do with it."

"I didn't say don't go there, I just said don't go *alone*. I wouldn't mind having a look at the house myself."

"You're assuming I would take you?"

"I knew this detente couldn't last."

Noah came in, and we managed to get through dinner without further mention of Allan's death. Mrs. Johnson had outdone herself. The stew was savory and thick, the rolls were crisped to perfection and the ginger cake moist and spicy.

"Maybe we could take a drive over to your new house to let our dinner settle before we tackle the chocolate," Green suggested.

My instinct was to keep him away from Allan's house, but I could think of only one ready excuse.

"I'm not real anxious to go back after my last visit," I said, hoping he would change his mind.

"With Noah and I there no one would dare to bother you, right Noah?"

"Put Sonny in his pen," I said to Noah with a sigh of defeat.

Sonny's dognapping earlier this year had been aided by his habit of digging holes under the backyard fence. When we got him back, I had a pen built behind the garage with a wire floor that was buried under a layer of sod. Mr. J had crafted a small doggie door in the back wall of the garage that entered under the workbench, so he could get inside when he wanted. Noah deposited him in the enclosure and then spent five minutes apologizing and assuring the little rat he would release him as soon as we got back from Allan's.

We went in Green's newly cleaned car. The drive across town took twenty minutes. It was nearly dark when we pulled in the drive. It looked peaceful enough. As we went up the sidewalk, I noticed a few weeds were beginning to appear in Allan's flower-beds — I would have to arrange to get them weeded. I opened the door and then paused when we heard a loud thump.

Green pulled a gun from the back of his waistband. It hadn't been there at dinner. He must have grabbed it when we got out of the car.

"You two wait here," he said and headed slowly into the house.

"Green," I said, "try the kitchen."

He motioned to me to be quiet. I turned back to Noah.

"The orange cat," I said. "I didn't do anything about the cat door. He probably comes in to see if his little friend is home yet."

Green came back into the living room and motioned us in.

"I think it was an animal," he said. "The pet door was swing-ing."

"I could have told you that," I said, and pushed past him.

I went upstairs and opened the door to Allan's office. Green followed me in.

"What are you looking for?" he asked.

"I don't know, but if there's anything to be found, it will be in here."

I sat in Allan's desk chair. The file drawer to the left was pulled open an inch. It wasn't much, but I was fairly sure it hadn't been that way when I last left. I pulled it open all the way. The files looked pretty much as they had when I'd looked in the drawer yesterday.

Green lifted papers that were lying on the desk, looked at them then set them back down. He moved one stack from the front of the desktop. It revealed a color photograph slipped be-tween the protective glass and the dark wood of the desktop.

"Do you recognize these people?" he asked.

Noah came over and looked as if he might have a clue. I got up and came around to the front of the desk. The picture was of a muscular, dark-haired young man with his arm around a slight fair-haired young woman. They were standing in front of a store of some kind, smiling. I scanned the young man's face, looking for any resemblance to Allan. You could see a jagged snow-topped mountain in the background. The picture was too small to be conclusive.

Noah went around the desk to Allan's computer.

"Is it okay if I look on the computer?" he asked.

"Good idea," I said. "Try the word processor files first."

He started it and opened the list of documents. Allan had been extremely organized. There were files for every aspect of living — his cats, his car, his garden, his mountaineering club, and on and on. He apparently documented everything he did. Everything, it would seem, except his possible paternity. There was no file labeled *child*, *son*, *daughter* or *paternity*. I would have to read each file just to be sure, but nothing stood out.

"I've got a flash drive," Noah said and pulled the gray plastic-covered stick from his pocket. "I could copy his documents onto it." He was looking at Green.

I spoke before Green could.

"Thanks, Noah. I'd like a copy of Allan's files. I need to figure out if he has someone who helps with his garden." Green looked at me. "He's getting weeds."

"I don't suppose you would give me a copy," he said. "I could get a search warrant, you know."

"How about I let you look after I look for his gardener?" I asked.

I could tell he wasn't happy with the compromise, but I suspected getting a search warrant for Allan's house might not be as easy as he was pretending. I had no intention of letting him look at the files until I knew what was there and whether it incriminated me in any way. I wasn't sure how it could, but then, I'd never imagined Allan would leave me all his worldly possessions, either.

"Let's get out of here," I said. "It gives me the creeps looking through his stuff this soon after he died."

"Will you let me come back again?" Green asked.

"That will depend on what happens with your case against me," I said, and walked out of the office and down the stairs.

Green and I were in the living room of my house in a chocolate bliss, eating ice cream out of the same carton. I still didn't trust him, but he did bring the ice cream, so what could I do?

"Harley," Noah called from his bedroom. He had taken a piece of ginger cake with him and plugged the flash drive into his computer, revealing the contents of Allan's documents file. Like most children of his generation, advanced computing was like breathing. Sam had bought him a computer system when he was ten, and he had pieced together several others from parts he'd ordered on the internet. Now he had one set up with Linux, one with Open BSD and another with something I'd never heard of. He also had networked all the computers, including mine, so we could easily share information. He had volunteered to search for the garden information, as well as any other regular home maintenance services Allan might use. "I think I found something good."

Green and I left our chocolate and went to his bedroom door.

"What have you got?" Green asked.

"It looks like some kind of loan agreement. He gave some guy named Ken Higgins ten thousand dollars. It says he's part-owner of Ken and Susan's grocery until the loan is paid back."

"What do you want to bet that picture on his desk is of Ken and Susan?" Green said. "I should be able to tell you exactly who they are by tomorrow."

Noah went back to searching the files. Green and I returned to our chocolate.

"Don't try to contact these people before I get back to you," he instructed.

"They hardly look like criminals."

"You'd be surprised. Not everyone looks the part."

There really wasn't anything else to discuss. We finished our chocolate frenzy, Green warned me a few more times to be careful and not go to Allan's alone. Noah was still digging through files when I went to bed.

⁓ ⌇ ⁀

The sun was shining in the clear blue Oregon sky when I left for work the next morning. The forecasters were predicting a warmer than average summer, but as Mr. J was fond of saying, no one forecasts the weather in Oregon except fools or foreigners. I looked west to the Coast Range, a ridge of hills that separated

Portland from the Oregon coast seventy miles away. The sky was clear as far as I could see. With luck we'd have a few warm days.

I stopped by Karen's desk on my way in.

"What did you end up doing about a memorial service for Allan?" I asked without preamble.

"We're having a service at the Unitarian church on Monday afternoon."

"Did he go there or something?"

"Harley, I think you know we have no way of knowing where he did or didn't go. I asked Jeanette, but she didn't know either. We figured the Unitarian church was fairly neutral. Do you know something about his religious preference?"

"No, but I've found some friends of his who might know. I can call them." I felt a brief flash of guilt about Green, and then retreated to my desk to make the call.

I'd copied the phone number from the check the night before. I really had planned to wait until Green called before I tried to contact them, but this was important—company business, really.

CHAPTER 18

A QUICK GLANCE IN the front of the phone book indicated that the area code was for Montana. The phone call was painful. It started with "You don't know me, but..." and went into "I've got terrible news..." Gentle probing revealed that Ken's parents had died in the same accident as Allan's, although Allan hadn't known Ken at the time. Their parents had been close friends, but Ken had been a late-in-life baby, a welcome surprise for a childless couple nearing middle age. He had been a small child when Allan had left home. After the accident, Ken and Allan reconnected.

Ken didn't know Allan's religious preference. He allowed that they had spent their shared time in bars, not church. Eventually, they both moved on. Allan returned to Portland, and Ken married Susan and moved to Montana.

I tried to think of a good lead-in, but after delivering this kind of news, nothing else you say will matter—you are now the enemy.

"This must be a terrible shock for you," I began.

"You have no idea," Ken said in a tight voice.

"We're all pretty stunned here, too. I'm trying to understand a few things about—"

"What's to understand?" Ken interrupted. "A guy is dead. And he shouldn't be. Not yet."

"Well, actually," I continued, "Allan left a few things unresolved." Even I could see what I was saying was offensive. "Just tell me this. To your knowledge, did Allan have a child? Or children?"

"Who are you?" Ken asked. "I thought you said you were a coworker."

"I am, but..." There was no other way. "Allan named me his heir. I inherited his whole estate."

There was silence.

"I see," he finally said. "So you were his..."

"I wasn't his anything," I said in a rush. "I mean, I was his friend, but that's all—just a coworker and friend. I don't know why he left his estate to me. We were talking about it when they handed out the forms at work, and he said he didn't have anyone to leave it to." The words were out before I could think about it. I couldn't call them back. "I don't think it was a well-thought-out decision."

"Well, if he left you his whole estate, clearly he thought enough about it to contact his attorney," he said.

"I don't know what to tell you," I said. "I didn't know what he'd done until he was gone." If it's any consolation, it made me the number one suspect in his murder, I thought, but wasn't cruel enough to say aloud. "That's why I'm trying to make certain he didn't have any children I don't know about, who would be rightful heirs."

"I don't know of any children," Ken said. "But then, we haven't been that close since I moved to Montana."

I thought about the notation on Allan's calendar. They had been close enough to stay with him in March.

There wasn't anything else to say. It clearly wasn't the time to question Ken.

I warned him that a Detective Green would be calling him, and offered to pick him and his wife up at the airport the day after tomorrow. He thanked me but said they would be getting a rental car at the airport.

Almost as an afterthought, I offered that he and his wife could stay at Allan's house.

"Thank you," he said in a softer voice.

I wished I was one of those people who knew just the right thing to say in these circumstances, but after a few moments of silence, I mumbled an awkward goodbye and hung up.

The rest of my day was spent in a meeting with two reps from one of our Japanese material suppliers. They had been midway through a cross-country trip visiting American customers when

Allan died. It was too late to reschedule, so we forged ahead with what proved to be a productive if awkward meeting. Jeanette turned out to be very knowledgeable about the problems we were having with the substrates being supplied by this vendor. I zoned out while she discussed volume discounts and shipping issues. My suspicions she had been the brain behind our purchasing department all along were reinforced.

One of the things that amazes me about the Japanese style of business is how we can be in a meeting where everyone engages in red-faced, raised-voice arguments, and then, when the deal is finally struck, everyone smiles, bows and goes out to dinner as if the previous interaction had never occurred. So, after four hours of relentless discussion, we went to dinner. Since these reps had a senior-level marketing manager with them, Mr. Iguchi joined us.

Mr. Iguchi's presence guaranteed we would go to an expensive Japanese restaurant in Portland. We were not disappointed. Bush Garden is a classic Japanese restaurant, with waitresses dressed in traditional kimono and obis. It has the low tables with hidden leg wells that allow you to sit on a pillow but still maintain your dignity and circulation. The best part was that it's located on Morrison Street in downtown Portland, which meant I would be halfway home when we were done.

Jeanette and I both declined to join the after-dinner migration to the bar.

"You were great today," I said to her as we left the restaurant.

She blushed. "I was very nervous," she said. "I've always prepped Allan for these meetings, and as you know, I sometimes sat in to take notes, but it was different having to actually talk myself."

"Well, your nerves didn't show," I said. "You got us a good deal on the substrates."

We walked down the block to where we had parked our cars on the street.

"Can I ask you something?" I said.

"Sure," Jeanette replied as she dug her keys out of her purse.

"Do you know anything about a Ken and Susan who were friends of Allan?"

"I know *of* them," she said.

"Do you know if they were close to Allan?"

"I wouldn't say close," she said after a moment. "I think Ken is the son of his parent's friends. They were all killed in the same car accident, so he and Ken had some kind of survivor thing going on, but I wouldn't say they were real friends. Why do you ask?"

"Karen's planning the memorial service and was trying to round up any non-work friends. Their names came up. I'd never heard of them before, so I was just wondering."

"Sorry, but I don't know anything more than that," she said. "See you tomorrow."

She continued down the block, and I watched her get into her car before opening my own door.

CHAPTER 19

IT WAS DARK WHEN I pulled into my driveway and parked in front of the garage. Mrs. Johnson met me at the back door. Her lips were clamped into a straight line. Noah was well past the age of needing a babysitter, but when Mrs. J knew I would be out in the evening, she packed her sewing basket and planted herself in the wooden rocker in my living room. She always claimed she had been trying to watch TV at home, and Mr. J had fallen asleep. She said his snoring was drowning out the sound. Noah and I knew better, but didn't argue. The fact that she wasn't in the rocker when I walked into the kitchen was not a good sign.

"*He's* back," she said and turned on her heel and marched to her favorite spot in front of the kitchen sink.

"Who?" I asked, hoping it wasn't who I thought but knowing in the pit of my stomach it was. I dropped my keys on the kitchen desk.

"Harley had nothing to do with it," I heard Noah say, his voice rising with anger.

"Where you're concerned, Harley has to do with everything," a familiar voice replied.

I felt a brief flash of joy. Sam was alive, and here. I instantly hated myself and then him. I hated that I still cared, and that he didn't, or at least not enough to put me before his craziness. I took a deep breath and tried to calm myself. Talking to Sam was like going into battle. I needed to stay composed. He could take Noah away, I reminded myself. I smoothed my sweaty palms over my skirt and went into the living room.

"You're back," I said.

I never knew what Sam would look like when I saw him. He was a master of disguise. If he really did it as part of his job, as he claimed, he was good. This time, his short hair was pale blonde and his eyes a robin's-egg blue I thought might be natural.

"What the hell are you thinking?" He turned his rage on me. "Do you know what he's been up to?" He didn't wait for me to answer. "He's got a cop searching for his mother—a goddamn *cop*!" He got up and paced the length of the small living room. He rubbed his hand over his short hair and stared at the ceiling.

"Dad," Noah started, "I have a right to know who—"

"You have no rights," Sam thundered. He faced Noah and I. I put my arm around Noah's shoulders. "I'm not the bad guy here," he said in a controlled voice that sounded more dangerous than his yelling. "I'm trying to keep you safe."

"Sam," I said, and took a deep breath to calm my nerves. "What or who are you trying to keep Noah safe from? You keep asking us to trust you, but you haven't given us much reason."

He focused on me. "This is between me and my son."

"Cut the macho crap, Sam," I said. "As long as Noah lives with me and I'm in charge of enforcing your edicts, I have a vested interest in knowing what's going on. I'm sure Noah would be more accepting if you'd just tell him something."

He paced again. I could tell he was reviewing what story to tell us.

"If you're about to tell us another fairy tale, don't," I said. "I'd rather know nothing than hear another bunch of lies."

Noah glared at me, a desperate look on his face.

"Noah, your dad can lie without even thinking about it. It's like breathing to him. If he *is* planning to tell you yet another fabrication, we don't need it. I don't know who your mother is and he does, but if he isn't willing to tell you, you'll just have to learn to deal with it."

"It's not fair," he said.

"Well, life often isn't fair," I said—to his back as he stomped away toward the kitchen.

Sam turned to me. He actually looked torn. "Harley, if I could tell you anything, I would," he said. "There are only three people besides me who know who Noah is. People have died to keep it a secret."

He looked so intense, I almost believed him.

"You have to know I haven't encouraged him in this," I said. "But you can't expect him to just keep blindly believing everything you say. He's not a little boy anymore. He's growing up. He needs to know why you make him go to military school. And why you make him study so many languages. His friends are studying computers and going to space camp and soccer camp and playing lacrosse. You choose everything for Noah, and it has nothing to do with what he's interested in. He has no autonomy."

Sam rubbed his tanned hand over his hair again, a gesture I remembered so well. My heart gave a small lurch.

"So, what are you saying? I let him go to soccer camp, and he'll lay off this mother business?"

"Are you seriously asking my opinion?"

He glared at me.

"I'm just saying. If you could let him choose an elective, or a summer camp—and I mean *really* let him choose it—he might feel like he had some independence."

"An elective course, as long as it's at his school, is fine. A summer camp is a whole different thing. I'd have to be sure I could keep him safe," Sam said.

"Maybe you could let him look at some options and see if there really is a problem or not. Seems like that would be easier to deal with than him working behind your back with Detective Green."

"Don't even get me started on that guy," Sam growled. "And don't think I've forgotten you're the one who brought him into our lives."

"*Me?*" I said, raising my voice. "I didn't ask my workers to start killing each other."

"That didn't mean you had to bring him home with you. Don't ever think I don't know what goes on in this house. I know that guy is spending time with my wife and my son."

"Hey, that was your choice. Noah and I didn't push you out. You left, of your own free will. If Detective Green wants to spend time with your son, and you don't, there's no one to blame but yourself."

"And my wife?" he said and looked directly into my eyes. He moved closer, and tried to pull me into his arms, but I ducked and stepped away at the last minute.

"I stopped being your wife when you sent me divorce papers," I reminded him. "It's no longer your business who I do or don't spend time with."

"It will always be my business."

"I'm going to check on Noah," I said and stomped into the kitchen.

Mrs. Johnson put a cup of tea on the table at my usual spot. I sat down and busied myself adding sugar from the pottery bowl she slid over to me. Noah glared at his glass of milk.

"I don't get it," he said. "Is it so unreasonable to want to know who my mother is? Or who I am? Did she commit a horrible crime or something? Is she a drug addict or a prostitute? Why won't he tell me?"

"Noah," I said, and took his hands off the glass and held them in mine. "If I knew anything, or could make your dad tell you anything, you know I would."

He searched my face for the truth.

"For what it's worth, I don't think your dad is doing this just to make your life miserable. I think he really believes what he's saying."

"But what if he's crazy?" he said. "I heard you tell Neva Dean that he might be. What if he took me away and left her the way he left us? What if my mother is out there somewhere wondering where I am?"

"First of all, young man, I don't appreciate you eavesdropping on my conversation with Neva Dean. Second, if you had listened to the *whole* conversation, you would have heard me say I didn't know if he was crazy or really works in intelligence, like he says. I also said it didn't matter. That's not the same as just saying I think he's crazy."

"Only you would say there's a difference," he said. "Can I go to Chris's house?"

"Call first and see if it's okay with his mom."

He pulled out the new iPhone I'd gotten him and was talking to Chris five seconds later. He headed for his bedroom, stopped briefly to hug Mrs. J and to plant a quick kiss on my cheek on his way past me.

"I'll walk over," he said as he left. "His mom is going to a yoga class and said she can bring me home after that so I won't have to walk in the dark."

"Okay. Have fun," I said.

"You're just going to let him walk out like that?" Sam said as he came in.

"Well, it didn't seem like you were accomplishing anything. You both yelled, which probably reduced your stress level a little, but you didn't tell him anything, and as a result, he doesn't understand any more than he did, except that continuing the search for his mom will make you mad. I can keep trying to get him to obey your edicts, but as far as his understanding them, I can't help you there. I don't understand them myself."

"Can't you just trust me?" he asked in the whispery voice that used to be my undoing.

"I don't have a choice now, do I?" I said.

Mrs. Johnson finished rinsing Noah's milk glass and put her faded cotton apron on its hook by the back door.

"I should go check on my Henry. You call if you need me, Harley." With a last long, silent stare at Sam, she followed in Noah's footsteps out the door.

"I'm not the enemy here," Sam said as he sat down across the table from me.

"You keep saying that. I hear you. But if you won't tell us who the enemy is, or if there even *is* an enemy, it doesn't mean much. 'Trust me' doesn't cut it with Noah anymore. He needs facts."

"I can't tell you any more than I already have. You just have to believe me."

"I can't have this conversation again," I said with a sigh. "We've been over this before. It's why we aren't married."

"Okay, let's talk about Noah, then," he said. "What's your plan for him when you're arrested for murder? Who'll take care of him while you're sitting in jail? *You're* supposed to be keeping him safe, too." He stood and paced. He stopped and ran his hand over his hair.

"I'm not going to be arrested for murder," I said. "How can you even think that?"

"Get your head out of the sand, woman. Homicide detectives questioned you at your workplace. You found the body, you had a pretty good financial motive, and you're more than strong enough to whack a guy in the head with a big stick and inject something into his IV in the hospital. Means, motive and opportunity, wrapped up and tied with a bow."

"That's ridiculous. I didn't know ahead of time I would be the second person on our team to cross the lake, and I certainly didn't know he had left his estate to me. I still don't know why he did. I'm also not sure I believe he left it just so I could provide for Noah. But whatever his reason, I *didn't* know."

A look I couldn't read flitted over Sam's features.

"So, if you didn't whack the guy, who did?" he asked after a long, silent moment.

"Do you care? Or is this just one more chance to find fault with me?"

He took a deep breath. "I'm sorry," he said and came back to the table. "I'm not trying to hurt you or make your life any harder than it obviously is. Things are a lot more complicated than you realize." He reached across the table and took both my hands in his. My skin burned where he touched it. "You have to believe I'm not trying to hurt you, Harley."

"But…?"

"I know you don't understand, but I can't risk Noah and the possibility of exposure another public incident could cause."

"What are you saying?" I could feel the blood leave my face.

"If you can't get this wrapped up, and I mean now, I'm going to have to send Noah somewhere else, away from you and your penchant for publicity."

I pulled my hands out of his grip.

"You can't," I said.

His very blue eyes had taken on an icy gleam. "I can and I will."

He got up and strode out of the kitchen.

CHAPTER 20

I COULDN'T MOVE. He was right. Someone had killed Allan and someone had pushed me down the stairs at Allan's house. The fact that it probably was the same person meant that, at the very least, a killer wanted me out of the way. Sam was right. I was exposing Noah to danger just by association. I covered my face with my hands, blocking out the world.

"Don't you worry, Harley," said Mrs. Johnson from the door. She came in, sat down in the chair beside mine and ran a hand over my tangled curls.

"I thought you went home," I said and uncovered my face.

"I left my knitting basket by my chair."

We both knew she did this all the time, especially if she thought her presence might be required.

"Have you been waiting outside?" I asked. "It's cold, even if it is summer. Do you want some tea?"

"I was waiting for that one to leave, but then I saw the light go on upstairs and figured he wasn't leaving." She paused. "And I would like a small cup of tea."

I got up, filled the kettle from the tap and put it on the stove. She fetched a plate of lemon sugar cookies and took the foil off. I set out our usual cups and choice of tea bags—Earl Grey for me and English Breakfast for her.

"He isn't all bad, you know," I said. "There was a time when he made me laugh."

"That one is nothing but trouble, for you *and* the boy. You would do well to steer clear of him."

"He might be paranoid and a little crazy, but he's fiercely protective of Noah. And he's right. It's not good for Noah. *I'm* not good for Noah. The police think I'm a murderer, and then there's the small problem of the real murderer, or whoever it was who pushed me down the basement stairs at Allan's house. Being with me puts Noah in harm's way."

"Nonsense, Noah loves you, and he hates being at that school without friends or family. Besides, you have that good-looking detective to protect you, and Noah likes him—more than his own father, I dare say."

"Whether Noah likes it or not, Sam *is* his father, and that means Sam gets to decide what is best for Noah. And I can tell you, if I don't find out who killed Allan and clear my name, Sam is going to take him away from me."

The Johnsons had lived in my neighborhood long before Sam and I had bought our house. She knew who was happily married, who was cheating and who was newly divorced. She hadn't come into my life until Sam left. I was an emotional mess and Noah was devastated by the breakup of our family. She held our hands and dried our tears, and to her, Sam was the cause of our trauma and therefore was and always would be the enemy.

I got up and took our empty teacups to the sink.

"I'm too tired to think about it tonight. I'm going to bed. Will you be okay, or do you want me to walk you home?" I asked.

"I've walked this block for forty years, I think I can make it this time, too." She pulled the two sides of her cardigan around her ample torso and buttoned it. "You mark my words, Harley, that man is trouble, and you'd do well to get him out of here as quickly as you can," she said as she left.

The warm water felt good on my hands as I washed our teacups and the cookie plate, so I lingered. Footsteps sounded on the stairs from the attic room.

"Has the old battle-ax left?" Sam asked.

Sweat glistened on his bare chest. He was clad in a pair of worn cotton-knit workout shorts. He had been doing his evening ritual of hundreds of sit-ups and pushups. He opened a cabinet, got a glass and reached past me to fill it from the tap. I held my breath, trying not to smell his sweaty, masculine odor. I couldn't stop feeling the heat radiating from his body. Images of us together came unbidden to my mind, and I hurried to block them.

104

"I take it you're spending the night?" I said, trying to fill the silence.

"At least I can be sure Noah will be safe for one night," he said. He drained his glass and set it in the sink. "This is serious, Harley." He went to the coat hooks by the door and fished in the pocket of the jacket he'd left hanging there. "I have something for you, and I'd rather not have a big fight about it."

For the first time, I noticed how drawn his face looked. He was exhausted, and not from his sit-ups. He pulled a small gun from the jacket pocket. He came back to the sink and put it in my hand, closing both of his over mine.

"Carry this with you at all times," he said. He handed me a piece of paper. "Here's your concealed carry permit."

"But..." I started to protest, knowing I'd never applied for, much less been granted, a gun permit.

Sam put a finger on my lips.

"Just take it. Until this murderer is caught or I can arrange a new situation for Noah, you need it to protect him. And yourself," he added.

He had insisted both Noah and I learn to handle guns safely. I had never carried or discharged one outside of a firing range, but I knew how, and could do it with accuracy. I kept the weapon.

My sleep was restless that night. During wakeful moments, I constructed excuses I could use to explain Sam's presence in my bed, but as it turned out, I didn't need them.

When I got up, there was no trace of Sam. I had become accustomed to his abrupt departures during our marriage—they were part of the reason we were divorced. I'd get up in the morning, he'd be gone, and I wouldn't know if he'd be back in a few hours or a few months. A simple goodbye would have gone a long way.

The gun he'd given me was still on my bedside table. I understood why he'd given it to me, but I just couldn't see myself carrying it into work in my purse. I considered putting it in a bag in my car, but as often as cars got broken into in parking lots, that didn't feel right either. In the end, I put it in the drawer of the kitchen desk.

Thursday was filled with the usual workday chaos. Our supplier had shipped the wrong clean room wipes, and to a person, my groups were furious. At least two people from each group had to come out to my desk to explain why having the wrong wipe would cripple them at their particular job. Jeanette was using all her connections, but the correct wipes couldn't be delivered until Monday afternoon. There was much discussion among the team about who should get their wipes first when the shipment came. I finally had to call a meeting of my lead ops and tell them to get their people focused on their jobs again. I could tolerate a little grousing, but missing schedule because they didn't like the brand of wipe they had to use was unacceptable.

The production supervisors in my department generally go to coffee after the afternoon shift change. We relax a few minutes and prepare for the several more hours we often put in. On sunny days in the summer we do an abbreviated version. We consume our drink of choice, pass on critical info to the evening supervisor and then we get out of Dodge.

This day, the main topic was the wipe crisis. We all passed on our best method of getting our people to stop obsessing about the missing wipes. I packed up my briefcase, grabbed my keys and phone and stopped by Jose's desk. Along with being a competent supervisor, Jose was a gourmet cook. He was always the hit of our company potlucks, which was saying a lot, considering the variety of cuisine we had available.

"Jose," I said, "my stepson had a Hispanic foster mother, and loves Mexican food. Where could I take him in Portland that would knock his socks off food-wise?"

In reality, Noah had been moved through a series of foster homes, and his recent penchant for Mexican food probably had more to do with the new information he'd gotten about who his mother was, even if Green didn't believe it was true. Jose didn't need to know the details of my nightmares; he had his own teen-agers to deal with.

"Well," he said, obviously weighing several choices, "you can never go wrong with Esparza's on southeast Ankeny, but lately, I've been favoring La Costita in Burlingame. Their nopales quesa-dilla is to die for."

I wasn't foolish enough to believe Sam wouldn't be skulking around in the bushes wherever we went. If he wanted to make something out of our dining choice, let him bring it on; but with any luck he'd keep his presence hidden.

CHAPTER 21

I CALLED NOAH on my cell phone and arranged to pick him and Chris up at home.

The drive into town from Hillsboro gave me time to think. By the time I reached Portland, I had decided to add one more diner to our party.

I drove by Neva Dean Willet's apartment. I don't really buy her "Angelologist" story—the idea that one can see the angels of departed loved ones and that they pass on insights into what is happening in the here and now is a little too out there for me. She is, however, a good sounding board, since she generally has a much more objective view of my world than people like Mrs. Johnson, who tends to be blinded by affection and loyalty. And Noah loved her.

Her apartment door opened as I raised my hand to knock. She was shrugging her arms into a lightweight tan car coat.

"Let me get my purse and I'll be good to go," she said, turning back and opening the coat closet door. "The angels indicated I would be going somewhere tonight, so I thought I'd get ready just in case we had to leave in a hurry."

"No hurry," I said. "I just thought you might like to go to Mexican dinner with the boys and me. I know it's one of your favorites."

"Well, thank you for thinking of an old gal like me," she said and punched a series of numbers into the keypad of the alarm system her son had installed after Neva Dean's neighbor had been murdered earlier this year.

We went out the door and down the steps toward my car.

"Maybe on the drive over to your place you can tell me why you really invited me along," she said and climbed into the passenger seat.

"Sam thinks I'm endangering Noah," I said without preamble.

"He *should* be worried," she said, and held her hand up to silence the protest she could see I was about to give voice to. "He is the boy's father. He should worry about everything that happens to Noah. It's his job. That doesn't mean he should take action on every little thing that enters his imagination. Our children would never grow up and leave home if we treated them like that. We just need to take reasonable precautions and then teach them how to avoid trouble when possible, and how to handle it if they can't avoid it."

"But a man has been killed," I pointed out.

"And that is very unfortunate, but it has little to do with Noah. Someone clearly wants to cause trouble for *you*, but again, it has no bearing on Noah."

"It wouldn't be too hard for anyone to figure out that the best way to get to me is through Noah," I said.

"But whoever did this wants to *blame* you. They're setting you up to take a fall. If they'd wanted you dead, they could have hit you on the head, too, when you found that man. They apparently don't want to physically hurt you. Whoever it is needs you alive."

"Yeah, they want me alive, alright—so Green can put me in jail."

"That may well be true, but it doesn't pose a threat to Noah. Besides, between Detective Green and that ex-husband of yours, no one would have much of a chance to get near the boy."

What she said made sense. Or at least I wanted it to. We rode the last few blocks in silence.

I parked in the driveway. Before I could get out, Neva Dean put her hand on my arm.

"I know you think I'm a crazy old lady, but believe this— Noah's angels indicate that his troubles will be of a completely different sort and are yet to come." She let go, got out of the car and marched up to the back door.

As much as I didn't want to believe in Neva Dean Willet's angels, my heart felt lighter as we all got into the car a few minutes later.

The trip was filled with lively chatter as the boys reported their week's activities to Neva Dean. I was glad Noah had someone he could talk to and jealous that it wasn't me.

Our group was seated in a booth after a brief wait at La Costita. I conveyed Jose's comments about the nopales quesadilla. The boys promptly ordered bean-and-cheese burritos, but Neva Dean and I opted for the recommended fare. We fell silent when our food arrived, and everyone began savoring his or her chosen delicacy.

Two male voices arguing loudly in Spanish broke our reverie. The sound receded as one man headed for the restroom and the other toward what had to be the kitchen.

"That didn't sound very friendly," I said. "I wonder what they were arguing about."

"I'm sure I don't know," Neva Dean said, "but their angels were sure agitated."

Noah got up without saying a word and headed for the restroom. I was about to send Chris to look for him when he finally came back to our table.

"That was really weird," Noah said.

"What?" we all chorused.

"I think the guy who went into the restroom is the brother of a guy who works at your company," he said to me. "Romeo? Or something like that."

"Romeo," I repeated.

"Yeah, his girlfriend is pregnant, and the family doesn't like her. Bathroom guy was trying to convince their dad to lighten up. Then he was telling his friend in the bathroom that if the parents won't accept the girl, Romeo is going run away with her."

"They can't do that," I said, selfishly thinking of the production schedule and our current shortage of experienced workers.

"I know—he would be walking out on a full-ride scholarship. His brother was upset that he was willing to throw it away when the baby isn't even his."

"*What?*" I said, in a louder voice than I intended. "What?" I repeated in a more reasonable tone. "Whose baby is it, then?"

"The brother doesn't know, he just said it isn't Romeo's," Noah said and sat back. He was obviously pleased with himself.

Sam's insistence that Noah become fluent in multiple languages did have its advantages. The new information was confusing. If Romeo wasn't the father of Mitsuko's baby, who was? And how did Romeo fit in the mix. Why wasn't she marrying the father of the baby?

Neva Dean paused and looked up. Previous experience told me this meant she was getting a message. I waited until she looked down again.

"The angels are indicating the baby's father isn't available. I'm not real sure what they're meaning by that. Maybe the father is married, or maybe he's emotionally unavailable. They don't exactly send me a telegram."

"I'm still having a hard time with the fact she's pregnant out of wedlock," I said as I slid out of the booth and held Neva Dean's coat for her. I handed Noah my debit card and he and Chris hopped up and went to the reception desk to pay our bill.

"You can't tell me you're surprised that a young couple could make a foolish mistake, can you?" she said.

Noah brought back the receipt for me to sign, and we headed for the door.

"I'm only surprised it happened to that particular young woman. She has a childlike quality to her. I didn't even know she dated anyone before Romeo."

"Who says it was before?" Neva Dean said as she got into the car.

"Oh, please, I can't even think about that possibility."

We drove home in silence. I was hoping Neva Dean might hear more from her angels, but if she did, she didn't share. I pulled to the curb in front of her apartment, and Noah and Chris jumped out as soon as the car stopped. Noah opened her door, and Chris offered his hand to help her stand up. I had seen Neva Dean in her yoga outfit and knew she was probably more limber than I am, but she put on a good show of needing help for the boys' sake.

Chris escorted her to her door while Noah followed along carrying her bag. When she was safely inside, I watched her hug each boy in turn. I knew they would be blushing, but they hugged her back in spite of their embarrassment. I wondered if I would ever reach the level of ease Neva Dean had with teenaged boys. I surely didn't have it now.

110

CHAPTER 22

GREEN'S ENTIRELY TOO-FAMILIAR maroon sedan was parked in my driveway when I turned the corner and pulled in front of the garage. The boys bounded over to him like hound dog puppies. The trio went through a bobbing, weaving play-boxing routine. It was the sort of thing that seems to come naturally to the male of the species.

After a few minutes, I heard the screen door slam as the boys ran into the house. I came out of the garage, where I had taken my time parking the car. I had hoped Green was there to talk to the boys about going to a baseball game or to come help out at the Police Activities League or anything that would mean he would be gone when I was done. His presence by the back door gave the lie to that idea almost as quickly as it had formed.

"What's up?" I asked, afraid to hear his reply.

"Nothing really," he said, "That's the problem. Can I come in?"

I wanted to say no, that I just wanted to come home once and not have a belligerent male waiting for me.

"Come on in," I said instead. I led the way into the kitchen. I dropped my purse and keys on the desk, went to the refrigerator and pulled out a can of diet cola. "Want one?" I asked.

"Do you have the hard stuff?" he asked.

I pulled out a Classic Coke and handed it to him.

"Thanks."

We popped the tops on our cans and drank in silence for a moment. Neither of us, it seemed, was eager to start what was sure to be an argument of some sort.

"We finished the interviews with your fellow campers," he said at last.

"And?"

"And...nothing. Every one of your people was accounted for. The staff at the ranch was either in view of your teammates or each other during the time in question. We're arranging to interview the people at the rifle range, but we did background checks on them, and there's no evidence they knew anyone in your group, or even that they knew you folks were there. It would be a long shot if one of them turned out to have anything to do with this. Seems like if one of them had a beef, they wouldn't set their gun down to pick up a stick."

"So, what are you telling me?"

He ran his hand over his hair in a gesture that reminded me of Sam.

"I'm not telling you anything," he said. "I *want* to tell you that I've cleared you as a suspect, but I can't. You still are the only person who was alone with the vic at the critical time, not once but twice. And there is still the insurance problem."

"You mean I'm the only person besides whoever did this," I said.

"I believe you." He sat down at the kitchen table. He wouldn't look at me.

"But?" I prompted.

"It doesn't do you any good if I can't prove it." He looked up at me then.

"I don't know what you want me to say. I didn't do it. I found Allan lying on the ground unconscious. And in the hospital he was fine when I left. Unconscious, but he was definitely alive. What do you want from me?" I paced across the kitchen, and I could hear my voice rising.

Green stood up and stepped into my path. He put his hands on my arms and guided me to the chair opposite his. I sat down.

"I'm not accusing you of anything. I know you didn't do it. I'm just frustrated. We have to be missing something — something big. I was hoping maybe we could just go over everything again."

He stared into my eyes, as if he could will the information out of me. I sighed.

"Okay," I said at last. "What do you want to know?"

"Why don't you just start by telling me everything you knew about Allan before this happened?" He took his small notebook from his pocket and pulled a pen from the loop at the side of the lined pad.

What I knew didn't amount to much.

"We worked together every day. I know he could be brash and boastful, but he could also be charming and sensitive. He was a master at being whatever or whomever he needed to be to get the job done."

"So, who had it in for him?" Green prompted.

"Well, it was obvious he had issues with Britt Langley, but then, Langley is a jerk and pretty much everyone has issues with him. Then there's the couple in Montana who owes him money. But they seem to have been on friendly terms with him, and sounded genuinely upset about his death."

"Don't think I don't know you called them, right after you said you wouldn't," Green told me. "Another detective might think you were trying to get to them before we could."

"But you don't believe that, right?" I said, trying to look innocent.

"Let's just say I've learned that you consider anything I say to you as an open invitation to do the opposite."

"That's not fair," I protested. "I had to call Ken and Susan about the memorial service. It's my job."

"I suppose you have a bridge in New York to sell me, too."

"Hey, it's the truth!"

"Whatever," he said, and turned back to his notebook. "Let's go over what happened in the forest again."

We reviewed the trip to the forest camp, but nothing new came out. We'd gone, and Allan had died. We tried a second time, but the facts didn't change. The third time through, I got to the part where I'd found Allan's broken body, and I stopped. Tears filled my eyes. I took a deep breath and tried to relax, but it was too late. Once the tears started, I couldn't stop them.

Green reached across the table and patted my hand. I knew he was trying to comfort me, but it didn't help. Finding Allan's beaten body and then having him live for a week before dying, then finding out I was his heir, and then suspected of his murder was all too much.

Green sighed and got up. He circled the table and pulled me into his arms. It was obviously awkward for him, but I was well past caring.

Noah and Chris chose that moment to come into the kitchen.

"What did you do to her?" Noah demanded.

Green let go of me and handed me the box of tissues from the kitchen counter. Noah pushed past him, grabbed the box of tissues and put his arm around my shoulders. He guided me into the living room and sat with me on the sofa.

"Are you okay?" he asked.

I blew my nose on a tissue and took another one to dab at my eyes.

"I'm fine," I said. "All the talk about Allan just got to me there for a minute. Everyone is so concerned about who killed him, and I want to know that, too, but they seem to forget he was a person. He was my friend. He got up that last morning thinking we were going on a fun adventure and scheming about how to win the activities, and then he was just lying there in the forest with the life leaking out of him. I don't understand."

Chris was standing in the doorway between the kitchen and living room.

"I'll call you later," he said to Noah. He turned back to the kitchen. "Maybe you should leave now, too," he suggested to Green.

Green hesitated, but in the end, he followed Chris out. I heard the screen door shut, and then it was silent. Noah sat beside me and rubbed my back.

"Do you want some tea or something?" he asked after a few minutes.

"No, thank you. You being here is all I need."

He got up and put a CD in the stereo. Soon the soft voice of Sting filled the room.

⁓ ⌣⤸

I woke up sometime after midnight. I was covered with the knitted afghan my mother had made when I'd bought my navy blue chairs. Noah was no longer sitting beside me. I turned off the CD player and went to bed.

The workday at Sil-Trac starts with a series of morning meetings. First, the supervisors pass critical information to the various team leaders and lead operators, and then drop in on whichever team might need help in enforcing any new procedures or policies. Usually, there's a frantic session of trading people around to cover unexpected absences that have been discovered. Only after our teams have started to work and we're sure the product will flow do we gather in our manager's office with the materials manager and the engineering manager to discuss the day's output.

You would think that, once product started its three-month journey through our production area, there wouldn't be much to talk about. The sad truth is that if one of our big customers called with a desperate need, we were not above snatching product designated for a small customer and giving it to the big guy. This set off a ripple effect that was felt from start to finish in the work area. It generally impacted multiple areas as well as the support staff.

Allan had been the one to represent materials management in these meetings. Jeanette was taking over, and doing a competent job, for the most part. She didn't have Allan's aggressive style, but she didn't let people push her around, either. Today she explained again why we still didn't have clean-room wipes and what she was doing about it. We would repeat this discussion every day until the wipes arrived. Our management believed this repeated bludgeoning tended to promote creative problem-solving. I'm not convinced they're wrong.

"Jeanette, can you explain why we can't get wipes from anyone? I thought that was why we had more than one supplier," I asked.

"There must be a problem with the source," she said. "They probably all order from the same factory. I'll check into it and let you know what I find."

The meeting was otherwise routine, and we were out in just under an hour.

Once the immediate chaos of changing shifts and morning meetings was over, the manufacturing area settled into quiet efficiency. Mechanical pickers and placers moved wafers along with only occasional human intervention. Absent any foreseeable disaster, I decided to drive to Allan's house again. Ken and Susan were arriving in a few hours and were going to be staying there, and I had no idea if there were clean linens or soap or any of the other necessities of daily living. On my previous visits to the house I'd had bigger fish to fry.

I stopped at the organic grocery store near his house and picked up bread, milk, orange juice and a couple of fresh bars of soap. On impulse, I picked up three votive candles that were labeled Refresh, Calm and Peace, along with a leaf-shaped pewter candleholder. These, I hoped, would help set the tone for the visit.

CHAPTER 23

AN OLDER WOMAN in a shapeless black cotton knit dress was watering a cluster of petunias at the front corner of Allan's yard. I pulled into the driveway and waved at her before I carried my bag up the steps to the porch. I stowed the perishables in the refrigerator and was relieved to find that Allan kept a tight ship. He had left no fresh food to spoil when he departed on his weekend adventure. There were two lemons still in good shape, a jug of drinking water, three sticks of butter and a carton of eggs with two missing. Assorted condiments lined the door, all with neatly closed and wiped lids. I closed the door quickly as thoughts of my own jumbled collection of chilled science projects crept into my consciousness.

I gathered the sheets and towels from the bedrooms and bathroom and headed toward the basement. I double-checked the latch before descending the stairs. This trip was uneventful, and I started my first load, set the timer on my watch and went back upstairs. Allan kept such a clean house, there was little to do. I didn't know if Ken or Susan would find it creepy to use a dead man's soap, so I threw away the partially used bars and installed the new ones I'd purchased, just in case.

The neighbor was still sprinkling plants in the area between the two yards. I went outside and joined her.

"Hello," I said.

"Good morning," she replied. "Are you a realtor?"

"No." This would be harder than I thought. How would I explain my position to people? "I'm a friend of Allan's."

"I don't think I've seen you around here before," she said.

"Allan and I worked together. At Sil-Trac," I explained.

"So, what are you doing here?"

"I'm checking out my new house." I wasn't in the mood for pushy neighbors.

"Allan isn't even in the ground yet, and they've sold off his property?" She turned back to the flowers on her side of the common space.

"Not that it's any of your business, but I inherited Allan's house. He left it to me in his will."

"Why would he do that?" she asked. "I've never seen you here before. I see who comes and goes on this street, not that I tried to spy on him. Can't help it — my kitchen window looks right out the front here."

"I've been here before." Once, I didn't add. Not counting my unexpected trip to the basement. "To be honest, I don't know why he left his house to me. But he did, with official papers filed with an attorney and everything." I wasn't sure why I was explaining anything to this shrew.

"Well, I suppose he had to leave it to someone, and he didn't have family, you know."

"I know he didn't. But he did have friends, and that's why I'm here. Allan was friends with a young couple in Montana —"

"Ken and Susan?"

"Yes, Ken and Susan," I continued. "They're coming for his memorial service Monday, and I told them they could stay here. They'll arrive later today, so I was just checking things out and dropping off some fresh food."

"They're such a nice young couple — they must be devastated. Not to speak ill of the dead, but Allan could have used a few more friends like them."

"He did have a variety of interests," I agreed, hoping that would keep her talking.

"That's the truth," she said. "If that's what you want to call them. Take that snippet he had on the side lately. She was a little young for him, if you ask me."

"Are you sure he was dating her?"

She looked over the top of her glasses at me. "I don't think she was coming to play chess. Friends don't spend the night, and then go home barefoot and in the same dress they arrived in the night before—and more than once, I might add. Friends don't come back a month later and sit in their parked car in front of the house for hours on end."

"You don't miss much, do you?"

She straightened. "Neighbors have to look out for each other."

I wondered where she'd been while I was locked in the basement. "I'm trying to make sure everyone is notified about Allan's memorial service. I suppose I should try to find this young woman," I said. "Do you know her name or how I might find her?"

"I don't believe I heard her name. Men don't usually introduce girls like that. She was a little thing. Asian, I'd guess. Dressed real smart, but then, it seems like those girls always do." She paused and seemed to be thinking. "No, I don't guess I can tell you any more than that." She returned to her watering.

I started back to Allan's house. The woman spoke without turning around.

"I did write down the license plate number. When that car was sitting out in front of his house for so long? I thought maybe she was planning on robbing the place or something, so I wrote it down. I can get it for you, if you want."

I retraced my steps. She handed me the hose and went into her house, returning a few minutes later with a number written on a piece of lavender notepaper.

"Will you let me know what you find out?" she asked before she released the paper from her grip.

I mumbled a reply she assumed was agreement.

Yeah, sure, was what I thought.

We parted ways at the curb. I gave her the hose and went in and put the load of sheets in the dryer. I'd have to come back later and make up the beds.

The neighbor had pulled her hose to the house and wound it up on a rack. She wasn't in sight when I left. I called Green on my cell phone as I eased my car down the quiet street, fumbling with my new handsfree earpiece.

"Just don't get ideas here, Nancy Drew," he said when I told him what I wanted. "The Portland Police Department isn't here for your private use, you know."

"Yeah, but aren't you curious about who was stalking Allan before he died?"

"Might be nothing," he said. "A small, young Asian woman doesn't sound like a good prospect for hitting a six-foot-plus male in the head. And we'd have to be able to place her in the forest."

"Still, it's something, isn't it?"

"I'll let you know when I find out who it is."

He called back as I pulled into the Sil-Trac parking lot twenty minutes later.

"That was quick," I said.

"I got friends. Are you sure you got the license number right?"

"That was the number the woman gave me. Why?"

"Well, that number belongs to a black Honda Accord registered to a Mr. Ichiro Komatsu, who is a forty-five-year-old male."

"Wait," I said, "did you say Komatsu?"

"Yeah."

"Geez," I said as the implications sank in.

"What?"

"I have to go," I said.

"Wait!"

I hung up before he could say more.

CHAPTER 24

MITSUKO KOMATSU AND ALLAN. It was hard to believe, but the pieces fit. He was asking his attorney about child support issues, she was definitely pregnant by someone and not, it would seem, Romeo.

If she *were* pregnant with Allan's child, he might have reason to want *her* to disappear but not the other way around. Why would she want him dead? It was clear Mitsuko's dad believed Romeo was the father, if his visit to the workplace was any indication. It was possible he had then found out the truth and gone to the forest in search of Allan, but that would assume he could come and go undetected and was able to overpower a larger and stronger man. Romeo was young and strong, and he clearly loved Mitsuko, but that didn't seem like enough of a reason for *him* to kill Allan. So, this could explain why Allan was asking his lawyer about paternity, but was it enough to cause someone to kill him?

It hit me then that, if Allan was the father of Mitsuko's baby, it was his rightful heir. I needed to talk to her.

Jose was in the breakroom. Like me, he was tired of listening to his workers complain about the missing wipes. We spent a few minutes commiserating.

"Jose, what can you tell me about Mitsuko Komatsu?" I asked when we finished.

"She's a good inspector," he said. "You're not trying to recruit her, are you?"

We sometimes made deals for operators that would rival major league sports in both their intensity and intricacy.

"No," I said. "I'm curious about her pregnancy."

"She hasn't been talking. I only knew because of her morning sickness. Even then, Donna told me, not Mitsuko. I assumed Romeo did the deed. He's the only guy I've seen hanging around her."

"That was my assumption, too." I said. "But apparently that's not the case. I was hoping to have a word with her."

"Why?"

I wasn't ready to tell anyone, even Jose, about my fears. "She stopped by to see me the other day, and we were interrupted by the news about Allan. It just seemed like she had more to say. I thought I'd drop by and give her a chance."

"Unfortunately, you just missed her. She had a doctor appointment this afternoon. She might come back to get her check. Do you want me to send her your way if she does?"

"It's not a big deal, but if you see her, I'd appreciate it if you could tell her I'm looking for her."

All was quiet back in my department. People were using a substitute clean-room wipe Jeanette had found. My new senior lead operator Pratima told me they were a lot like using wax paper in place of paper towels in your kitchen. The group understood there was no better option for the moment and were doing the best they could.

The Japanese contingent was busy with some sort of social visit from the Japanese consulate. There seemed to be a great deal of ceremonial social obligation required for Japanese companies doing business in Oregon. I took the opportunity to go back to Allan's and finish the laundry. Traffic was heavy on the Sunset Highway, but it kept moving, so I got there in under a half-hour. The neighborhood was quiet when I pulled into the driveway.

I wasn't sure which bedroom Ken and Susan would want to sleep in. There was one obvious guest room, and then a smaller bedroom with a single bed that seemed to be more for storage. I assumed they would use the guest room and not Allan's bedroom, so I had washed those sheets first. I'd left the linens from Allan's bed in the dryer when I'd gone back to work. They now smelled like meadow-fresh fabric softener instead of after-shave lotion. One more trace of Allan removed from this earth.

I carried the bedding upstairs and entered Allan's room. I'd been in a hurry earlier, but now I looked around.

There was dark wood furniture in a style I thought was called Mission. The dresser looked like it had been a family hand-me-down. The top was draped with a length of silk that looked like it had originally been an Indian sari. There were three pillar candles of varying heights at the back of the dresser top. A string of dark beads snaked around their base. I picked up the beads and let them cascade from one hand to the other. I'd never heard Allan say anything that suggested any Buddhist inclinations, but it just proved that you never know about a person's private life. I hoped the Unitarian Church included those with Buddhist leanings.

A postcard-sized picture in a black frame sat on the right-hand nightstand. It showed a couple standing by a nondescript blue sedan. The man was the image of Allan in build, but his face was different. There was no mistaking the nose on the woman. These had to be Allan's parents. It seemed to be the only picture on display.

A cedar chest sat at the foot of the bed. A pale-lavender chenille afghan was neatly folded on its top. I opened the closet door. Freshly dry-cleaned slacks and shirts hung in their plastic bags from the wooden closet pole. Dress shoes in the usual brown, black and cordovan were lined up beside an equal number of tennis shoes on the floor. In one corner were several pairs of bedroom slippers. A fuzzy blue pair in a decidedly feminine size seemed out of place. I picked one up. The bottom was well worn. These were definitely someone's old friends. Maybe Allan was one of those guys who kept a trophy to remind him of past loves.

When I finished making the bed, I replaced the comforter. I took it back off and flipped it over so the striped side was replaced by a large floral print. It wasn't much, but it didn't look quite as masculine as it had.

I took one last glance around the room and stepped out into the hallway, shutting the door behind me. I'd reached the top of the stairs when I heard a key rattling in the back door lock. I reached into my pocket for my cell phone, my finger poised like a gunfighter's over the 911 autodial button.

"Hello?" I called down as the door opened.

"Hi, it's just us, Susan and Ken," a feminine voice replied as I arrived at the bottom of the stairs.

A short, wiry blonde woman stood just inside the kitchen door. Her khaki cargo shorts were topped with a faded purple T-shirt that advertised Ken's Mountain Mercantile and Grocery.

"Ken's getting our bags," she said, and looked at the floor as if suddenly interested in the linoleum pattern.

"I'm Harley Spring," I said. "I'm sorry we have to meet under such difficult circumstances."

We were standing in awkward silence when Ken entered the kitchen carrying two large nylon duffel bags.

"You must be Harley," he said.

He set the bags down and extended his hand. I clasped it in a business handshake.

"Nice to meet you, although I wish it had been under better circumstances," I said. I realized I was repeating myself, but I didn't know what else to say.

Another strained silence followed.

"I'll leave you two to get settled in, then," I said and headed for the door. I turned back, intending to point out the note I'd left on the dining room table listing the address for the memorial service and giving them my phone number. They were standing where I'd left them, and looked so forlorn I spoke without thinking. "Why don't you come to my house for dinner tonight? You can meet some of the people Allan worked with."

Ken's expression softened, and I knew I had stumbled onto the right thing to do.

"That would be real nice," he said quietly. Susan murmured her assent, and I added my address and a simple map to the paper I retrieved from the dining room.

"How about seven?"

"We'll be there," Susan said.

CHAPTER 25

MY FIRST CALL AS I got into my car was to Mrs. Johnson. I explained the situation to her, and she assured me she could handle it. She complained on a regular basis that she was the most underutilized housekeeper in Portland. Any excuse for her to spend time away from "her Henry" was cause for celebration.

"I'll pop a couple of those pre-seasoned pork tenderloins in the oven, and we can slice them and serve them with crusty rolls. We'll set it up buffet-style with condiments and maybe slices of a mild cheddar or Gouda, and people can make little sandwiches. I can cut up a tray of carrots and celery and some of those sweet yellow peppers Neva Dean's growing on her patio. And maybe you can stop on the way home and pick up a quart of assorted olives from the olive bar at New Seasons. I've got some Dubliner cheese and a nice Havarti we can put on a tray with crackers. I'll have my Henry pick up some things to drink and the paper goods at Costco and we'll be all set."

"Mrs. J, you're a wonder," I said and rang off. I immediately dialed work and, even though it was Friday afternoon, found Jeanette at her desk. I explained the situation, and she assured me that not only would she come to my house but she was sure she could get Tim to come, too.

Karen was my next call, and she, too, agreed to stop by. Neva Dean Willett hadn't known Allan, but she was the kind of person who knew the right thing to say in any situation, so I added her and her peppers to our group. Finally, in an attempt to appease

Detective Green, I called and left a message on his voice mail inviting him to the evening's festivities.

My car had barely started rolling when my phone rang.

"Is there something you'd like to tell me?" Noah demanded. "Mrs. J is running around like a chicken with its head cut off, and she has Mr. J here, too."

"We're having a small gathering at our house tonight."

"And I guess it was too much trouble to tell me?" he complained. "Am I even invited? Or are you sending me away, like you always do?"

"Let's just calm down," I said. "This came up kind of suddenly."

"Yet somehow, you invited people and told Mrs. J," he said. "That doesn't sound too sudden."

"Noah, please. This is hard enough. Some people Allan knew are staying at his house. I was there making the beds when they arrived, and they don't know anyone here and I invited them over. It's not like it's a major party or anything. They just seemed a little lost, so I invited them, okay?"

"So, who-all is coming over?" he asked, a little of the anger leaving his voice.

"The couple—Ken and Susan, the two purchasing people who worked directly for Allan, the HR lady from my work—you met her at the company picnic two years ago."

"Is that all?" he asked.

"Well, that's all from work. Then I invited Neva Dean, because she can talk to anyone, and that might help, since we don't know these people."

"Anyone else?"

"I invited Detective Green."

"Yes! I knew you were starting to like him."

"I'm not 'starting to like' anyone," I said. "It just seems easier to invite him than to have to try to tell him what everyone said afterward."

"Whatever," he said.

I assured Noah that Chris was invited, and that I was on my way home.

New Seasons Market is a grocery store chain in Portland that is trying to give shoppers the best of both worlds. It has a full selection of organic products that are shelved alongside those old

126

favorites you can't do any other way, like Kraft Macaroni and Cheese and Coca-Cola. It's brightly lit and has knowledgeable department staff, and can always be counted on for good food samples. It was always an enjoyable escape to shop there.

The front-featured sample for the day was a soy drink that did not tempt me, so I went straight to the bakery and its bread bowl. Once I was fortified with a generous sample of Kalamata olive bread, I made my way to the olive bar. The international selection of olives was daunting. In the end, I filled my quart container with a combination chosen by size and color and hoped for the best. A quick trip down the chocolate aisle completed my trip. I follow the chocolate theory of shopping. The idea is that any shopping trip that ends with a couple of chocolate balls will be a success, no matter what else ends up in your basket.

A lime green teapot caught my attention. I turned away from my cart and picked it up to check the price. At twenty-nine dollars it was less tempting than I had first thought. I returned it to the shelf and went back to my cart. Two bottles of red wine were now sitting in its front corner. A slip of paper was wrapped around the neck of the Napa Valley Merlot. It was held in place with a thin rubber band. I pulled if off and flattened it in my palm.

"Put these in your wine cellar," it said.

I looked up. The aisle in front of me was empty. I turned and looked behind me. A small dark man in a pinstripe suit lifted his black-lensed sunglasses, winked at me and disappeared around the end of the aisle.

The months of therapy that followed my divorce from Sam allowed me to take the bottles of wine out of my cart and set them on the nearest shelf without a second thought. Whatever game he was playing, I was out.

Friday night traffic took my attention on the drive home. My neighborhood was quiet as I parked in the garage. Noah and Chris met me at the door.

"Can we go to Burger King?" Noah asked.

It was a bit of a walk, and Mrs. J was undoubtedly cooking an army's worth of food, but I agreed.

"Just make sure you are back before seven," I said.

Mrs. Johnson was peeling carrots at the sink when I entered the kitchen.

"How are we doing?" I asked.

"Don't you worry," she said. "We'll have a fine party." She knew how nervous entertaining made me under the best of circumstances. I could hold my own in a roomful of angry assemblers but making small talk in a social setting made me break out in a cold sweat.

"Someone left a box with bottles of red wine in it on the back step," Mrs. J said. "There was a note that said 'Put these in your wine cellar.' Do we have a wine cellar?" she asked.

"Where are they?" I asked. "You know as well as I do we don't have a wine cellar. It's probably fine, and if I know Sam, expensive, but I'm still not going to serve wine that was anonymously dropped on our doorstep. I'll put it in the basement and deal with Sam later."

Mrs. J pulled the box of wine from under the kitchen table. I took it and headed down the steps to the basement. Cher was pacing across the shelf we'd built at the back of the stairwell. Her food dishes sat on the shelf—a person could reach it from the second stair. We'd built a narrow walkway along the top of the wood trim that circled the stairwell so Cher could reach it, but Sonny couldn't come anywhere close, insuring she could eat in peace. Sonny was an ill-tempered pet, and only his deep devotion to Noah insured his continued place in our family.

I stroked Cher's back and scratched her ears and walked down the remaining stairs.

"Mrs. J," I yelled. "Could you come down here?"

The back wall of my basement had shelves that held large storage tubs. I kept things like Christmas decorations, ice chests and suitcases on them, too. Someone had removed a section of the lower shelf and installed one of those dorm-refrigerator-style wine cellars with the smoke-glass doors. It was about half-full of wine bottles.

"Where did that come from?" Mrs. J asked.

"That's what I'd like to know. Who was here today?" I opened the door and discovered Sam had stocked a selection of both white and red wines.

"No one was here," she said. "Noah was at my house in the morning, helping Mr. J change the oil in his truck. I was baking bread."

"So, what about after we talked?" I shut the door and latched it.

"I had to wait for my bread to finish baking. That was about twenty minutes. I pulled the pork loin from my garage freezer, packed my basket and came over."

"I hate this. If I call my lawyer, Sam will take Noah away. If I don't, we're stuck with him doing this kind of nonsense." I started to run my hand through my unruly hair but stopped when I realized it was Sam's gesture.

"I have carrots to cut," Mrs. J said and stomped back up the stairs. She didn't have much patience for fence-sitters.

I went back to the cellar and took a closer look at the wine. I had to give him credit—he had picked good ones.

Voices interrupted my wine survey. I put a fine-looking Allende 1998 Rioja Aurus back in the cabinet and went back upstairs. Green stood in the middle of the kitchen dipping a freshly cut carrot stick into Mrs. J's dill dip.

"Hey, Harley," he mumbled through his mouthful of carrot. He swallowed and wiped his hands on the paper towel Mrs. J handed him. "I thought I'd come early and find out what's going on here."

"What do you mean?"

"Well..." He paused. "As you are so fond of pointing out, we aren't exactly friends, and when it comes to my job, you generally do whatever it takes to make things more difficult. So, I'm wondering what I'm doing here."

"It's simple," I said. "I feel bad about calling Ken and Susan after I said I wouldn't, so I'm making it up by handing them to you. You can talk to them all evening if you want."

"Nothing is simple with you, lady. Let's try again. Why am I *really* here?"

"I have no other agenda. Unless, of course, you count the part about how if you don't find a better suspect I get charged with murder. A murder I didn't do, I might add."

"You must be getting desperate if you're even thinking of co-operating with me," he said. "No, I'm not buying it."

"Look, Green." I gave him my best sincere look. "I'd rather have a root canal than entertain people I don't really know. This wasn't a well-thought-out plan. Ken and Susan got into town, and they just looked so forlorn, I invited them to my 'dinner party' before I knew it."

"That I can believe," he said. "You seem to be fond of the 'ready, fire, aim' way of doing things. Whatever your reasons were for inviting me—and I don't think you've told me the real one yet—I'm glad you did. I have to agree with you. Things aren't looking good."

"Thanks for the reminder," I said.

Mr. J pulled his Ford Explorer into the driveway, and Green went out to meet him and carry the boxes of paper goods into the kitchen. Mrs. J assured me things were under control and I could go freshen up.

Noah and Chris came home while I was changing. I put on a pale-avocado linen tank top and natural linen slacks. I'd contemplated a pair of linen-trimmed sandals I'd bought on sale and had yet to wear. In the end, I slipped my feet into worn Birkenstocks. Tonight was going to be painful enough without adding sore feet to my problems.

The boys were at the kitchen table with Detective Green. Mr. and Mrs. J were busy at the sink. There were still thirty minutes before the guests would arrive, and I seemed to be the odd person out; so I grabbed Sonny's leash and clipped it to his collar. He started bobbing up and down and whining.

"I'm going to walk him around the block and let him stretch his legs, since he's going to have to be locked in the basement all evening," I said to the room.

I made it to the corner of 25th without incident. I had started down Stanton Street when I passed a man in a dark-grey suit bent over rummaging in the trunk of a silver late-model BMW. I was almost clear of the car when a voice said, "Meet me at the wine cellar at eight p.m."

I didn't even look.

"Sam, I'm asking you nicely. Please don't do this to me tonight. I'm having a hard time, and I really can't cope with your games right now."

Sonny took advantage of my hesitation to lift his leg on a small shrub in the strip between the sidewalk and the street.

"This is dead serious," he said. "Be there." He slammed the trunk lid, walked around the car and got in the driver's side. He drove off without another word, leaving Sonny and me standing at the curb.

"I'm not going to have to worry about jail," I said to Sonny. "I'm going to be in a mental hospital, and Sam will have put me there."

Chapter 26

WE COMPLETED OUR WALK around the block without incident. This was a big feat for Sonny, who was prone to nipping the ankles of anyone who looked at him wrong.

I was ready to bite someone by the time we arrived home. My mood didn't improve when I walked into the kitchen. I could see two figures in the living room. Detective Green was talking to a man whose back was toward me. Mrs. J took Sonny downstairs while I hung up his leash.

"Harley," Green said. "Mr. Stange was just telling me how he and Allan knew each other." He sounded deceptively calm. "He says he and Allan were in the marines together."

The man with Green turned around. It took every ounce of strength I possessed not to explode. His hair was dyed, he had on dark-brown contacts and a really good prosthetic nose, but I'd lived with Sam and his disguises too long not to recognize him.

"I'm sorry?" I said lamely, not knowing what fiction Sam had told Green to explain his presence.

"I was just telling him how fortunate it was that I called while you were at Allan's today."

"Yeah," Green said. "It must have been a real shock hearing about Allan that way. One thing I was wondering, though..." He looked at Sam.

"What's that?" Sam asked, smiling but not meaning it.

"Well, if you didn't know Allan was dead, how come you called a working man in the middle of the working day?"

"I was just leaving a message on his machine. A couple of guys were putting together a card game. I was checking to see if he wanted in. It wasn't worth bothering him at work."

"You must have an understanding boss that lets you arrange card games during the working day," Green said. "What is it you said you do?"

"I didn't say," Sam shot back.

"Mr. Stange works in corporate security," I said, naming a job I'd heard Sam use when we were married. I sounded a little formal, but I had no idea what first name he'd given Green. "Can I get either of you a drink?"

Green raised a nearly full tumbler of Perrier. Sam asked for a microbrew. I went back to the kitchen.

"What is Dad doing here?" Noah asked me in a stage whisper. Sam's changing appearance never fooled him, either. He believed his father worked in a security job that involved undercover work. Maybe he did.

"I don't know. He wants me to meet him in the basement later, so I suppose all will be revealed then. Since he's in disguise and pretending to be a Mister Stange, you probably shouldn't call him Dad."

"You guys are so weird," he said. "I don't know which is worse, the fact that Dad lives in a fantasy world, or the fact that you're willing to go along with it."

"Noah, you of all people should know by now that confronting your dad with reality does no one any good. At least this way he stays calm—most of the time, anyway."

Noah rolled his eyes skyward. "Whatever," he said. He grabbed two cans of Coke and headed back to his bedroom, where he and Chris were waging video game war.

The doorbell rang while I was getting Sam's beer. By the time I got back into the living room, Jeanette and Ken and Susan had come in and were chatting like old friends. I introduced Green.

"Alex Stange," Sam said, and shook hands with Ken. He was smooth, I had to give him that.

Tim and Neva Dean arrived, followed shortly by Karen. Our party was underway.

Mrs. J circulated with a tray of cheese and vegetables. I took drink orders from the new arrivals and delivered their requests.

When I'd handed off the last one, Green took me by the elbow and steered me into the kitchen.

"I thought we just agreed you weren't going to do any more end runs on me in this investigation," he said.

"What are you talking about?"

"As if you don't know," he said. "Mere moments ago, you were apologizing for calling Ken and Susan and promising to never do anything like that again."

"I didn't," I said. "I swear. He just came out of nowhere. Like he said, he called, and I told him about Allan and it only seemed right to invite him to this." I didn't like lying, even to Green.

"That sounds innocent enough, except we both know you only planned this party *after* Ken and Susan arrived, *after* this joker is supposed to have called."

"I called him back after I knew about the party."

"And then you just forgot to tell me, when you told me every-one else who would be here?"

"Yes, I forgot, so shoot me." I said.

"There's something about that guy that isn't right."

"I'm afraid I can't help you. He says he was Allan's friend, and I really have no way of knowing if he was or wasn't, although it would be a little weird for someone to go to a pre-funeral party for a total stranger." I left him in the kitchen and went back to my guests.

Ken stood at the fireplace, leaning his arm on the mantle. He was intently listening to Tim, who was explaining something that involved a lot of hand gestures. Karen and Jeanette were clustered around Green, who sat on the overstuffed arm of the blue chair. Sam was looking at my collection of CDs as if he'd never seen it before.

Neva Dean got up from her spot next to Susan on the couch.

"She's a tough nut to crack, that one," she said. "Even her an-gels are drab, if you can imagine that."

She went into the kitchen, where she would undoubtedly tell all to Mrs. J. I was glad they enjoyed each other's company, but if I wasn't careful, Mrs. J would find other ways to escape her Henry besides hanging out at my house.

I made my way over to the sofa and sat down in the seat Neva Dean had just vacated.

"Hi," I said. "This must be hard for you."

"You're very nice to invite us to your…" She hesitated. "… gathering," she finished and blushed.

"I though you might like to meet some of Allan's friends. At least you don't have to just sit in his house and be reminded."

She looked at her hands and twisted what was left of a handful of Kleenex.

"Has anyone spoken to you about the memorial service?" I asked.

"Nothing besides your phone call."

"Karen is organizing the service, but I know she would like to hear from anyone who could give her some guidance about what Allan might have found meaningful. I can call her over, if you want." I started to raise my hand to get Karen's attention.

"Miss Spring," Susan said and pulled my arm down. "That won't be necessary. The truth is, you probably know Allan better than Ken and me."

I must have had a puzzled look on my face.

"I know we stayed at his house and all, but we weren't really friends. Kenny's parents and Allan's parents were friends—after Allan was away from home. Our only real connection was the accident." She held up two fingers on each hand and made quotation marks in the air as she said the word *accident*. "Allan's parents were taking Kenny's parents to the airport when they were all killed. The police said it was Allan's dad's fault. I think Allan felt guilty. His parents were older, Kenny's were still relatively young. Allan's parents left him insurance money and property he didn't need. Kenny's parents left him with a house mortgaged to the hilt and cars that weren't paid for. Allan paid to bury Kenny's parents, but Kenny wouldn't take anything else from Allan at the time. He was young and angry."

"I take it they mended their relationship before Allan died," I said.

"I wouldn't say it was mended, but they were doing better. Allan made an effort to stay in touch and to come see Kenny every now and then. Eventually, he convinced Kenny to take some money to start the store. Kenny insisted it be a loan, not a gift. We would stay with Allan when we were on buying trips to Portland, but only because we couldn't afford to stay at a motel."

"That must have helped, didn't it?"

"I guess," she said, and her eyes filled with tears. "Kenny was just so angry, and Allan was so understanding. Now, it'll never change."

I looked around. Where was Neva Dean when I needed her? I could hand over a box of Kleenex without missing a beat when my workers were in tears, but this was different.

"How often did you come to Portland?" I asked.

She dabbed at the corner of her eye with her Kleenex shred. "I only came a few times. Ken came every season—he liked to buy handmade stuff at the Saturday market here. That way, he wasn't just another gift shop with the same doodads everyone else in town has. And he's trying to make an arrangement to sell cheese and pepperoni snack packs from the Tillamook Cheese factory, too."

"When was the last time you were here?"

"Well, *I* haven't been since March."

"What about Ken?"

"I thought you knew," she said. "He had just gotten back when we got your call about Allan."

Susan and I were each lost in our own thoughts when Neva Dean came back carrying two plates. She handed one with cheese and bread and olives to Susan.

"The man in the kitchen wants to talk to you," she said to me. "He wants to ask you something about the wine. Funny, though…"

"What's that?"

"I watched him. He's been nursing the same bottle of beer all night."

She took my place when I stood up.

"So, tell me about that store of yours," I heard her say to Susan.

CHAPTER 27

THE KITCHEN WAS EMPTY when I went in. I could hear the faint sound of canned laughter coming from the upstairs attic room — Mr. and Mrs. J were probably watching their favorite sitcom on the portable TV. I opened the door and went down to the basement.

"You're late," Sam said from the shadows. He was sitting on a step stool. Sonny was curled up by his feet, the little traitor.

I pulled a wooden crate over and sat on it.

"So, what is so important that we had to do all this cloak-and-dagger stuff?" I asked.

He didn't rise to the bait, which was a relief but scared me at the same time.

"What is it?"

He rubbed his hand slowly over his short dark hair. "Harley, my contacts in the department told me the DA is pressuring them to arrest someone for your friend's murder."

"That's not a big surprise, is it?" I asked. "Isn't that what DAs do?"

"This isn't a joke, Harley. He's talking about *you*. They're preparing paperwork on you."

I felt the blood drain out of my face. My vision started clouding. My face felt hot and clammy at the same time. Sam jumped up and came to my side. He put his hand on my back and pushed my head down between my knees.

"Breathe deep," he said. "Look, I'm sorry." His hand made slow circles on my back. "I'm not trying to hurt you here. I've looked at what your buddy upstairs has got, and he's hasn't found anything that points anywhere but right at you."

I raised my head up to argue, but my vision started swimming, so I dropped my head down again.

"Come on, breathe. Slow. That's right." He crouched down beside me. "I'm not telling you this just to torment you. I know you think I am, but I'm not. I just need something to work with. Tell me everything you can think of, no matter how small it seems."

"I've been through all that with Green. Allan was lying on the ground when I came out of the trees. I saw him at the hospital, but he wasn't awake, so I just sat a while and then left. I didn't know anything about him leaving me his house. Stop me if you've heard this before."

"What about work?" Sam asked. "Has anything out of the ordinary been going on there? Remember that people kill people for all kinds of reasons. It's rarely because of the big stuff."

"Well, one of our workers is pregnant, and Allan could be the father."

"Jesus, he slept with one of his employees? That's kind of slimy."

"Well, she didn't work for him directly, but yeah, not one of his better moves. And her dad showed up at work the day we left and was out for blood. He didn't seem to know about Allan, though. He was after her current boyfriend."

"Is he the father of the baby?"

"I don't think so, but who knows. I don't know for sure Allan slept with her, but the neighbor did see a young Asian woman coming and going and she took the car license and Green says it's our worker."

"Okay, that's something." He pulled a small spiral notebook and a pen from his inside coat pocket. He wrote down Mitsuko's and Romeo's names.

I raised my head slowly. Nothing happened.

"I did learn something interesting tonight," I said. "Allan's alleged friends Ken and Susan weren't exactly bosom buddies. Ken, especially, might have had and ax to grind with Allan." I told him the story about the death of their parents. "Susan just told me tonight that Allan's dad was identified as having caused the accident. I'm sure it didn't help that Allan benefited while Ken lost everything. Also, I think Ken might have been at least in Portland and maybe Tillamook while we were at camp or shortly after we returned."

Sam made more notes. "What else?"

"Isn't that enough?"

"I don't know. Is there anything else?"

"Nothing real unusual is happening at work. Our schedule is behind, and we're pretty sure our customer has double-booked the order and will cancel if we don't deliver on time. We always have schedule-related problems, though. And frankly, if our competition wanted to mess up our production, there would be more critical people than Allan to take out."

"I'll check it out, but I agree, it doesn't feel right."

"Other than that, we can't seem to get our hands on our favorite clean room wipes, but I can't quite see that as being a motive, either."

"If you think of anything else, let me know right away." He stood and pulled a bottle of wine out of the wine keeper. Sonny jumped up and ran up the stairs.

Sam put the bottle beside my perch just as Green came down the basement steps, Sonny dancing around his feet, his tail beating a staccato rhythm on Green's pant leg. Sam held my arm as I got up.

"Are you going to be okay?" he asked softly.

"That's what I'd like to know," Green said. "You were gone so long; I thought I'd better see if something had happened. You do have a thing about basements, lately. Seems like I was right."

"Harley was showing me her collection of red wine, and she had a dizzy spell," Sam said.

"I'm fine," I said. "I'm just tired."

"Are you sure that's all? I can take you out the back door and run you over to the ER and let them have a quick look-see."

His concern was kind of touching.

"That won't be necessary. I'll get some rest when everyone goes home, and I'll be fine."

"I know you're under a lot of pressure right now, but you would let me know if it was something more. Something I could help you with. Wouldn't you?" he asked.

"The only thing you can do for me is find out who killed Allan."

"Let me help you up the stairs," Sam said, brushing past Green. He held my arm. Green followed us.

Green got me a glass of water, and then Sam guided me to the living room sofa, where Neva Dean was sitting alone.

"Honey, you look awful," she said. "What happened?"

I was getting tired of people telling me how awful I looked. I was going to have to do something. Perhaps a new lipstick would do the trick. Maybe they had one called "Innocent."

"I just had a little dizzy spell while I was in the basement."

She took my hand in her warm clasp. "What is it, Harley?"

My eyes filled with tears. Neva Dean handed me a soft linen handkerchief. She shifted to the edge of the sofa and turned her back to the room, effectively blocking me from anyone's view.

"Now, you tell Neva Dean what's going on, and we'll just see what we can do."

"I don't think you can fix this one," I blubbered. "They're really going to arrest me for Allan's murder."

"You didn't murder anyone," Neva Dean said indignantly. "Detective Green knows you didn't kill anyone."

"Knowing it and proving it are two different things. The DA is pressuring the police to arrest someone, and I'm the only one they've got."

"Well, we know you didn't do it, so you just have to find out who did."

"I know, but this isn't TV. I'm not some colorful and witty citizen sleuth who solves the crime at the end of an hour. This is real life — my life. If something doesn't happen, and soon, I'm going to jail."

"Honey, you are not going to jail. Your angels just don't indicate anything of the sort." She looked up for a moment. "Okay, they think you have the information you need to figure this out."

"I've been over it a thousand times. There's nothing there."

"Why don't you try *not* thinking about it for a while? Sometimes, that's the best way. When these people leave, maybe you could take a nice bath and have a cup of tea and relax."

A bath did sound like a great idea. I wasn't holding out much hope for a bath time revelation, though.

"Thanks, Neva Dean, I'll try that."

I got up and went to the bathroom to wash my face off. When I came back out, Jeanette got up from the blue chair and intercepted me at the end of the hall.

"Harley? Is it true?" she said.

"What?" I asked, although I suspected I knew what.

"Well, Ken said he heard that the police were close to making an arrest. And I think we all know who suspect number one is. I don't mean to sound harsh, but you *are* the one who benefited most from Allan's death. And you did find him—twice."

"Except I didn't have any reason to kill Allan. Yes, I inherited his house and money, but I didn't need it. Well, I mean, everyone can use more money, but I'm not in any kind of financial trouble or anything."

"We don't know if you had some reason to want the money, though. Maybe you have a sick relative or something."

"Jeanette!" I protested. "How can you think that?"

"Oh, well, I don't. I was just trying to think what the police must be thinking."

"Thanks for sugar coating it."

"Seriously, is there anything I can do to help?" she asked. "I could be a character witness. Tell them that you probably wouldn't do something like this."

"*Probably* is the best you can do? I think I need a little more confidence than that."

"I'm not saying I suspect you, but wake up and smell the French roast. It's going to be someone we know. I mean, how likely is it that some strange maniac was roaming around in the woods and happened upon Allan and was able to overpower him and hit him? Then that selfsame maniac was able to sneak into his hospital room? I don't think so."

"When you put it that way, I have to agree. As much as we don't want to believe it, it probably is going to be someone we know. It just happens the someone isn't me."

"Well, I better go," she said. I wished I could dismiss my problems as easily as she did. "My cat doesn't like it if I stay out too late."

"Thanks for coming," I said. I wanted to say "Take your suspicions and go away and don't ever come back," but I didn't. She lacked finesse, but I could count on her to tell it like it is.

Jeanette picked up her sweater and purse and headed for the door, Tim followed along like the underling he was.

"Well, she's just a breath of fresh air," Karen said when Jeanette was out of earshot.

"Yes, but it's that same bluntness we appreciate so much when she's getting parts out of our vendors," I said. "Besides, she's right. Whoever killed Allan is probably someone we know."

"That may be true about whoever hit Allan, but Steven told me whoever killed him had to know their way around a needle. He thinks it will turn out that someone shot air or something worse into his IV with a syringe."

"Anyone could have that knowledge. How would we know? People have all kinds of secrets in their private lives." The image of Karen and Steven groping each other came to mind.

"Well, I took a look at the personnel files of everyone on the trip. Just to see if anyone was a nursing school graduate or a medical school dropout."

"And?"

"And nothing. Not even a hint of medical knowledge. Whoever did it either isn't one of us, or they got their knowledge elsewhere."

"Do you happen to know what Mitsuko Komatsu's father does?" I asked.

"No, but I might be able to find out. He and Mr. Iguchi seem to be buddies. I'll get back to you on that." She glanced at her watch. "I've got to go. Thanks for putting this together, it was nice." She pulled her keys our of her Coach bag. She turned back, gave me a brief social hug and left.

Ken and Susan were the next to leave. Susan stared at the wall behind me as Ken made a stiff thank you and goodbye. I could see her eyes were again filled with tears. I knew now it was more for the lost opportunity than the actual loss, but it was touching just the same.

I took a deep breath and headed for the kitchen and my remaining three guests. The room was divided. Green was speaking to Mrs. J at the sink, but his attention was on Sam, who was across the room sitting at the table with Neva Dean.

"Mr. Stange, would you mind dropping me by my place on your way home?" Neva Dean asked Sam. "I don't live far from here."

"Sure, no problem," he said and looked at me. "Thanks for inviting me. It was good to meet some of Allan's other friends."

Neva Dean fetched her purse and cardigan. Sam took the sweater and held it out for her to slip her arms in like the gentleman he was — sometimes.

"Harley, I'll call you tomorrow, and you try that bath," Neva Dean said, and slipped her hand into Sam's bent elbow.

He guided her slowly through the living room and out the front door. She could play the helpless granny role to perfection. It was hard to tell who was conning whom.

When they were gone, Green took my hand and led me out onto the front porch without saying anything. We sat on the porch swing. Neither of us spoke for a few minutes.

Finally, he broke the silence. "Harley, I don't know what to do."

"What do you mean?"

"You know what I mean."

I was afraid I did, but let the silence fall between us again.

"Okay, let's start with who Mr. Stange is. And don't even try to tell me you just met him. That little scene in the basement proves that's not true."

"He was just helping me," I protested.

"Harley, the dog said otherwise."

"What do you mean?" I tried to sound innocent but missed the mark.

"That dog barks at everyone he sees. And he bites anyone who moves quick. I should know — I still have the scars. But this new guy comes, and nothing. No show of teeth, and not a sound. I'm just a dumb cop, but if you ask me, the dog knows the guy."

I didn't say anything.

"And since when did you get a wine cellar? I searched your whole basement after your break-in last spring. You didn't have a wine box. You don't even drink wine. A mini-fridge full of Diet Cokes I could believe, but not wine. Help me out here."

"I know you're trying to help me."

He leaned forward in the swing, his face in his hands.

"Mr. Stange is just some guy." I said to his back. "There's no mystery there. I don't know why my dog likes him — maybe just because he's weird."

"Harley, I'm trying to keep you from being arrested, but you're not helping," he said, his voice muffled by his hands. He sat back up. The moonlight illuminated the creases around his eyes. He looked tired.

"I understand the stakes here. It's my life. I'm scared. If I get arrested, what will happen to Noah?"

"You know I won't let anything happen to Noah."

"You won't have a choice. Sam will come and take him away, even if I'm cleared."

"I've got people going through Allan's life with a fine-toothed comb, but so far, we aren't getting anywhere. The guy seems to have lived an ordinary life, right up until someone hit him in the head."

"Well, there is one thing," I said. "Maybe."

"Jeez, don't keep me in suspense here"

"When I spoke to Allan's lawyer, he said Allan had recently asked him some questions about paternity."

"Go on."

I knew if I stopped, I wouldn't tell him everything, so I plunged ahead, talking faster now. "I know it's a stretch, but one of the associates at work is pregnant. We thought it was her boyfriend, but he says he isn't the dad."

"This wouldn't happen to be a young Asian stalker, would it?" Green asked.

"According to the neighbor. But I'm not sure she saw Mitsuko Komatsu in that car. She saw her coming in and out of the house, and then a month later she saw the car."

"Let me guess—the car is registered to her daddy?"

"According to you."

"So, Nancy Drew, have you talked to her?"

It was dark, so he couldn't see my face flush. "I tried, but she was gone to a doctor appointment."

"Why don't you let me do my job for once? I can question her about her relationship with Allan," he said.

"I know you don't like my input, but she isn't going to talk to you about her relationship with Allan, if she had one."

"This may surprise you, but many people find me easy to talk to."

"With all due respect, Green, I know my work force. A young Japanese woman is not going to spill her guts to you about an out-of-wedlock pregnancy. She has caused her family great shame in their community. Daddy isn't going to *let* her talk to you. Believe me, I've met the man."

"Daddy isn't going to have a choice."

"Could you just let me try talking to her on Monday? You could talk to Daddy in the meantime and find out if he was in front of Allan's. He did show up at work uninvited, you know. He was after the wrong guy, but he was plenty mad."

"I can try to stall Harper until Tuesday. She has Monday off, so it shouldn't be too hard, but that's all I can promise. The DA is really pressuring us on this one. I don't mean to rub it in, but the clock's running."

Tears filled my eyes again. I'm not usually prone to such displays of emotion, but I was starting to feel trapped. Noah was depending on me, and I was betting our future on one conversation with Misuko Komatsu.

Green put his arm around my shoulders and pulled me to his chest. He leaned back in the swing and kicked it into motion. For just a minute, I let myself lean on him. His chest was strong and warm, and I felt safe wrapped in the circle of his arms. I also felt weak. But if I was going to jail in three days, I deserved a weak moment.

We were still in the swing when Noah and Chris came banging out the back door. They went past the front porch and were at the street before they stopped, spun around and came back.

"Whoa," said Noah. "I didn't even see you two kids." His grin went ear to ear. "I'm spending the night at Chris's. Mrs. J said you wouldn't mind." He didn't wait for a reply. He and Chris jumped the front fence and went off down the sidewalk.

I broke away from Green. "We need to nip that in the bud," I said.

He pulled me back to his shoulder. "Why?" he said. "We're just two people taking a little comfort where we can find it."

"You know he'll read more into it than that."

"Would that be so terrible?"

"His situation is so complicated with his father. I have to be really careful."

"I do understand. I'm not asking anything here. I'm truly just offering a shoulder to cry on." He started the swing moving again.

"We can't un-ring the bell tonight, so you might as well make the most of it."

I knew this was all wrong, but I stayed where I was anyway.

CHAPTER 28

MY SLEEP WAS RESTLESS that night. I dreamed I was a trapeze artist at a circus. Two male figures were on the swings. One wore black and one white. I would twine my limbs with first one man and then, with perfect timing and a graceful twist, switch to the other guy. I wore a blood-red leotard. A clown with blue fuzzy slippers marched a pattern across the ring, a shotgun held loosely in its large white gloves. On my last pass, the black figure let me go, but when I twisted around the white figure was gone. The clown raised its gun as if it were shooting skeet...

I awoke with a jolt. My heart was beating like a hammer. I sat up, dislodging Cher from her perch on my chest. She reached her paws to their full extension and performed a slow stretch. I did the same.

I hadn't taken the relaxing bath Neva Dean suggested the previous night but decided it would be a perfect way to start my Saturday. Mrs. J wasn't due to come over, and Noah was at Chris's, so I had breakfast duty for the animals before I could indulge in a long hot soak.

I opened my bedroom door and was hit in the face with the smell of fresh-brewed coffee. Too many people had access to my house for me to be completely panicked by this, but Mrs. J and I drank tea, and Noah thought coffee was disgusting. I went back into my bedroom and pulled on a pair of sweatpants to go with my Minnie Mouse sleepshirt. I grabbed my cell phone and again poised my finger to speed dial. I tiptoed down the short hallway and peeked into the kitchen.

"Oh, for crying out loud," I said, and stepped into the middle of the room. "Don't you ever knock?"

"Not while my kid lives under your roof," Sam said. "And good morning to you, too."

His hair was the white-blonde color it had been a few days ago, so the dark must have been of the washout variety. His eyes were back to their more natural-looking robin's-egg blue. The hooked nose was gone, and only a slight red line on either side of his face caused by his sensitivity to prosthetic glue remained.

"Did you find anything out that can help me?" I asked.

"I'm flattered that you think I'm superman, but no, I slept last night, just like you. Although I thought I was going to be up all night waiting for your friend to leave so I could come in."

"You slept *here*?" I said, my voice rising in an unattractive way. I wasn't sure why I felt as if I'd been caught cheating. We were divorced, after all.

"I wanted to ask you a few more questions about Allan, but it was so late by the time Green left, and you seemed shot, so I figured I'd just sleep over and ask you this morning."

"You can't keep doing this, Sam. We're divorced. You don't live here. You can't just keep coming and going as you please."

"When you stop bringing trouble into our lives, you won't see me, if that's what you want. Until then, I'm keeping an eye on you."

I didn't have the energy to fight this battle. Not now, anyway.

"So, what did you want to ask me?"

"Tell me everything you know about this Japanese girl," he said.

We talked for an hour. I recited the conversations I'd had with Mitsuko and Romeo, and what Noah had heard in the restaurant bathroom. I also filled in a few blanks regarding Susan and Ken. The copy of Allan's hard drive yielded the loan agreement for Ken's store as well as the name and address of the business. We did our best to construct a crude timeline of Ken and Allan's relationship based on the bits and pieces we had.

I wasn't sure what Sam learned from this exercise, but it felt good to be doing something, however small, to help figure out who killed Allan.

"Okay," Sam said at last. "I'll go see what I can find out. Is your friend coming back? Or can I crash here again tonight?"

"First of all, Detective Green is not that kind of friend, and second of all, even if he were, I wouldn't have a guest staying over when Noah was home."

"He didn't stay over last night, but he—"

"Sam, I'm not having this conversation with you. I'm going to go to the place that's boarding Allan's cat and see if I can make a longer-term arrangement and then I need to swing by work. I've got a few people working overtime I want to check on. Then I'm coming home alone to my quiet, *empty* house and see if I can think of anything I might have missed that could save my neck."

"That's good. I'll come over around seven with a Pizza from Pizzacato and see if you've come up with anything." He got up and was out the back door before I could say anything. My traitorous eyes evaluated the close fit of faded denim on his muscular rear. I shook my head. Forget the relaxing bath—I needed a cold shower.

I wasn't sure what I should do about Allan's cat, but I figured he at least deserved a face-to-face meeting before I decided his fate.

CHAPTER 29

THE PURR TENDER LODGE was located in southwest Portland. It was a three-story pink Victorian home set back from the road and surrounded by old growth Douglas fir trees and one large spreading oak with a tire swing hanging from its lowest branch. I pulled into the circular driveway and got out of my car. A sign on the entrance read "Open," so I went up the stairs, across the broad porch and entered.

The entry hall had been divided into a series of chambers with a central booth that seemed to have interlocking doors not unlike those in our clean room air shower at work. You entered the first chamber and could hang your coat on a coat tree, or leave your umbrella in a rack. Once you were in the center booth, you had to close the entrance door before the exit door would open. This was to prevent any unintentional cat releases. Or so the older woman behind the counter in the third area explained. There were four Siamese cats lounging in front of her.

"The front parlor is one of our community rooms," she said. "We have several different areas, depending on how interactive your cat is. And of course, we have private accommodations, if you prefer. Cats are social creatures, though, so most of our guests prefer the company of others. Do you have a friend you'd like to place with us?"

"My name is Harley Spring," I said. "I spoke to someone a few nights ago about Mr. Allan Sayer's cat, Cyrus."

"Oh, I was so sorry to hear about Mr. Sayers. I'm Lydia Lewis, I own the Lodge," she said, and proffered her hand. I shook it, and she continued. "Cyrus was a regular visitor here, so we felt like we knew Mr. Sayers, too. You know, a cat can tell you a lot about what kind of person their owner is. Mr. Sayers must have been a nice fellow. Have you decided what to do with him? Cyrus, that is," she added.

"Not yet," I waffled. "I thought I'd come meet him and see what he's like. As I mentioned on the phone, I have a cat and dog at home already, so I have to consider what's best for everyone."

"I think you'll find that Cyrus is flexible. He enjoys his friends in our active cat room. Well, what am I thinking? Come on back and meet the little guy."

I went around the counter and followed her through a doorway into a wide hall. A large black cat with gray whiskers on its muzzle was stretched out on a pink overstuffed chair; the arms of the chair bore the evidence of many sharp claws. A staircase rose at the far end of the hall, with a solid door on its far side. Four doors, two on each side, were to our left and right. These doors were glass, and were followed by a viewing window for each room.

"Our guests are grouped according to activity level," my hostess explained. "The rooms are decorated accordingly."

She paused by the first window. This one had an elaborate carpet-covered structure on one wall that featured a dozen lounging platforms. About half of these featured unconscious feline forms draped on their surfaces. Four fleece-lined fabric igloos sat on a table on the opposite wall. An extended paw protruded from one. If the others were occupied, I couldn't tell.

"This room is for the more leisurely crowd. They enjoy their naps."

We moved to the next room. It was filled right up to the window with a maze of large living houseplants. Closer inspection revealed several large, strategically placed tree limbs angled across the space. I could just make out the forms of two cats perched amongst the greenery.

"Some cats are a little shy and prefer a jungle atmosphere, so they can see you before you see them. At home, they hide behind sofas, but we find this a little more natural for them." She stepped across the hall. "And here we come to Cyrus and his playmates."

This was clearly a high-activity room. Six-inch-wide ramps zigzagged from floor to ceiling on all walls. Suspension bridges crisscrossed the room. What looked like a train track spanned the room a little open cart poised on a platform at one end. Two tree trunks rose from the center of the floor. They were just close enough that a cat could leap from one to the other if he chose.

A blur of yellow fur followed by a similar one of black sped across the room, up one tree, down the other, and up one of the wall ramps. They finally came to rest on a platform near the ceiling.

"The golden one is Cyrus," Ms. Lewis said.

"Gosh, he's definitely active," I said.

She must have heard the doubt in my voice. "He's not like that all the time, but he does like his exercise. Isis, there, is his special friend. They seem to bring out the devil in each other. He can be quite loving." She opened the door to the active room and motioned me to follow her inside. "Cyrus," she said in a firm voice. "You come down here and meet your new mistress."

To my surprise, the golden-colored cat came right down the ramp and sat at her feet.

"Is he always that well-behaved?" I asked.

"If you're firm with him. He can smell a pushover a mile away."

"Is he, ahhh…"

"Neutered?" she finished for me. "Yes, he was altered before Mr. Sayers brought him home from the cattery. That's one of the requirements when you buy a registered cat that is labeled pet quality. He's a perfectly healthy cat—he just doesn't meet the breed standard for the show ring. In his case, he has a white spot on his chest. You aren't allowed white spots if you're a show Abby."

"Well, I'm sure he doesn't care what color his chest spot is," I said.

"If you'd like, you can bring your cat over here to meet Cyrus. We have a small room off the kitchen where we introduce new cats to one or two of our regulars, just to see how they do. That way, neither one of them would be on their home turf."

"That's very generous of you. I'll do that, but is it possible to leave him here for another few days?" I asked. "Mr. Sayer's memorial service is Monday and things are going to be a little hectic until that's over." I was more worried that I would be arrested Tuesday and not have a home for Cyrus—or Cher, either, for that matter. "If for some reason it turns out Cyrus doesn't like my house, do you have any kind of bulletin board where I could arrange a placement for him?"

"I shouldn't think that would be necessary," she said. Her insistence that Cyrus would work out was getting annoying. "The lady who has been dropping him off and picking him up lately seems pretty attached to him. In fact, she's been to see him twice since Mr. Sayers died. I'll bet she'd take him."

"What lady?"

"Mr. Sayer's lady friend, I assumed," she said. "I don't know her name. She usually came if there was an early morning drop-off. My nephew Randy works the early shift. He just mentioned it in passing. He said she didn't look like your typical Abyssinian owner. He had her pegged for more of a Persian or Himalayan type. He's not wrong very often, so he asked her. Sure enough, she was just dropping Cyrus off for Mr. Sayers. Her cat is a smoke gray Persian."

"Can you tell me anything about her? It's important." I tried not to scare the woman with my desperation.

Her smile faded. "No, Randy didn't say anything about her—just the cats."

"Could I possibly talk to Randy?" I asked.

"I suppose you could. He's not due to work again until Monday night, though. I can give you his cell phone number, but I wouldn't count on him being around on the weekend. He and his girlfriend usually go backpacking if the weather's nice."

"He didn't happen to mention anything about her being Asian, did he?" I asked.

"No, he didn't say, but like I said, he's a real cat person. She could have had two heads, but if one of them didn't have pointed ears and whiskers he wouldn't have noticed."

We walked back out to the lobby, where I paid Cyrus's bill and thanked her for her time and trouble. She gave me Randy's phone number, and I sat in her driveway and dialed. She was right, his phone wasn't on. I left a message asking him to call me as soon as possible.

If Mitsuko was bringing Cyrus to the Purr Tender Lodge, then she must have had more of a relationship with Allan than I thought. He wouldn't have trusted Cyrus to a casual friend. I needed to talk to her.

CHAPTER 30

I DROVE TO SIL-TRAC and checked on my workers. They were making some headway in catching our schedule up. My test group had commandeered an extra tester from process engineering, and my inspectors were using every available microscope to do visuals. If nothing else happened, it was beginning to look like we might make the deadline. The wipes were still on everyone's mind, but they didn't affect these functions as much as they did those in the fab area.

I was on my second circuit through the work areas when Pratima stopped me.

"Harley, I don't mean to be rude, but you're just slowing people down, asking them how they're doing every five minutes. They just want to get their parts tested and looked at and get out of here. I've got all your phone numbers, and if anything happens, I'll call you."

She was right. I was there to solve problems and encourage people, not to cause problems and annoy them. I decided to go see Skip at the Blue Whale.

Skip slid a Diet Coke down the counter as soon as I walked in.

"Pratima kicked you out, didn't she?" he asked.

"How'd you know?" I asked.

"Cause she knows how to kick butt and take names," he said. "She doesn't need you there slowing things down. She'll call you if she needs you."

"That's exactly what she said."

He gave me a smug look. "I know your people better than you do."

"I doubt that, but if you know so much, tell me about Allan. And I'm not talking about his tennis game."

"What do you mean?" he asked, trying to sound naive and not succeeding.

"Who was he sleeping with?"

"I don't know," he said.

"Oh, come on," I said. "You know everything that goes on across the street. Don't try to tell me at this late date that you don't know who sleeps with whom."

"The reason people tell me things is because I don't gossip."

"Oh, please," I said. "People use you like a telephone."

He turned his back to me and started wiping glasses that were already clean.

"Come on, Skip, I need you. I'm in real trouble. If I don't figure out who really killed Allan, I'm going to go to jail. I'm suspect number one, and if my sources are right, I've got until Monday to figure it out."

"For reals?" He turned around.

"For reals," I said.

He pulled up his stool and leaned on his elbows across from me. "Well, in that case," he said then hesitated.

"Come on, Skip, I'm counting on you."

"Well, I don't know for sure, but I think he did the horizontal mambo with Mitsuko Komatsu a while back."

"Is he the father of her baby?" I asked.

"He didn't say and I didn't ask. My job is not to judge."

"Did he have any other girlfriends?" I asked. "Anytime in the last year or so?"

"Not that I know of."

"Doesn't that seem a little weird to you? A single adult male, with no woman in his life? And don't tell me he was gay. I know he wasn't."

"Are you sure?"

"Pretty sure, why?"

"I don't know, but he just struck me as one satisfied dude. When we were at the rec center, hot babes would fall all over themselves to get to him. They'd prance around him with their legs up to here, sticking out of those skimpy little skirts they wear.

158

Babes would rub up against him, and he would walk right past like they were made of wood. If he's not gay, then he's getting it in a big way somewhere else."

"But who?"

"I don't know, boss. When it came to his private life, his lips were tighter than my mama's pantyhose."

"You sure that's all you know?" I asked. He gave me his "oh, please" look.

I laid a five-dollar bill on the bar. "Thanks, Skip. Let me know if you hear anything, okay?"

"Sure thing, Boss."

It was just after noon, which meant Noah and Chris would be waking up soon. Tiny raindrops gathered on my windshield as I drove home. There were just enough to make it hard to see, but not enough to keep my windshield wipers on continuously. I wished the weather would make up its mind.

The phone was ringing when I walked in the door.

"Harley?" the caller said.

"Hi, Karen. What's up?"

"I thought you would like to know what I found out about Mitsuko's dad."

"Did you talk to Mr. Iguchi?" I asked.

"No, I figured if he was a medical practitioner he would be in the yellow pages, and I was right."

"Are you sure it's him? Komatsu is a fairly common name."

"His home phone was listed for after-hours calls, and it's her address. I looked it up on the employee database. I thought you'd want to know."

"Thanks," I said and rang off.

I didn't have long to think about it. The phone rang again almost immediately. Noah and Chris were up and were more than willing to go to the Original Hotcake and Steak House for a late breakfast. I arranged to pick them up in ten minutes.

Cher was on her food shelf, and I gave her a second bowl of food. She would need her strength if we were going to add another pet to the family. She and Sonny had a love-hate relationship that was in one of its cool cycles right now, and she still wasn't over the trauma of the orange cat I'd brought home. They hadn't been together, but she'd known there was a usurper in her domain.

The drive to Chris's house took just under a minute. I arrived early, but the boys were already at the sidewalk. They got in the car as soon as it stopped moving.

"I take it you guys are hungry?" I said.

"Harley, I think you can safely assume we're always hungry," Noah said.

"Well, you'll be happy to know we're having pizza tonight."

"What's the deal?" Noah asked.

"What do you mean?" I asked. "No deal, just pizza."

"There has to be some reason. I always have to talk you into pizza. You never suggest pizza on your own."

"Okay, you're right. Your dad is coming over and bringing pizza."

"Why?" he asked. "You don't even like Dad."

"Noah, I don't dislike your dad, I just can't live with him."

"You said he drives you nuts — and what about Green?"

"He does drive me nuts sometimes, but he is your father, so he's going to be around for the rest of your life. And I know you thought you saw something with Green and me but don't read more into it than there was. You know I've been under a lot of stress, and he was just offering a little friendly comfort, no more and no less."

"It's a start," he mumbled to Chris.

"I heard that," I said.

CHAPTER 31

DINNER STARTED BETTER than I'd hoped when Sam showed up with a large pepperoni pizza and a box of cheese bread from Papa John's for Noah and Chris, as well as our artichoke, black olive and feta cheese pie from Pizzacato.

"Get us some glasses and ice, kid," he said to Noah as he walked in the front door balancing the three boxes on one arm and carrying two six-packs of pop in the other.

Noah and Chris jumped up and went for the kitchen without comment. Pizza was, indeed, a powerful bribe. Sam set the food and drinks down on the big blue ottoman between the two easy chairs in the living room, and I was reminded of the happier times we'd had as a family. Pizza had been a Friday night tradition when Sam was home. This wasn't Friday, but he did still remember everyone's favorites. It was a thoughtful touch that he had replaced three of the Cokes in one six-pack with Minute Maid Orange, which was Chris's favorite.

The boys sat on the rug and made careful small talk with him, mostly about the latest innovations in computers, while they inhaled their pizza. Sam and I were still on our first pieces when the boys excused themselves and went back to Noah's room.

"Okay," Sam said, and set his pizza down. "I've done a little checking. There are a finite number of places you can get a paternity test taken in Portland, and I can't find any record of either our dead guy or the Asian chick being involved in one. I've got people checking in Seattle and San Francisco too, just in case they went out of town, but that will take a day or two. Green has talked to the dead guy's neighbors, and if his reports are up-to-date, they aren't telling him anything useful. A young woman out riding her bike heard what sounded like an air horn going off near the house a few nights after he died. Green didn't make a note if he followed up on that one."

"I might know about that," I said.

Sam set his glass of Coke down on the floor.

"Harley, I can't help you if you don't tell me everything you know."

"I didn't think of it," I said. "A lot has happened since then." I told him about my tumble down the stairs and my following entrapment.

"Does Green know this?" he asked.

"I think I may have mentioned it."

"So, he's being cute, too. There isn't any mention of the incident in his reports. But it does explain why they didn't follow up on the girl's report."

"He probably didn't report it because he wasn't there when it happened."

"Is there anything else you've told him that I should know about?"

"You know, this jealous husband routine doesn't become you. This isn't about you or Green or who solves the case first. This is my life. I don't have time to play games with you two."

Sam leaned back in his chair. "I'm sorry," he said. "It's just that I can't help feeling this would have never happened if I'd been here."

"So, this is about *your* guilt?" I said. "What arrogance. You couldn't have done anything about this. I was in the middle of nowhere on a company trip. There was no way for anyone to know that Allan had left me his house and money. What would you have done? Provided me an alibi? That would have been easy to explain. 'Hi, Detective Green, my ex-husband, who skulks around in the bushes and wears disguises and has at least seven passports—yes, that man whose real name I don't even know. He'll vouch for the fact that I didn't kill Allan.' I'm sure that would have cleared it up for everyone."

"My name really is Sam," he said quietly.

I sat, mute, my anger spent. Sam sulked in wounded silence.

"There is one thing we could check out," I said after a few minutes.

"I'm listening."

"Right after Noah let me out of the basement, I went up to Allan's office. It was totally trashed. Later that night, Noah and I went back to return the wrong cat we'd taken." Sam raised his eyebrows but remained silent. "I went back upstairs and when I looked in the office, it was completely normal. Everything was back in place."

Sam ran his hand over his head. I could tell he was carefully measuring his words.

"It could still be useful if I had a look," he said at last.

He didn't say how much more useful it would have been if I'd told him sooner. He didn't have to.

I called Allan's house, and Ken answered. I explained that I needed to get some papers from Allan's office. He told me he and Susan were going out to dinner and a movie and would be gone before we got there. I thanked him and hung up.

We told the boys we were going out, and Noah insisted that he and Chris would like nothing more than to come along. He still didn't like it when I was out of his sight, even if I was with his dad. Sam insisted on driving my car. The boys climbed in the back seat and buckled up in silence.

Sam instructed the boys to stay in the same room with us at all times and to not touch anything in the office. He then made a call to someone he referred to as Bud. Bud would be meeting us at the house.

We parked in the driveway, and the boys and I got out of the car and went inside. Sam waited outside and then followed us in after a little while, accompanied by a short, dark man in a blue jumpsuit. He had a thin beard and clutched a small black case to his chest.

"Show us where the office is," Sam said.

I gave him my best annoyed glare but complied. The boys and I stood out in the hallway while he and Bud made a methodical search. Bud dusted surfaces with something that looked like a makeup brush. He would then lay a cellophane patch over the dusted area. I assumed he was taking fingerprints. He worked for less than a half-hour and then left without ever saying a word to me. I had a flashback to high school when I had once walked into a classroom where a group of boys was playing some kind of role-playing game that seemed to be a cross between *Dungeons and Dragons* and *The X-files*. I hoped we weren't doing the post-adolescent version tonight.

"You can come in now," Sam said from inside the room. "Tell me everything you remember about where things were the first time you came in here."

I described the previous scene as well as I could remember it, but that was admittedly lacking in detail.

"Look," I told him. "I had a brief look after I'd fallen down the stairs and been locked in the basement. I wasn't exactly taking notes."

"Okay," he said. "Close your eyes and think back. Not about the details, but tell me what your first impression was when you opened the door."

"Frankly, my first thought was 'Here we go again.' It looked a lot like our house did when we were robbed last spring. Wait a minute," I said. "It did look like someone was looking for something. Drawers were open, and papers were spread out. But things weren't damaged as much as...examined, if that makes any sense."

"That's good, Harley. If someone were mad at the vic, there would have been purposeful damage. It sounds like someone was looking for something specific."

"But what?" I wondered. "What would Allan have that someone would want bad enough to kill him?"

"We can't assume the search was done by the killer," Sam said. "Your buddy might have been into something with someone who didn't want their business made public after he died."

"I find it hard to believe he was doing anything illegal out of his home. He was a marine, for God's sake."

"I didn't say it was illegal. We already know he had a fling with one of your employees. Maybe someone didn't want her name in the papers."

"That makes no sense. He slept with her. I highly doubt he documented the deed. I suppose anything is possible. I guess there were a lot of things I didn't know about Allan." I sat down at the desk and pulled the right-hand file drawer open. Sam opened the closet. A white coated-wire shelf held a box of blank floppy discs, a stack of read-write CD's and a USB cable. Two boxes on the closet floor held a ream each of laser printer and inkjet printer paper.

The desk drawer held neatly labeled files. I riffled through them, but nothing seemed out of the ordinary. I pulled the drawer to its full extension and raised it up. The drawer came off its sliders with a thump.

"What are you doing?" Sam asked.

"This drawer was partly open when I was here before. I can't see anything unusual about the files in it, so I thought I'd look at the outside. Isn't that where they always find stuff on TV?"

"Good idea, Harley," Noah said and joined me. He helped me lift it up and set it on the desktop. His straight black hair covered his eyes as he tipped his head sideways to look at the end. "There isn't anything here," he said then rubbed his hand over the smooth wood. "But it's sure sticky."

Sam came over and looked. Indeed, sometime in the recent past something had been stuck to the end of the drawer.

"If the adhesive had been exposed to the dust and air in the room for very long it wouldn't be this sticky," he explained.

"Yeah, but what?" Noah asked.

"Well, that would be the question," I said.

Among the four of us, we must have looked at every item in the office at least twice. Nothing seemed unusual. There were personal files with bills and receipts, and several work files that were part of a project Allan had been working on, comparing the cost of various Teflon tools from different vendors.

"What about these shreds in the wastebasket?" Noah asked. He scooped up a handful of crosscut paper shredder output.

Sam and I stood up and looked into the basket. Someone had clearly emptied it but, in their haste, hadn't noticed that the liner bag had a large fold in the bottom that had trapped several handfuls of shredded material.

"We could glue them back together," Chris suggested.

"That's sweet of you, Chris," I said, "but these pieces are like confetti. Coming from the bottom of the basket like that, they're probably from a mixture of documents."

"Have you got something better for us to do?" Noah argued.

"You're right," I said, and handed him the basket. "Live it up,"

He pulled the garbage bag from the wastebasket and tied a knot in the top.

"I think we've done as much damage as we can here," Sam said. "Who wants to go to Baskin Robbins for some ice cream?"

Noah and Chris looked at him like he'd grown a third eye in the middle of his forehead, but they were never ones to turn down food of any sort, even if it came from unexpected places. After a moment's hesitation, they agreed, and we locked up Allan's house and headed for frozen heaven.

The boys jumped out of the car and ran into the house the minute we arrived back home again, the garbage bag of shreds held between them. Sam went into the living room and started cleaning up pizza leftovers. I went upstairs and got my sewing lamp that has a magnifying lens attached to its stem, and took it to Noah's bedroom.

"Don't forget to call your mom and tell her if you're staying over tonight," I said to Chris.

"Thanks for the lamp," Noah said and smiled at me.

Sam was in the kitchen rinsing glasses when I came out.

"I know you were making an effort with the boys tonight," I said.

"I do care about the boy."

"Maybe you should tell him that occasionally."

"How about you," he said. "Should I tell you, too?"

"Sam—"

He turned away from the sink and caught my hands in his. He pulled me to him. I could smell the faint familiar mixture of lime and sandalwood that was his after-shave.

"You know I didn't leave because I didn't care," he said and wrapped his arms around me in a gentle hug. His chin rested lightly on my head. "If I thought it was safe, I would come here and never leave."

"Our problems were never about caring enough, Sam. We did that part fine. It was all the other stuff that got in the way."

I pulled away from him, and he didn't stop me. I turned and headed for my bedroom. It took all the remaining strength I had to make it inside and shut the door.

❧

Noah and Chris stayed up all night, carefully arranging shreds of paper on a leftover piece of green felt they'd found in my sewing stuff. For his first Halloween after Sam brought him home, Noah had been Robin Hood. I'd used the felt to make his hat. Now the two boys were hunched over the ragged piece of green, intently placing small scraps of paper with tweezers. After the third time I'd asked them to turn the music down, I gave up and went into the kitchen to make some chamomile tea.

Sam was sitting at the table drinking coffee. The dark circles under his eyes told me he hadn't been able to sleep through the music, either.

"Do they have to have the music up that loud?" he complained.

"Apparently," I said, and set about filling the kettle and heating it. I sat down across from him. "At this point, I choose to not fight the music battle. Lord knows Noah and I have enough other issues."

"So, I guess me going in and making them turn it off is out of the question?"

"Welcome to the world of parenting a teenager."

Sam rubbed both hands over his face and head.

"I suggest a small snack, a warm drink, and a second pillow placed strategically over the ears," I said. "And thanks."

"For what?" he said.

"For not yelling at him. For respecting my wishes and parenting style."

"I'm trying," he said with a sigh. He got up and rummaged around in the fridge. "You want some of this leftover pork?"

"No," I said, "I'll stick with my tea."

I poured hot water over the tea bag then drizzled some honey from the plastic bear on the stove into the hot liquid. Sam made a pork sandwich and drank more coffee. I drank my tea. The clock said three a.m. At three-thirty, I put my cup in the sink and said good night to Sam. I looked in on Noah on my way to my room.

"How's it going?"

Both boys looked up. Their eyes were red from the strain of staring at the little bits of paper.

"I think we're making progress," Noah said.

"Well, don't stay up too late," I said. I knew my request was falling on deaf ears, but I had to say it anyway.

The boys took mercy on me and turned the music down without me asking. I returned to my bed and tossed for a few more hours before falling into an exhausted sleep just as dawn was breaking. It was after nine when I finally got up. The boys were asleep, and Sam was gone.

CHAPTER 32

I SPENT THE DAY paying bills, doing laundry, making lists and generally getting my affairs in order in case I was arrested on Tuesday. The boys got up sometime after noon and came out of Noah's room only long enough to toast a box of PopTarts and pour a couple of glasses of juice. When I checked on them in the late afternoon, they had three partial documents, each about the size of an index card. They appeared to be copies of some kind of order form, but so far they hadn't found anything identifiable. It was quite possible they were just old audit copies of purchasing records Allan was shredding. I didn't have the heart to stop them.

Other than a brief break to take Noah and Chris to Taco Bell, I worked on my preparations till bedtime. Green called at ten.

"You want to be my date tomorrow?" he asked.

"Do you know what time it is?" I asked. "I'm in bed."

"Yeah, but you're not sleeping now, are you? You're tossing and turning and worrying about whether you've planned for everything in case things don't go well tomorrow. Am I right?"

"I'm not sure what's more depressing, the fact that you know me that well, or that I really am that worried."

"How about it—can I take you to the memorial service?"

"Why do you want to go with me?"

"I know how upsetting it will be for you. I want to be there for you," he said.

"You are such a liar."

"I do want to be there for you. I know how upset you've been."

"Keep it up, and I'm saying no."

"Okay, so it would help me watch people close to the victim if they thought I was there to support you. And I *would* be there to support you, too."

"Fine," I said. "I don't have the energy to argue about how insensitive it is that you are using me at a really horrible time to solve your case."

"Listen to yourself," he said. "I'm not trying to solve my case. I'm trying to keep your butt out of jail, figure out who killed your friend and, oh, by the way, keep you safe in the process."

"I'm sorry," I said. "Everything is just so unreal. I spent my day preparing to go to jail. I haven't done anything bad. I pay my taxes, I don't jaywalk...most of the time...but if I don't get some major miracle by Tuesday, I'm going to jail. I'm having a little trouble with this."

"Look, it's not going to come to that," he insisted.

"Tell me one reason it won't. You've been telling me for days that I'm going to be arrested if I don't tell you everything. Well, guess what? I told all, and I'm still going to jail."

"It won't come to that. I don't know what will break this, but you won't go to jail. I won't let them take you."

"Now you're sounding like Sam. If we don't find out who killed Allan in the next twenty-four hours, I'm going down and there is nothing you can do about it."

"Do you want me to come over?"

"Thanks, but I don't think I can take the rubber hose treatment tonight. We've been over everything a million times and nothing changes. I'm just going to try to get some sleep and hope Mitsuko Komatsu can tell me something tomorrow."

"If you change your mind, call me—doesn't matter what time."

I didn't say anything.

"Okay, then, I'll pick you up at one."

"Thanks," I said and hung up. I turned off my light, but sleep wasn't my friend that night.

CHAPTER 33

WHEN MY GREAT-UNCLE WARREN died, the family had a memorial service. We all shared memories of his long, productive life. There were creased pictures, brown with age, from a simpler time and of a younger man. Old men with faded mustaches and canes hobbled into the church, glad it wasn't their turn but secretly envious that Uncle Warren had made it through without suffering too many of the indignities of extreme age. Aunt Hayden laid out a display of his medals from World War Two. The church women provided coffee and tea in the basement. It was a fitting tribute to a life well-lived. Even his death had been elegant. After 87 years, he went to bed one night and never got up again.

Allan's case was entirely different. He hadn't even made it halfway that far, and his end hadn't been the gentle transition from sleeping in his bed to sleeping with the angels. Allan's end had been violent. I only hoped he hadn't been aware enough to know what happened in his hospital room.

There was no family to prepare pictures or tell funny stories. When we reached the church, Pastor Sumerlin was circulating among the first arrivals trying to get a sense of whether he could call on anyone to speak during the service. Allan's neighbor was there with another woman I didn't recognize. I later learned she lived across the street. Mr. Iguchi had granted a day off for the purchasing department. Other employees were allowed half a day if they requested it in writing. Mitsuko and Romeo stood at the back of the church, speaking only to each other. Jose and Scott were in a pew with Skip, who for once wasn't dressed in white.

171

Britt Langley was sitting with Barbie. Steven was there, but was careful to stay away from Karen. Whatever was going on with them seemed trivial these days.

Noah had offered to come for moral support, and though I loved him for offering, I knew Sam would not appreciate the sentiment. Sam himself was there in his Alex Stange persona, introducing himself to anyone who crossed his path.

I couldn't bring myself to sit in the rows customarily reserved for family, even if I was Allan's heir, so Green and I sat in the third row, letting the purchasing department fill the front two. Dave walked in dressed in a somber black wool suit and sat down on my other side without saying anything.

In the end, Pastor Sumerlin delivered a moving if slightly impersonal service. An older woman in a black flowered dress sang "Amazing Grace," and it was over.

"I was hoping someone else would show up," Green said.

"You mean like some mysterious stranger in a black trench coat and slouch hat? That would be a little obvious, don't you think?"

"Perpetrators often like to attend the funeral. I was sort of hoping someone new could be added to our list of suspects." He looked around. "We're pretty much back where we started. I even ran background checks on the neighbors and—nada."

"I'm going to catch Mitsuko before she and Romeo leave."

I started for the back of the church. Mr. Iguchi rose from his place two pews behind Green and I.

"Harley-san," he said, and looked pointedly at Green.

"You remember Detective Green, " I said, and gritted my teeth while Mr. Iguchi stumbled his way through stilted questions regarding the investigation into Allan's death. I watched helplessly as Mitsuko and Romeo slipped out the back door and left.

Mr. Iguchi spent ten minutes grilling Green and then made small talk about American funeral ceremonies for another five. It became clear he thought Green was with me as a way of keeping an eye on suspect number one. Green did nothing to change his opinion.

"Why did you let him think I'm your main suspect?" I asked him when Mr. Iguchi moved on to speak to Karen.

"Well, technically, you are," he said. "But I'd like our perpetrator to think he's home free. If he thinks we're focused on you, maybe he'll slip up."

"What's to slip up? He doesn't have to do anything else. He can return to his regular life while I go to jail."

"Bad guys don't work that way," Green said. "They generally can't leave well enough alone. They aren't patient enough to let things play out. You mark my words — our perpetrator is going to make another move. I can feel it."

"Well, I'm going back to work and talk to Mitsuko."

"Not so fast there, Nancy Drew," he said, and grabbed my arm. "I drove, remember?"

CHAPTER 34

I HADN'T REMEMBERED.

It took me almost an hour to get back to Sil-Trac. Green drove me home; I did a quick change out of my black crepe dress and into black pants and a dark-gray print silk blouse. My intention had been to go straight to Jose's area and find Mitsuko. Pratima was waiting at my desk with other ideas.

"I was just trying to call you," she said.

I pulled my cell phone out of my pocket. I had no power left.

"What's up?" I said as I pulled my charger out of the left-hand desk drawer and plugged it in to the power strip at the back of my desktop.

"Lot oh-thirty-four is failing at audit."

"One hundred percent?"

"No, twenty, but that's enough to require a one-hundred-percent inspection, and we probably should recheck oh-thirty-three, too, just to be sure. There's no reason for them to be different."

"How much time are we going to lose?"

"That depends on whether you can get us some time on Engineering's tester or not. If you can get us on it right away, I'll get some people to work over and we may be able to catch up without much loss. Of course, that's assuming we don't find a major problem, in which case, all bets are off."

"Let me go talk to Nathan and see if he feels like cooperating today," I said.

"Thanks, boss." She headed back to the air shower entrance.

It was after four by the time I had convinced Nathan, our process engineer, that he needed to not only give up his tester but needed to see why our parts were failing. I left him in Pratima's capable grasp and headed for Jose's desk.

"If you're looking for Mitsuko, she just headed for the locker room. You might catch her if you hurry," he said without turning away from his computer.

Sil-Trac provided metal lockers with combinations for employees to store their coats, purses and lunches while they were in the clean room. At end of shift, people tended to linger there, exchanging gossip, making plans for afterwork activities and generally making the transition between their work lives and their homes and families. The room was arranged in u-shaped bays with lockers on three sides and a bench running through the middle. I stepped into the first bay.

"Hey, Willie," I said to a tall young man who worked in my diffusion area, "have you seen Mitsuko?"

The younger men in my work group played basketball together during lunch. Willie and Romeo were core members of the hoop set.

"Hey, Harley. She was just here a few minutes ago, looking for Romeo. I think he's working OT, though. Her locker's down at the other end. She might still be there—she was here, like, two seconds ago."

"Thanks, Willie," I said and went to the last bay. No one was there.

There are exit doors on each end of the locker room. I went into the hallway and looked out the window onto the parking lot. Mitsuko backed out of a parking spot, accelerated down the aisle and drove out the exit.

I continued down the hallway, planning to go back to the office area. I could feel my freedom slipping away. I needed some good news.

The purchasing department was next to the locker room, so I stopped by to check on the wipe situation. The area was deserted. Apparently, they didn't subscribe to the work is the best medicine theory of grief management. They were clearly taking advantage of their day off—Allan would have been disappointed in them.

I hurried back to my cubicle and dumped my mug full of pens and pencils. Allan's desk key fell out onto my desktop. I hurried back to his desk and keyed the center drawer open. I lifted out a black spiral-bound calendar and located the paperclip box. The file keys were just where I'd left them.

I turned to the row of file cabinets behind his desk and started opening locks. I wasn't sure what I was looking for but decided the clean room wipes were the logical place to start. I was more than a little curious how the crisis had developed.

For everyday supplies, we generally use a formula for automatic reordering. The number of wipes used per day is multiplied by the number of days it takes for the supplier to deliver. That quantity is then multiplied times two. Whenever our stock dips to that level, wipes are ordered. If we have a minority supplier for an item, ten percent of the quantity is diverted to that supplier. Those order times are offset from the main order, so we have a steadier supply of material coming in.

I located the files for Peterson's Supply. Peterson's is a distributor—most of our supplies come through wholesale distributors. Peterson's took up a whole drawer. There was a labeled folder for each individual supply we ordered. Product specification papers were included, along with a log of orders placed and orders received. An orange file contained all correspondence related to the current crisis—the department was definitely well-organized. I wasn't sure how much impact Allan and Jeanette had actually had on the problem, but it was well documented.

It took a while, but I read everything. The orange file didn't reveal any secrets. The wipe manufacturer had experienced a problem with one of their raw materials. Peterson's didn't have enough wipes in stock to ride out the crisis. Everyone expected it to be resolved in another week.

At the end of the Peterson files was a signed contract with signatures of both the Peterson rep and Allan.

A quick audit of the remaining files showed the same pattern—item files and logs followed by a signed contract. A few more orange files were scattered throughout the drawers, but no others addressed anything with the impact of the wipe problem. I sat back. Nothing here.

I was about to lock the drawers again when it hit me. The red files. I opened the drawers one at a time and ran my hand over the folder tabs. It took a few minutes to go through all the drawers, but there was no mistake. The files for the minority suppliers were missing.

I glanced at my watch. I'd been at Allan's desk for almost two hours. It was possible Tim or Jeanette had taken the files home to update documentation or adjust order quantities or whatever else it was they kept busy doing all day. I'd have to wait until tomorrow to ask them...if I wasn't in jail.

Jose wasn't at his desk, so I helped myself to his employee phone roster. We all kept our phone lists on our desktops to facilitate easy shift cancellation in case of prolonged evacuation. I looked up Mitsuko's number and dialed. The phone on the other end rang five times and then was answered in what I assumed to be Japanese.

"Hello?" I said. "Is Mitsuko Komatsu there?"

"Mitsuko not home," the feminine voice said. "You call back later." The phone disconnected.

This could not be happening. I returned to my desk. I called Green.

"Have you gotten anything for me?" I asked without preamble when he came on the line.

"Hello to you, too," he said. "I take it you didn't get anything from the girl."

"I haven't been able to catch up to her yet. I called her home, but she wasn't there. I'm going to keep trying to get hold of her. Romeo is working OT tonight. She may be out getting him dinner. They seem to eat together a lot."

"I haven't done much better," he said. "I've been checking into Mr. Komatsu, who by the way is currently MIA. It seems like he's involved in a malpractice suit that may end his career if it doesn't go his way—at least in America. He apparently owns a couple of quickie plastic surgery clinics, one here and one in Mexico, where he is reported to be at the moment. Only catch is, he's not a plastic surgeon. And he doesn't seem to have anyone on staff that is."

"What does that have to do with Allan?" I asked.

"Maybe nothing, but it's all I've got. I got a guy working on it. Maybe something will turn up. You want me to come over there and wait with you?"

"No, I'm fine. I'm just going to wait another half-hour and then I guess I'll go home and pray for a miracle."

"Okay, maybe I'll swing by there later."

The receiver was barely back in the cradle when the phone rang. I lifted it to my ear.

CHAPTER 35

"*MEET ME ACROSS* the street," Sam said and hung up.

Instinct said "run the other way," but at this point, I was grasping at straws. I grabbed my purse and keys and crossed the street to the Blue Whale. The room was empty save for a couple of rugged-looking guys standing at the pool table, cues in hand, and a hard-looking woman in a plaid flannel shirt and frayed jeans with a hole in the rear bent over the table, setting up a shot.

Skip handed me a Diet Coke and nodded toward the back booth without saying anything. I could only imagine what Sam had said to render *Skip* speechless.

"Oh, geez," I said when I saw him.

Sam's hair was silver-gray and jelled up. His eyes were a pale blue that was almost white. He was wearing tight jeans and a dark silk T-shirt, which draped over his washboard abs. The effect was completed by a blue-grey leather biker jacket. He looked like the villain in a futuristic movie.

"So much for blending in with the locals," I said.

"My contact called from Seattle."

"And?" I leaned toward him, as if that would make him tell me quicker.

"It's not much, but a single pregnant Japanese girl came in two weeks ago. She had two samples to compare her baby's DNA to. A Caucasian and an Oriental. I'm still trying to get a positive ID on the girl. The address she gave is a rented mailbox half a mile from the clinic."

"What were the results?"

"Well, if this is our girl, your guy is off the hook. The Asian guy is definitely the father of the baby."

"That doesn't make sense. What Asian guy? There wasn't an Asian guy in the running."

"I wouldn't be so sure about that. How well do you know the girl? She could have been sleeping with ten guys. How would you know?"

"She just seems so sweet."

"Yeah, well."

"But if Mitsuko's baby isn't Allan's then why would her dad kill him?"

"First of all, we don't know if her dad did kill Allan, and second, I'm pretty sure he doesn't know about the paternity test. The lab hasn't released the results to anyone yet."

"So, wait. If the baby isn't Allan's, but Mitsuko doesn't want it to be the other guy's, could she be thinking she could get her hands on Allan's money if she killed him?"

"Who knows what she's thinking. People who kill their lovers are rarely rational," Sam said. "She would have to think she could make people believe it was Allan's baby. When she gets the DNA results, she's going to know that's not going to help her—unless she plans on counterfeiting it."

"Allan was asking his attorney about paternity, so they must have at least discussed the possibility, but Allan hadn't changed his will or anything," I said. "What else could she think she has to prove paternity? I doubt Allan hand-wrote a new will. Why would he? He had no idea he was about to die."

"If it exists, she must have it. There wasn't anything like that at his place. We searched, and I'm sure Green did, too."

"Well, if she did it, it looks like she'll get away with it," I said.

"We know she isn't the one who hit him in the head in the forest. Green checked the attendance at Sil-Trac to see if anyone interesting was gone from work that day. Your gal was at there all day. You'll have to check attendance for the day he died. Maybe she finished him off with a shot to his IV."

"You mean she took advantage of someone else trying to kill him and failing?"

"No," he said. "Either her daddy or boyfriend hit him and she finished him, or someone else did all of it. It's all speculation at this point. We have more important things to worry about right now."

"What could be more important?"

Sam took my hands in his across the table. "We need to get you out of here," he said, "before they can arrest you."

"I can't just leave," I protested, and pulled my hands back and put them in my lap.

"Yes, you can. It's the only way. They're going to arrest you tomorrow. Why do you think Green is sticking so close to you? When they arrest you, they'll stop looking for other suspects. You'll be their solution to the problem. You'll go to jail. You will not pass go or collect two hundred dollars." Sam pulled a packet from the inside chest pocket of his jacket. "Take this." He thrust it at me.

I didn't mean to, but I took it. Inside were a passport and driver's license, both with my picture on them, a plane ticket to Switzerland and a second, smaller envelope. The smaller envelope contained a bundle of cash and a prepaid debit card.

I resealed the envelope and set it on the table between us.

"I can't do this," I said. "I can't just leave my life. What about Noah? And my workers? I have a critical order to fill. If we don't deliver on time, we lose a million-dollar order."

Sam grabbed my shoulders. "Harley, listen," he said. "You aren't going to be there for Noah or your workers. You are going to be in jail. That life is gone."

I picked up the envelope and fought off a new round of tears.

"It's not forever." He moved his hands up and held my face, his thumbs tracing small circles on my cheekbones. "I'm not going to give up. This will make sure you're safe while I figure out who really killed your friend. And you won't be alone. You'll stay with a family. You'll be their cousin visiting from America. It'll be like a vacation for you."

"I don't want a vacation," I said. "I want my life back. I want Allan back. I want this to have just been a horrible nightmare."

"It is a nightmare. I can't bring your friend back, but I sure as hell can find out who killed him."

"I can't believe this is happening to me."

"You just be on that plane tomorrow afternoon," Sam ordered. He got up, laid a twenty on the table and left.

Skip sidled over to my booth and sat down as soon as Sam was out the door. He set a fresh Diet Coke in front of me. "Yowza, yowza. Who was that?"

"You don't want to know," I said.

The pool players held up their empty beer pitcher, and he left to refill it for them. I drank my Diet Coke in silence. It might be my last one for a long time. When my glass was empty, I carried it back to the bar, said goodbye to Skip and went back across the street.

CHAPTER 36

MY CELL PHONE WAS ringing when I got to my desk. I unsnapped it from the charger and pushed the green answer button.

"Hello?" I could hear static in the background.

"Harley?" a garbled voice said.

"Yes?" I answered.

"Come to the Scotch Church."

"Who is this?" The connection was bad, and I wasn't sure what the person said next. It sounded like the stilted English spoken by many of my workers. It could have been Mitsuko, but before I could be sure, the line went dead.

I grabbed my purse and keys and headed for the parking lot. It might have been wishful thinking, but I couldn't take any chances—if it was Mitsuko, I had to talk to her.

The Old Scotch Church is one of the oldest continuously used churches in the state of Oregon. Founded in 1873 by twelve Scottish settlers, it is one of the most photographed buildings in the state. The church lies on a ten-acre plot, four miles north of the city of Hillsboro on a road that bears the church's name. The churchyard includes a pioneer cemetery where eight of the twelve founders are buried, along with noted Oregon pioneer Joseph Meek, the first US Marshall of the Oregon Territory.

The sun was setting as I drove out of the Sil-Trac parking lot and headed for the highway; Scotch Church Road was just two exits down. It took all the self-control I could muster to not drive ninety. A lone car sat at the far end of the church parking lot. I pulled in beside it. It was Mitsuko's. I got out and looked around.

"Mitsuko?" I called. No one answered. I looked in the car. A purse sat on the passenger seat. I tried the door. It was locked. I climbed the steps to the church and pulled on the door handle, but it didn't move, so I walked around to the back.

The trees cast shadows on the walkway. I looked back over my shoulder and didn't see anything, but I couldn't shake the feeling I wasn't alone. I heard a shuffling noise.

"Mitsuko?" I called again. I returned to the front of the church. The noise seemed to be coming from the cemetery. "Mitsuko? Anyone? Are you there?"

I started toward the cemetery. A guttural animal noise came from that direction. I tried to hurry, but I stumbled on a tree root, so I had to slow my pace. As I got closer, I could just make out a dark form slumped at the base of what must be a headstone. I ran over to it.

"Mitsuko? Are you okay?" I turned her over. She was not okay.

I pulled my phone out of my pocket and dialed 911.

Her face had dark smears across it. Whoever had attacked her had been met with resistance. The edge of her left hand was grotesquely swollen, as if it had been used in an unsuccessful attempt to protect her face from whatever had hit her in the head. Her hair was matted with what could only be blood. Her breathing was ragged, and a dark line trickled from the corner of her mouth. I implored EMS to hurry.

"Harley!" Romeo yelled. I hadn't heard him arrive. "What did you do to her?" He ran to her and pushed me out of the way. "Mitsuko," he said. "Say something, baby."

He pulled her limp form into his arms and began to cry. I could hear the sirens now, getting louder as they approached. A fire truck arrived, followed by an ambulance. I stood and watched helplessly as they worked on her battered body and then whisked her away. A Hillsboro patrol car pulled into the churchyard. I explained the phone call, my arrival and that I was a manager where Mitsuko worked. They seemed to buy my story, so I decided not to complicate things with my possible ranking on Portland's most-wanted list. They'd find out about that soon enough.

Romeo followed the ambulance to the hospital, and I assumed he would be questioned there. It probably would seem mercenary to anyone who hasn't worked in the world of high tech manufac-

186

turing, but every moment counted; and if he was going to be at the hospital all night, I needed to get someone else on the test equipment he had vacated. I mentally reviewed the substitutions on my return trip to Sil-Trac.

On my way back to the cleanroom, I stopped at my desk, tossed my keys in the drawer and plugged my phone into the charger cord. Pratima met me in the hallway.

"Willie called me," she said. "He said Romeo didn't come back from his dinner break. He was worried. Maxine was here working on documentation, so she's going to test until he comes back or the next shift arrives.

"I don't think he'll be back," I told her. "There's been an accident."

I explained my finding of Mitsuko, and Romeo's arrival as we headed for the test area. Maxine agreed she would stay until the next shift arrived.

"Willie said Romeo got a phone call and left here like he'd been shot out of a cannon," Pratima said. "He's pretty hot for her, so Willie assumed it was Mitsuko...you know..." Her face turned red. "...playing him."

"Is Willie still here?" I asked.

She went to find him, and I went back to my cubicle and answered my cell phone, which had started ringing.

"Get out of there," Sam ordered.

"What?"

"You heard me. You have got to get out of there *now*. The Hillsboro police didn't arrest you because they haven't talked to Portland yet, but it's only a matter of time—minutes, probably. Get your stuff and meet me out front. Don't tell anyone where you're going."

Pratima arrived with Willie.

"Do you know who called Romeo?" I asked, trying to keep my voice calm.

"Sorry, Boss. His cell phone rang, he listened and then he was out of here."

"Thanks, Willie." I turned to Pratima. "Call me on my cell phone if anything happens. I'm going to go check on something else."

Willie started back to work, then turned and came back to my doorway. "Jeanette was looking for you a little while ago. Right

187

after Romeo left. She said she'd leave you a note. I think she was on her way out."

I thanked him again and picked up my keys and phone. I glanced at my desk and didn't see a note, but I didn't have time for a more thorough search. I reached for the pink mohair sweater I'd left on the back of my chair but then left it where it was. I had a feeling I wasn't going to need pink mohair where I was going.

I felt like everyone was watching me as I left the building. A green Ford Taurus pulled up as I walked toward the curb. The door swung open, and I got in. Sam was behind the wheel.

"Where are we going?"

"Hide and watch," he said and accelerated out the driveway and toward Sunset Highway.

We drove in silence.

"I don't suppose you know how Mitsuko is doing?"

He turned and looked at me.

"I've been a little busy cleaning up your latest mess," he said.

"My what?" My voice rose up to the unattractive range.

"You couldn't just leave for Switzerland until I could figure this out. No—you had to go find another victim. You were the last person to see this one, too, weren't you?"

"I saw her leave the parking lot. She obviously saw someone else before I was set up to find her in the cemetery. Someone who nearly beat her to death, I might add. I can't believe you think I did this on purpose."

"No, Harley, you just seem to be able to dig your grave deeper without even trying."

I turned to the window and watched the lights slide by in a blur.

"I have a right to know where you're taking me," I said.

He was silent for another few minutes. "I'm taking you to a quiet house in a quiet neighborhood out near the airport. It belongs to a man who is out of the country. That's all you need to know."

Sam drove for another thirty minutes. We crossed Portland and headed north on I-205.

"Lie down on the seat," he said.

"I beg your pardon?"

He reached over and pushed me down.

"I don't want anyone seeing you come in here."

He turned the car onto an exit that immediately put us on a neighborhood street. Old fir trees towered over both sides of the dead-end road he turned onto. What I could see of the modest homes, looking up through the window from the seat, looked like they had been built in the thirties or forties. He pulled into the driveway of a pink two-story house with white trimmed windows. The garage door opened, and he pulled in beside a dark-gray Honda Accord.

"You can get up now," he said.

CHAPTER 37

I GOT OUT OF THE CAR. The garage had three wooden steps that led to a door that went into the kitchen. Sam held the door open, and I went in ahead of him. Neva Dean and Noah were sitting at a Formica-topped table.

"What are they doing here?" I asked Sam.

"I couldn't leave him home. He'd be a sitting duck for your detective buddy. I can't trust you not to try to call and check up on him, and that would be that."

"What about Neva Dean?" I asked.

"*She,*" he said and glared at Neva Dean, "showed up talking crazy and making a scene about angels. The kid wouldn't come with me unless I brought her along, and I didn't have time to sedate them both, so here we are — one big, happy family. You..." he added directly to her, "...give me any problems whatsoever, and you'll be sleeping with the fish where even your angels won't find you."

"Dad!" Noah said. He knocked his chair over as he stood up and put his arms around Neva Dean's shoulders.

She patted his hand.

"Don't you worry, honey. He isn't going to do any such thing."

An hour later, I was wearing a new-looking pair of sweatpants and a gold Purdue University T-shirt and seated at the table with a subdued Neva Dean and Noah. Sam was nowhere to be seen.

Neva Dean got up and made a pot of tea.

"Whoever lives here has good taste in tea," she observed.

"Sam can't expect us to sit here and wait forever," I said.

"What choice do we have?"

"We could look at my papers," Noah suggested.

Neva Dean and I looked at him.

"Chris and I used that Post-It glue and stuck the shreds to a piece of paper and copied it at Kinko's. Then we turned them all over and stuck them down again and copied them."

"How many pages do you have?" I asked. It was hard to imagine the time and patience it had taken.

"There are three pages that are pretty complete and two more that are about half-pages. Want to see?" He pulled folded papers from the buttoned side pocket on his cargo pants. He spread them out on the table and smoothed them with his hands. We all leaned forward to examine them.

Two of the larger pages were order records from Peterson's. I picked one up and looked at the item numbers and quantities.

"This is weird."

"What?" Noah and Neva Dean said in unison.

"Well, it shows a part number here on the left, then a total quantity here on the right, but then below it splits the quantity into two groups. The larger group shows a delivery address of one-nine-zero-three-zero Evergreen Parkway. That's Sil-Trac's address, so that makes sense. But then there's a second, smaller quantity that has a drop-ship order to a Tigard address." I picked up the second paper. "Wow," I said. "I'd recognize this part number anywhere. This is for clean room wipes. And this order is split the same way. The majority goes to the Sil-Trac address, and the smaller quantity to the same Tigard address. It makes no sense."

"My son's company has offsite locations that are supposed to simulate a startup business," Neva Dean said. "Do you suppose your company has something like that?"

"Anything is possible, but those sorts of operations are more usual for products that are less reliant on capital equipment. A clean room is expensive to set up. Peterson's is our clean room product supplier. Besides, I'd know about it. I'm on the chemical recycling committee. We would have to be making arrangements for their waste. No, I think this is something else." I picked up and studied the remaining papers, but didn't learn anything else.

We drank tea for another half-hour. I picked up my cell phone and checked for messages. There were three from Green. He had heard about Mitsuko and wanted to know where I was. Well, he was just going to have to wonder. As much as I hated Sam's craziness, I couldn't think of a better alternative at the moment. At least Noah was with me.

I was nervously punching buttons on my phone, wondering too late if I'd identified my location by turning it on. I wasn't sure how tracking a cell phone worked. As I went to shut it off, I passed over my call log and Randy's number. He should be working the night shift at the Purr Tender Lodge.

"Neva Dean, do you have a cell phone in your purse?"

"Yes, my son got me one. If I carry it he doesn't insist I have that alarm thing around my neck all the time."

"Can I use it?"

She agreed, and I called Randy.

"It's your dime," he answered.

I explained my earlier visit.

"Yeah," he said. "My Aunt Lydia told me you were going to call. She said you were asking about the woman who brings Cyrus."

"Yes. Can you tell me what she looks like?"

"I been racking my brain," he said. "All I can come up with is average. Average height, mousy hair, not thin but not too fat."

"How old is she?"

"I don't know. Not a young chick or anything, but not an old woman, either."

"Can you remember *anything* distinctive about her?" I asked.

"No," he said. "That's why I knew she couldn't be an Abysinian owner. Ordinary people don't own Abbys."

"Thanks, and if you think of anything, let me know." I gave him Neva Dean's number. "That didn't help much," I said to Neva Dean and Noah. "Some woman brings Allan's cat to the kitty hotel, but she could be anyone. The description could be Susan, Ken's wife, although she claims to not be here that often. It could be one of Allan's neighbors, or it could be someone we don't even know about. The only thing we know for sure is that it wasn't Mitsuko."

"Well, we aren't going to solve this tonight," Neva Dean said. "Let me brew up a soothing tea from this cabinet and then maybe we can try to get some sleep."

I agreed and drank the brew she came up with. It was chamomile-based and tasted good. I was tired, but doubted I could sleep. I went upstairs to the bedroom Sam had directed me to when we first arrived. A queen-sized carved cherry sleigh bed dominated the space. My intention was to lie on top of the covers, but there was a feather bed on top of the mattress and a summer-weight down comforter. I pulled off my sweat pants and slid between the cool cotton sheets. I was asleep before my head hit the pillow.

Sunlight streaming in the bedroom window woke me up. I glanced at the clock on the bedside table. It was seven a.m. I got up and put my sweats back on. I stepped into the hallway and was faced with three closed doors. The second one proved to be the bathroom. A basket on the countertop contained travel-sized toiletries. I made use of them to freshen up and went downstairs.

Neva Dean was sitting at the table with Sam. He had a mug of coffee in front of him. She got up when I came into the room.

"Would you like some tea, honey?" she asked and got a large blue ceramic mug from the cabinet. She poured hot water into it and selected a bag from the tea cabinet without waiting for my reply.

"Thanks," I said. "Sam, have you heard anything about Mitsuko?"

"No, they're keeping a tight lid on things. Green's been out at the hospital. I can't risk being seen by him. He's too smart to be tricked by a disguise too many times. I'm getting a Japanese guy down here, but he's in Seattle right now following up on the DNA. He's the only one who isn't going to seem out of place."

"So, what am I supposed to do?" I said. "Sit here like a fugitive? Oh, my God, am I a fugitive? Sam?"

Neva Dean put her hand over mine.

"You know you didn't do anything, honey. Just take a deep breath. Sam, here, has good angels—let's listen to what he has to say."

Sam glared at her. He evidently didn't appreciate the endorsement of angels.

"They are definitely looking for you, but a warrant hasn't been issued yet. My guy says Harper's pushing for it, though."

"Are they at my work?"

"They probably called or went by Sil-Trac, but I called in for you this morning."

"What did you tell them?"

"I said you had a family emergency that was taking you out of town and would call in when you knew when you'd be back."

"Great," I said. "On top of everything else, I'm going to lose my job."

"You aren't going to lose your precious job," Sam said.

"By the way," I said. "I called the guy at the cat place."

His face turned white. His lips tensed into a straight line. "Tell me you didn't use the phone here," he said.

"I used Neva Dean's cell phone."

"Don't make any more calls," he said. "If Green's as smart as you think he is, he's going to be checking with your friends, and when he discovers Neva Dean is missing, he'll put two and two together."

"So, what are you going to be doing while we're sitting here twiddling our thumbs?"

"I'm going to go rattle Ken's cage. Find out where he was last night. I'm not sure how he would have known about the baby, but Allan may have told him about it. He may think he can make a claim on Allan's estate and wanted to eliminate a rival. Maybe he's going to be the one who is going to try the handwritten will. Or maybe he's planning a wrongful death suit for his parents."

"Do you think that's likely?" I asked. "That's been quite a while ago."

"Not based on what we know, but I don't like the way he happens to be around whenever someone gets attacked. Maybe this is his idea of a wrongful death action. It wouldn't be the first revenge killing."

He got up, rinsed his cup and wiped the handle and set it in the sink. It was an unconscious gesture. You'd never find his fingerprints left behind anywhere. He grabbed a caramel-colored denim workman's jacket from a peg by the door and put it on over his plaid flannel shirt and jeans. He was just another construction worker today. He was out the door and into the garage without so much as a "See you later."

CHAPTER 38

"SO, WHAT ARE WE supposed to do all day?" I asked Neva Dean.

"Honey, you just have to be patient," she said. "One of those two men is going to find out who killed your friend and attacked that girl. Then you can go home and get on with your life. Until then, we just have to wait."

Waiting patiently wasn't my strong suit. I got up and paced the length of the kitchen a few times. Noah's shred copies were on the table where we'd left them last night. I sat, picked them up and read each one carefully.

"Is there any writing paper in this place?" I asked Neva Dean.

She pulled a yellow lined tablet from a drawer near the wall phone and handed it to me along with a cheap stick pen. I made notes about each page—the quantity ordered, the number of items, the cost of the items and the percentage of the total order that went to each address all went into columns on the notepad. I studied the result.

Neva Dean had been silent. She washed mugs, wiped counters and took stock of the food cupboard.

"So, does it mean anything?" she finally asked.

I leaned back in my chair. "Just one thing stands out so far," I said. "Each one of the offsite orders is for close to ten percent of the total order."

"Is that significant?"

"I'm not sure. The only other ten percent I can think of is that our minority vendors provide ten percent of our supplies on Federal contracts. That's probably a coincidence, though." I reread the papers. "Can I use your phone again?"

"You know Sam doesn't want you making any calls."

"Let's go to a pay phone then," I said. "There's bound to be a corner store or gas station around here."

"A little walk wouldn't hurt us, I suppose."

We rooted around in the closets of the bedrooms and found men's overalls and flannel shirts. Neva Dean discovered a knitted hat to cover her white hair. I stuffed mine into a baseball cap that said "Jubitz" on the front.

I scratched a note to Noah, although it was unlikely he would get up before we got back. Neva Dean got out the phone book, but since we didn't know the address, it didn't help much. In the end, we went out into the back yard and cut through the neighbor's to the street behind. We walked three blocks and looked around. I spotted a gas station sign two blocks to the east of our location. We circled the block slowly. There were no parked cars with people sitting in them. No strangers lingered on the streets. The kid working the pumps didn't even look up from his comic book when we finally stopped at the phone booth.

Neva Dean pulled out two quarters and handed them to me. She shook her head.

"I remember when you could make a phone call for a nickel," she said.

I felt like Lucille Ball with Neva Dean as my Ethel Mertz. I took the coins and dialed Peterson's.

"This is Brenda Short, at Sil-Trac," I said, using the name of one of Allan's clerks. I got myself transferred to the rep who handled Sil-Trac's orders. I explained that, with Allan gone, I was taking over some of the accounts and was wondering about the split orders. All the rep could tell me is that a number of orders were split, and it was generally ten percent of the total order. She said it wasn't unusual for Peterson's customers to drop-ship supplies to subcontractors. I thanked her and rang off.

"Neva Dean, this just doesn't make sense. Integrated circuit manufacturers don't use subcontractors. Or if they do, it's at the end of the process and it's offshore, not in Tigard. I need to go to this address and check it out."

"You aren't going alone," she said. "Besides, how are we going to get there? We can't walk to Tigard."

"Let me think."

"I do have my taxi coupons," Neva Dean said. "It couldn't hurt if we took a cab and had a little look-see."

She called the taxi dispatcher and had them send a cab to a corner a few blocks farther east. It wasn't a driver who had picked her up before, and if he thought our outfits were weird, he kept his opinion to himself.

We had him drop us in the old downtown area of Tigard. Neva Dean went into a grocery store and purchased two four-packs of toilet paper. She had one put in a brown paper bag and the other in a white plastic shopping bag with handles. She handed me the plastic bag.

"Take this," she said. "This makes us look more like bag ladies. No one will notice us."

We walked the half-mile to the address.

"You know, Neva Dean," I said. "Sam gave me a gun, complete with concealed carry permit."

"Honey, that's great," she said. Her face brightened. "Where is it?" She looked me up and down.

"Well, that's the tricky part. I didn't think it was wise to carry it into the workplace, so I left it home in my desk drawer. And, well, I guess it's still there."

"Sure would have been handy about now," she said.

"I know how to shoot at a target, but I'm not sure I could pull the trigger on a real person."

"Honey, if they were coming at us with trouble in their eye, I could shoot. That's one of the most important lessons you learn when you have a child. If someone threatened my child, I could kill them and not bat an eye."

I would have never believed my gentle friend was capable of such violence, but one look at her expression convinced me.

The house at the delivery address was a pale-green box. The white paint on the trim looked like it had been applied with a shovel. It was probably twelve hundred square feet. The driveway and tin-roofed carport were empty. The cement was cracked, and weeds were growing between the pieces.

"Honey, you wait up at the corner and I'll go to the door," Neva Dean said. "If someone comes, I'll say I'm collecting clothing for the school drive."

I didn't like this plan, but Neva Dean had a better chance of pulling it off than I did. She went up the crumbling sidewalk to the small cement porch and rang the doorbell. There was no response. She knocked on the edge of the aluminum storm door and then opened it and rapped on the painted wooden door. Nothing. She leaned over the black iron porch rail and looked in the window. She turned back and shook her head.

I joined her.

"No one is responding," she said. "It doesn't look like anyone is in there. There isn't much furniture in the living room, either. I don't think anyone lives here."

"I'll check the back. Whistle if anyone comes."

She stepped behind a bushy arborvitae that had grown over the left side of the porch. I went through the carport to the back yard. There was no sign of life. A hedge protected the area from view. I checked the back door. It was locked. The windows were shut, but I went along the back of the house and pressed on each one anyway. I hit pay dirt on the third one—I pressed and slid, and it moved to the left an inch. I slipped my hand in and pushed and it opened.

I went back through the carport and whispered to Neva Dean, "I'm going in. Make a racket if anyone comes."

She agreed, so I pulled a dented aluminum garbage can from the carport to the back yard and pushed it up against the house under the window. I wasn't sure it would hold my weight, but I climbed on it anyway. The dent in the bottom got deeper, but it held long enough that I was able to boost myself through the open window.

Checking the house didn't take long. I'd climbed into one of two bedrooms. A bathroom sat between them, and a short hallway connected those rooms to the living room. Behind the living room were a dining room and a kitchen separated by an island bar. The bedrooms had no furnishings. The living room held a card table and two chairs. Stacked against the living room wall were empty boxes from Peterson's. The dining room area held unopened packages of boxes and labels. One set of labels said "Northwest Supply." A bundle of boxes said "King Clean" on a white label attached to the binding strap. There were several more bags and bundles with equally neutral-sounding names.

The red file folders from Allan's cabinets lay on the card table. The box of labels from Northwest Supply had a packing slip stuck to its flap in a clear cellophane sleeve. I was prying it off when I glanced out the front window and saw Neva Dean's head poking out from her leafy hiding place next to the porch. She waved her hand across her throat in a slicing gesture.

I abandoned the packing slip, stepped quickly to the card table, grabbed the top file and ran back to the bedroom. My fingers slipped as I tried to pull the window open. I could hear a key in the front door lock. I used both hands and the window pane finally gave way. I went out the opening headfirst. The garbage can cut painfully into my side as I landed, twisting into an upright position. I reached up, slid the window shut and pushed through the back hedge. I found myself in the First Fellowship Church parking lot. I looked around. The lot was empty. A moment later, Neva Dean came around the hedge from the side.

"That was a little too close," she said. "A white car was coming up the street real slow like it was going to turn in. As soon as I signaled you, I went off the porch into the bushes. The car pulled into the drive and I came around the house out of sight, and then eventually I saw you go through the hedge."

"Start walking," I said and took her arm. I guided her around the church and down the sidewalk away from the green house. We carried our grocery bags and walked slowly. When we'd gone half a dozen blocks, we stopped at a pay phone and called a taxi. My hands were shaking when we got out of the cab and went into the safe house.

"I think we need a nice cup of tea," Neva Dean said as she pulled the cap off her head and fluffed her hair with her hands.

"I need to check Noah." I said and put the red file folder on the table.

She put on the kettle, and I put my hat, overalls and flannel shirt back in the closet. I went upstairs and peeked into the bedroom Noah had been assigned. He was sprawled diagonally across the bed. The covers were tangled around his waist. He hadn't missed us.

CHAPTER 39

THERE WAS NO SIGN that Sam had come back to the safe house while we were gone.

"Could you see who was driving the car?" I asked when I came back to the kitchen. Neva Dean was pouring hot water into our mugs.

"I was too scared to look into the car, and I didn't see who got out." She handed me a green mug that said "Remember to Floss Daily!" followed by the name and address of someone's dentist, and sat down opposite me with her tea. "I was running for my life," she added. "I'm sorry. I guess I don't make a very good detective." She looked into her teacup.

"Neva Dean, the best detective is the one who lives to detect another day," I said. "Let's look and see what we got out of our adventure."

I opened the red folder. The papers inside were copies of order forms for supplies that were ordered and delivered from Northwest Supply.

"Oh, my God," I said and laid the folder back on the table. I leaned back in my chair.

"What is it, honey?" Neva Dean said, leaning forward, her brow pulling into deep ridges.

"I get it—or at least, I think I get it. The papers Noah found shredded in Allan's office were order forms that showed ten percent of several orders that went to an address in Tigard that I'd never heard of. The house has packing materials and labels for a variety of business names, including Northwest Supply. Then we have the red folder. In the Sil-Trac purchasing department, a red folder is used to denote a minority supplier. As a company that makes products for federal projects, we're required to buy at least ten percent of the materials used in those products from minority vendors. It looks like someone is ordering the full amount of some supplies from our main vendor, having ten percent dropped in Tigard, then repackaging the supplies under a dummy minority company. Then, they are charging Sil-Trac an inflated price for the repackaged supplies."

"Wouldn't your company notice if they were paying for the same thing twice?" Neva Dean asked.

"I've been thinking about that," I said. "I would have heard if the purchasing department had a big discrepancy at audit time. That means the person running the dummy company must have been somehow paying Peterson's, for example, so that Sil-Trac wouldn't be billed for materials they didn't officially receive *from* Peterson's. If our dummy company told Peterson's the Tigard location was a subcontractor, they could then set up a checking account with the subcontractor name to pay from — big companies share their volume discount with subcontractors all the time. So, our embezzler or embezzlers are buying supplies using Sil-Trac's discount, and then turning around and selling them to Sil-Trac as a minority vendor at an inflated rate."

"Would that amount to enough money to be worth all that bother?" Neva Dean asked.

"Well, they aren't going to become an instant millionaire, but you could create a tidy little supplemental income." I said. "Clean room supplies are expensive. Some of the clean room wipes are as much as fifty dollars a box. A five- or ten-percent hike to that cost is dollars per box multiplied times a lot of boxes. Sil-Trac processes thousands of wafers per month and uses a lot of disposable materials to do it. This is one folder. Who knows how many more dummy companies there are, or how many kinds of supplies they're repackaging? If they're clever, they won't be skimming off every item. They would probably target things like the wipes that are reasonably high-priced and used at a high volume. I don't know — you might make a thousand or two a month."

"Could someone outside your company pull off a scheme like that?"

"The whole scam starts with the order to the primary supplier. I suppose someone could impersonate a Sil-Trac employee and call the primary and add to an order, but the change would show up on the receipt the vendor sends back to Sil-Trac. I'm thinking it has to be someone inside the company."

"Who would or could do such a thing?"

"Well, that would be the question," I said. "Plenty different people have access to the supplies and their paperwork along the way. Shipping and receiving people handle the materials as they come in. They usually handle the packing slips and shipping forms. Some of our materials go through a quality assurance check, so those people have access to some items on their way in. Not usually general supplies, though. The materials management people—Allan's people—are the one's who have access to all material movement of any sort. And last but not least, the building janitors and security people have access to everything."

"Wouldn't the office people notice if the janitor or security people were changing papers in the file?" she asked.

"I'm not sure. It depends on how they have the tasks organized. They could each end up thinking the other person in the department had done it. They move a lot of material each month."

"Well, whoever is doing it, seems like they have a motive for Allan's murder," Neva Dean said.

"Unless it was Allan who was the embezzler," I pointed out. "Maybe he had a partner, and they had a falling out. Or Allan had an attack of conscience."

"Do you really think your friend could do such a horrible thing?"

"I don't think so, but then, I would have never guessed he was sleeping with our young Japanese worker, either."

"So, what's our next move?" she asked.

"I don't know." I got up and started pacing. "I need to think." My pulse was racing and wouldn't calm down. I felt like a car with its engine revving. "Just because we found what appears to be an embezzlement scheme doesn't mean I'm not still suspect number one. We don't even know if the embezzler has anything to do with Allan's murder. They could be two totally separate events."

"I think we need some food. That young'un is going to be getting up soon, and you need to eat something to calm your nerves." Neva Dean got up and opened the refrigerator. "There's not much in here," she said. "Eggs, milk, cheese." She slid a drawer open. "Looks like some kind of bacon or sausage meat. I could make a nice omelet."

"I can't even think about food," I said. "Sam gave me a plane ticket out of the country. I can't imagine getting on a plane and just pretending I'm on vacation. I don't even know what the extradition rules are between Switzerland and the US. And won't it just make me look guilty if I run?"

"I think he's trying to protect you, honey," she said.

"How do I know he really knows what he's doing?" I argued. "Maybe he's just some kind of paramilitary spy wannabe."

"Do you really believe that?"

"Yeah, Harley, is that what you believe?" Noah said from the archway that led to the stairs. His dark hair stuck straight up on one side. He was wearing a Ducks Unlimited T-shirt and baggy plaid flannel pajama pants. His feet were bare.

"I don't know what to think, Noah," I said. "I don't know how much you heard, but your dad thinks I should leave the country. That requires a really big leap of faith on my part. At this point, I'd *like* to believe your dad is some kind of super government operative who can make everything better if I just do what he says."

"But if Dad is some kind of government guy, why does it feel like he and Green are on different sides?" His dark-brown eyes stared into mine, looking for answers I didn't have.

The lilting chime of Neva Dean's cell phone broke the silence. She looked at me.

"See who it is," I said.

She looked at the display. "It's a southwest prefix," she said and pushed the answer button. "Hello?...Hold on." She held the phone out to me. "It's Randy, looking for you."

"Hi, Randy," I said. "What's up?"

"The woman you were asking about came in to see Cyrus this morning."

"Were you able to get her name?"

"It was kinda weird," he said. "I asked her who she was. I said she had been coming all this time, and I didn't even know her name. And now that Allan had passed away, she should be on Cyrus's records. I didn't think it wise to discuss who owns Cyrus at this point. She looked at me like I was crazy and said 'I'm Allan's wife—Mrs. Sayers,' just like that, like I was supposed to know that."

"What did you say?"

"I just joked with her and said Allan had told me no one would ever get him to the church. Which happens to be true," he said. "Allan always used to joke about he and Cyrus being confirmed bachelors. Then she said they didn't go to a church, that they were common law. It was a very strange conversation."

"Did you get a better look at her?"

"I went one better than that," he said. "I took a picture with my camera phone. Can you receive pictures on your phone?"

I asked Neva Dean. She shook her head no.

"I can't receive them on the phone, but could you send it to my e-mail?" I wasn't sure when I could access my e-mail again, but at least I would have it. It might not help my current problem, but if Allan had a legitimate common-law wife, and I managed to stay out of jail, I needed to know. I told Randy my e-mail address, thanked him for his quick thinking and rang off.

"This just keeps getting weirder," I said.

"What now?" Neva Dean took a dozen eggs and a brick of cheese from the refrigerator. She bent to retrieve a fry pan from the bottom shelf of the cabinet by the stove.

"Well, Randy said the woman who has been coming to see Allan's cat came in, and when he asked for her name, she said she's Allan's common-law wife. I don't understand how Allan could have been with a woman long enough to have a common-law marriage without me knowing about it. I ate lunch with the guy every day, for crying out loud."

"Well, honey, sometimes people keep different parts of their lives in different compartments and never mix the sections up," Neva Dean said.

"That house didn't look to me like a woman lived there," Noah commented. "There wasn't enough junk."

"There are tidy women," I said. "On the other hand, we only have her word that they had a relationship. She might have been a stalker. Apparently, Mitsuko stalked him for a while after their fling. Maybe he inspired that sort of reaction in his women."

"Yeah, maybe. Anyway, there's always something that gives it away if a woman lives in a house. You know, lacy or flowery things, lotions and potions in the bathroom, something pink or purple."

My mind flashed back to the lavender throw on the cedar chest. Noah was right, though—we had searched the house pretty well, and while there were a few items, there weren't enough feminine touches to convince me that a woman lived there.

"Am I allowed to watch TV in this prison?" Noah asked.

"I don't think that would be a good idea," Neva Dean said, and gave him a meaningful look.

"Right," he said, understanding dawning on his face.

"What?" I said, and then realized Neva Dean didn't want us to see the news in case I was the headline story.

She pulled a loaf of wheat bread from a drawer in the kitchen. "How many pieces of toast does everyone want?" She turned back to the refrigerator and got the butter dish out.

"I'll have a couple of pieces," Sam said from the door to the garage. He held a six-pack of Coke in one hand. He put the cola in the refrigerator and sat down.

"Where have you been?" I asked. "What's happening out there? How's Mitsuko? What about Switzerland?"

"Slow down," he said. "Noah, go find something to do."

I sat down beside him. Noah came over and stood behind my chair, his hands on my shoulders.

"I'm not leaving," he said.

Sam looked at him and me and then looked away and ran both hands through his short dark hair. He was annoyed but controlling it for once.

"First of all, I don't know what's happening with Green," he said. "My contact got stuck researching Ken and Susan. Green didn't tell my guy where he was going, so I don't know what he's been doing. My guy from Seattle got here and has been at Emanuel Trauma Center. It's not looking too good for the girl, and the parents don't seem to know anything more than we do at this point. It looks like someone jumped her from behind with a blunt object. As far as we can find out, the crime scene people haven't found the weapon yet. My guy is sticking close to the girl's room so we don't have a repeat performance by whoever finished off your friend. And they've collected that pink thing you left hanging on your chair at work."

"My sweater? What does that have to do with anything?"

"Your sweater fibers were all over Mitsuko Komatsu, according to the criminalists."

"I didn't even wear my sweater yesterday. It was on my chair from the day before," I said.

"Maybe Mitsuko was in your office and sat in your chair, or maybe the person who beat the girl wore your sweater to do it."

"My sweater was on my chair when I came back from the Scotch Church. I know it was because I thought about taking it home, but then in the rush I didn't."

"I'm just telling you—your fibers were on Mitsuko Komatsu. Green will have it tested for blood splatter, but even if he doesn't find any, they'll say you're the one most likely to transfer those fibers. The fact the police went to your office tells you the two departments are talking to each other. By the way, I rescheduled your flight for tomorrow night. I'm not going to risk driving to the airport in broad daylight." He looked at Neva Dean. "You and Noah are going to have to stay here until Harley is on foreign soil. I want her out of reach before the police question you."

"Did you find out anything else about Ken and Susan?" I asked.

"Not much that we didn't already know. He was definitely nearby when Allan was killed. And they're both still in town, with no alibi for last night."

"So, what do we do now?"

"We don't do anything," Sam said. "You three stay put. Don't go outside for any reason. I'm going to go check with my guy at the hospital again. The only link there seems to be between the two victims is that baby. I want to know who that baby's daddy is and what he has to do with this. Then I'm gonna find out if Green's surfaced. I don't like not knowing what he's up to."

Neva Dean served our omelets, and we ate in silence.

"I'm outta here," Sam said and stood up. He carried his plate to the sink then left through the garage door.

"So, what are we supposed to do all day?" Noah wondered.

"There's a bookshelf in the living room," I said. "Check out our host's taste in reading material. Maybe he has something you'd like."

"If you two don't mind, I'm going to find a book and go lay on my bed," Neva Dean said. "All this excitement is tiring for an old gal like me. Come on," she said to Noah, "let's see what we can figure out about our missing homeowner from his taste in reading."

I sat at the table with the tablet and pen. I wrote Allan's name at the top of one page and Mitsuko Komatsu's on the top of the other. I could hear Noah's voice crack as he laughed at something Neva Dean had said. The woman was a wonder. She could have been safely sitting in her own apartment sipping tea and talking to her angels. Instead, she was helping me chase an embezzler, cooking omelets and charming the socks off a surly teenager.

Neva Dean and Noah found books, and I heard them go upstairs, followed by the sound of two doors shutting. I filled the tablet with scribbles. I listed the facts we knew for sure. It was a simple sentence on each page. They had each been attacked. Allan hadn't survived his trip to the hospital, and Mitsuko was barely hanging on. Beyond that, my notes were all speculation. Allan was either an embezzler, or the victim of an embezzler. Mitsuko was pregnant by Allan, or some unknown guy. There were reasons for her or her parents to want Allan dead, but they certainly wouldn't attack her. And who was Allan's common-law wife and what did her claim have to do with anything? Could Ken and Susan know about Mitsuko's relationship with Allan?

I was going in circles. There had to be something I was missing. I tore the two pages off the tablet and folded them. When I was young and had a big test coming up, I would sleep with my textbook under my pillow. Maybe if I took a nap with the notes under my pillow, something would come to me.

CHAPTER 40

MY CELL PHONE LAY on the kitchen counter by the sink. I wondered if Green had left me any more messages. I had a brief internal debate. Sam probably wouldn't want me to turn the phone on, but on the other hand, he was anxious to know what Green was doing. I took a deep breath and pushed the power button.

My phone greeted me, displayed its name and fell silent. I waited. I stared at the screen for what must have been a minute, but I still jumped when it vibrated and chimed that I had messages. There were several voice messages and one text.

Both voice mails were from Mrs. J—Sam had called her to say Noah and I would be away from home for a few days. She reminded me again how much she didn't trust him and wanted me to call and tell her myself that we were okay.

Noah occasionally sent me text messages when he was afraid I would say no to whatever he was asking if he spoke to me in person. He knows I'm too intimidated by the punctuation buttons to write back. This was definitely not from Noah. I took a deep breath and pressed the show message button.

"I've figured it out, you're cleared," the text said. "Meet me at your house" It was from Green.

Relief washed over me. My nightmare was about to be over. I just had to figure out how to get to him.

Soft snores were coming from Neva Dean's room. I pushed the partially opened bedroom door farther open. Her book lay on her chest. Her head was turned to the side. She looked so peaceful I couldn't bring myself to wake her. I backed out and pulled the door closed.

I could call a taxi, but I didn't want take the time to walk to the gas station and wait. I was sure that, even if my crisis was over, Sam wouldn't want me to use the phone or have a taxi pull up to his "safe" house. That left only one option. The keys to the car in the garage had to be somewhere.

I went back down to the kitchen and into the garage. The grey Honda was unlocked. I searched under the floor mats and in the glove compartment. I flipped the sun visors down on both sides and looked in the center console. The keys were not in the car. I went back into the house and opened each drawer in the kitchen. I ruffled quickly through the contents. Whoever lived here was not a junk collector, so it went quickly. No keys.

I stood in the center of the kitchen. Where could they be?

The house was from the era when all the bedrooms were the same size. I dashed up the stairs. The one I was staying in had a definite male feel to it. Hunting prints adorned the dark-green walls. A bottle of Brut after-shave sat on the dresser next to a boar's bristle hairbrush. I couldn't be sure I was in the master suite, but I looked through the drawers anyway. I learned that the regular occupant preferred boxers, size medium, and V-neck T-shirts but did not leave his keys in his dresser when he traveled. I went back down stairs.

Where could he keep his keys? Since they weren't near the garage, maybe he came in and out the front door when he was home.

A small closet was to the left of the front entrance. Bingo. A brass key rack was attached to the inside of the door; several keys hung from the hooks. They weren't labeled, but the H symbol on the black plastic end of one key identified it. I grabbed it and hurried back to the kitchen.

I wrote a quick note to Neva Dean and Noah, telling them about Green's message. I told them I'd call them from home and be back later to get them. I wrote down the time and signed the note.

The automatic garage door opener was in the console of the Honda. I pressed the button and backed out of the garage as it opened. Portland is an easy town to navigate. The downtown is built along the banks of the Willamette River, which runs north to south. Hills circle the city, the taller ones sporting unique radio towers. If that isn't enough to guide you, Mount Hood to the east and Mount St. Helen's to the north lend their snowy glaciers to the landscape. I quickly determined that I was slightly northwest of my own neighborhood. I drove on surface streets for a few blocks and got my bearings then was on the freeway and on my way in moments.

Green hadn't said who had killed Allan, but all that really mattered right now was that it wasn't me. All I had to do was drive home and I could have my life back.

Green's maroon sedan wasn't in my driveway when I rounded the corner onto my street. I didn't see it parked on the street, either. I hesitated, but then realized Harper must have dropped him off. She was probably processing Allan's killer right now.

"Green!" I called as I got out of my car. He wasn't sitting on the porch swing—he must still have the key from when he stayed with Noah while I was on my work trip.

I opened the back door and went into the kitchen.

"Green?" I called again.

The room was silent. I could hear the muffled sound of Sonny barking from his fenced kennel area in the back yard. I set my purse and keys down on the kitchen desk and walked into the living room. "Green," I said, "come on, this isn't funny." I opened the door to the basement. "Green?"

I felt the brief sensation of falling before the lights went out.

CHAPTER 41

I WOKE WITH A SHARP pain in my side. My face was pressed into the concrete floor. My hands were pulled behind my back. I tried to move them, but they were bound. I tried to move my legs. My ankles were tied loosely to each other. I would be able to take small steps, but kicking and running were out of the question.

The foot poked my side again.

"Wake up, Harley," a singsong voice said.

I opened my eyes, but the light was painful, so I shut them again.

"I know you're awake, so stop pretending. You have work to do."

"Jeanette?" I croaked. "Help me. Someone hit me in the head."

"Help you? Well, that would be counterproductive, now, wouldn't it?"

I opened my eyes again. "Jeanette," I repeated with a cough. The coppery taste of blood filled my mouth. "What are you doing here? Where's Green?"

"I don't know where Green is, Harley. Trying to figure out who killed Allan, I suppose."

My head was killing me, but I pulled myself into a sitting position. My left arm hurt.

"I can't believe you fell for the old push down the stairs again. Fell," she repeated, and laughed. "I crack myself up."

"What are you doing in my house?" I asked again.

"Hold your horses, there, girlie," she said. "You're always in such a rush. You need to learn to relax. Well, I guess you don't need to worry about self improvement right now."

"Jeanette," I said, louder this time. "What's going on?"

She had been pacing in the small space. She turned to face me. I could see a gun in her hand. My gun.

"I should think that would be obvious. I'm solving Detective Green's case for him."

"Jeanette," I said, trying to steady my voice, "I didn't kill Allan. Green knows who did. It wasn't me. Harper is arresting them right now. Let the police do their job. And what are you doing with my gun?"

"You are so naive, Harley. I know you didn't kill Allan. You don't have the nerve to kill anyone."

My head was starting to clear. She kicked at me again.

"Get up," she said. "We're going upstairs." She grabbed my bound hands and wrenched them upwards.

I jumped to my feet as pain shot up my arms into my shoulders. She pushed me, and I stumbled to the stairs and up to the kitchen. She shoved me into a chair at the table. I took slow deep breaths, trying to calm myself.

Jeanette crossed the kitchen and turned on Mrs. J's small countertop television. She flipped through the channels and then turned the set toward me.

"Look, Harley," she said, and turned up the volume.

A blue banner across the screen proclaimed "Special Report." The banner dissolved and cut to a scene in front of City Hall. I could feel the blood drain from my face. Green and Harper were on the steps. The public information officer was in front of them, speaking into a bank of microphones.

"An arrest warrant has been issued in the murder of Allan Sayers. Harley Spring, a coworker of Mr. Sayers, is missing and should be considered dangerous." The image of me that Sil-Trac had taken for my security badge flashed onto the screen. "If you see Ms. Spring, do not approach her, dial nine-one-one."

A reporter came on screen and was talking, but Jeanette cut the volume.

"But Green knows it wasn't me," I said.

"Don't be thick, Harley. Green doesn't know anything. He can't detect his way out of a paper bag. He isn't going to help you.

I'm just going to have to solve the case for him. Let me spell it out for you. You are going to put an end to this. And yourself." She laughed again. "Here," she said and handed me a tablet and pen from my desk. "Take a memo."

I sat and stared at the pen and paper.

"Oh, yeah." She used her left hand to pull a knife from the wooden knife block on my stove and cut the binding on my wrist. "Don't get any ideas," she said, and pointed the knife at me. "Write exactly what I say. 'I can't live with my self anymore.' Write that down." She jabbed my arm. I started writing. "'I can't live with myself anymore. I killed Allan when I found out I would inherit his money.'"

"But I didn't," I protested. "I didn't know I would inherit his money and house."

"Harley, you're starting to try my patience." She jabbed me with the knife again. "'I can't live with myself any longer.'" She prompted again. She looked at the ceiling. "I suppose it would be over the top for you to pass his estate directly to me at this point. Read it back to me."

I read what I'd been forced to write.

"It doesn't have much flair, but it should do the job."

"Jeanette, I didn't kill Allan. Don't you care that someone is getting away with murder?"

"Well, that would be the point, now, wouldn't it?"

"Oh, my God!" I said as realization finally cleared my pain-clouded brain.

"Now, you're cooking with gas. Oh, that's a good one. I just crack myself up."

My mind was racing. Help wasn't coming. Help didn't know where I was. Keep them talking. Isn't that what they always say on TV? Mrs. J would come to feed Sonny and Cher, but it could be hours. Sam might come looking for me but only after he went back to the safe house and then verified Green hadn't sent me a message. Neva Dean would probably start calling when she woke up and read my note and realized I hadn't called her with the details. She could sleep another hour, though.

The truth was, no one would come looking until it was too late. I didn't know what Jeanette had planned, but I did know I wasn't intended to survive it. I had to try to distract her.

"Why are you doing this? I've never done anything to you."

"Well, I do feel bad about that. I wouldn't have chosen you if it weren't necessary — that lying slut Karen would have been a better choice. You've always been supportive of me at work. But you couldn't let it go, could you? You've been asking questions, talking to people. I can't have that. And I know it was you and that crazy old bat who showed up at the Tigard house. Then, there's the money. My money."

"What are you talking about?"

"Allan was my husband," she said. "That money is mine. At least, it will be when I come forward as his common-law wife."

"How can you be his wife? He never mentioned you, no one ever saw you at his house." Now I was curious.

"We were very discrete. *Very*." She turned and walked across the kitchen. I rubbed my left arm. Jeanette whipped around and came back to my chair. She grabbed my left wrist and pulled it behind my back. She put what felt like a cable tie around it then pulled my right wrist back and bound them together. "Don't get any ideas," she said.

"I was very careful to document our relationship," she continued. "I mailed postcards to myself at Allan's address. You know, making it seem like friends were sending them. I even sent myself bills. And I have a checking account in the name of Jeanette Sayers."

"What about Allan?" I asked. "Didn't he notice his coworker was getting mail at his house?"

"I picked them up when I brought his mail in."

"So, you took care of his place when he was gone?" I asked. "And sent yourself mail?"

"Harley, I was his wife in every sense of the word. I took care of his manly needs." Her face turned pink.

"Then why kill him?"

"I think you know."

"No, Jeanette, I really don't." I was telling the truth. In all my analysis of Allan's murder, not once did Jeanette figure into the equation.

"That little slut Mitsuko tricked him into getting her pregnant. She was going to have his bastard and then take him to the cleaners. He was supposed to take care of *me*. I deserved to be taken care of. I've been taking care of him for years — doing his laundry, cooking and cleaning. I slept in his bed — and I was good at it. We were going to grow old together. Then that little slut thought she would swoop in with her bastard child and take it all away from me."

"That explains why you beat her up," I said. "But why Allan?"

"He was going to leave me. He said it had nothing to do with Mitsuko, but I knew better. He was going to leave me for her. I gave him the best years of my life, and he was going to throw me away like yesterday's trash."

"Jeanette, you need help," I said.

"I think we both know it's a little too late for that."

The phone on my desk started ringing. We both looked at it.

"Get up," she ordered.

I didn't move.

"Get *up*," she repeated, and stabbed my thigh. Then, slowly, she pulled the knife out, giving it a slight twist.

Searing hot pain shot down my leg. I screamed. My stomach lurched. I could feel sweat beading on my forehead.

"Do you really want to play tough girl with me?" she said.

I lowered my head to my chest.

"I can't hear you," she yelled.

"No," I croaked through the haze of pain.

"Get up, then. We're going to the garage. It should be just about ready by now."

She grabbed my bound wrists and pulled me to my feet. I stumbled into the table as the strain of standing hit the cut in my leg. I shuffled to the back door and fell down the steps when Jeanette shoved me. She pulled me upright and hauled me through the side garage door. We were engulfed in exhaust fumes. Jeanette reached past me to set the note on the tool bench then backed out and closed the door.

Sam must have brought my car home from Sil-Trac after he dropped me at the safe house. It was running. I stumbled over to the driver's side door. The keys were in the ignition. I started coughing. I could see that the door locks were down. I looked around the garage. There was a hammer on the tool bench by the door. My hands were bound so tightly behind my back, I wasn't sure if I could raise them up high enough to grab it. I had to try, though.

I limped back to the bench. I could feel blood running down my leg and into my shoe.

It was getting harder to breathe. My head was starting to spin. My hands and feet started tingling. I made it, but forcing my bound hands up to bench height behind me was just too hard. I dropped to my knees. Pain shot up my leg from the cut in my thigh, but I found I didn't really care anymore. It was my last conscious thought.

My leg didn't hurt anymore. My hands and feet were free. My limbs were light. I was floating. Whatever this drug was, I wanted more. I didn't have a care in the world. I opened my eyes. I could see my body lying on the garage floor. I was somewhere up above. I felt good.

The doggie door that came into the garage under the workbench flapped open. Sonny came in and started licking my face. Pain returned in a rush. I gasped. Sonny went back to the doggie door and pushed the flap open so his face was outside and his rear end was facing me. Air rushed in around him. With all the energy I could muster, I crawled toward the opening. I twisted my face toward the opening.

"Help," I croaked. Sonny began howling. "Don't move," I said, more to myself than to the dog. If he went out through the door, the flap would shut, and with my hands bound, I'd have no way to open it. He stayed in place, being largely unable to howl and walk at the same time.

He finished a particularly long soulful note and went outside. The flap shut behind him.

"Sonny!" I called. Tears slid down my face. I was going to die on the dusty floor of my own garage, and Jeanette was going to get away with murder…again.

"Harley?" Mrs. J's voice boomed. Sonny barked and came in through the flap again. I took a deep breath.

"Help!" I yelled. "In the garage!"

"Harley?" Mrs. J called again. I could hear her pounding on the garage door.

"I'm in here," I said. "I can't get to the door." I heard her footsteps retreat. She returned in a moment with the key. She opened the door and stepped back as the fumes hit her in the face. "Mrs. J," I rasped. "Down here."

She gasped when she saw me lying half under the bench, hands and feet bound. She immediately assessed my greatest need and pulled me firmly outside by my bound legs.

I screamed. She looked at her blood-covered hand.

"What has happened to you?" she said and crouched down to inspect me. "Wait here." She got up and went into the house.

I wasn't capable of movement. I was still lying where she'd left me when she came back with a pair of scissors and a clean dishtowel. She quickly cut my bindings and pulled me up against the step into the house. She pressed the clean towel against my leg. "Hold this," she ordered and pressed my hand against the towel.

She pulled the cordless phone from her sweater pocket and dialed.

"I need an ambulance," she said, and gave my address. "And send that Detective Green here, too." She hung up. "For God's sake, they don't need to know who I am," she muttered as she turned back to me. "Tell me what happened," she demanded, but the phone interrupted before I could answer.

"Hello?...Yes, Harley is here, but Detective Green is *not* here and something has happened to Harley."

"Who is it?"

She handed me the phone. It was Noah. I explained that the killer had tricked me into coming to the house. I told him I had been slightly hurt, but that I was fine and I really needed to speak to Sam.

"Dad gave me a phone number to use in case of extreme emergency," he said.

"When did he do that?"

"A couple of years ago. He made me memorize it."

He recited the number to me. A part of me hated Sam for yet another secret. Another part of me was really glad to have a way to contact him. I instructed Noah to stay put with Neva Dean, and that I would call when it was safe for them to leave.

I hung up and dialed the secret number. An answering service picked up on the first ring.

"Sam?" I said before I realized I was talking to a computer. "Sam," I said again, "I know who killed Allan and attacked Mitsuko Komatsu. It was a woman named Jeanette Malone. She's insane. She tried to kill me. I'm okay, but the paramedics are here and taking me to the hospital. Noah and Neva Dean are still at the house you took us to. Call me," I added.

I could hear the siren of the ambulance drawing nearer. It slid to a stop in front of the house, and the EMTs rushed into the driveway carrying their orange boxes of equipment.

"What happened here?" a muscular young blonde asked. A detached part of my brain wondered why paramedics were always young and beautiful.

"I found her locked in the garage with the car running," Mrs. J said. "There's a nasty cut on her leg."

"Jeanette," I whispered—it had taken all the energy I had left to talk to Noah and call Sam. "She pushed me down the basement stairs and then stabbed me in the leg. She tied me up and put me in the garage with the car running."

The first paramedic had wrapped a blood pressure cuff on my right arm and was threading an IV needle into my left hand. A second man cut the leg of my pants open with a pair of blunt scissors. He poked gently at the cut with a latex-covered finger. I took a deep breath and passed out.

CHAPTER 42

"HARLEY, WAKE UP. You have to wake up."

It was Green's voice. He was slapping me gently on the face. I opened my eyes. I was in an ambulance.

"You have to tell me what happened," he said. "Mrs. J told me what she knows, but I need you to fill in the blanks. Quick."

I recited my story one more time. I was hiding at a friend's house, I got a text message that was supposed to be from him, I came home, Jeanette was here. She threw me down the stairs and tied me up. She made me write a suicide note and stabbed me in the leg when I refused to move. She put me in the garage, where my car had been running with the door closed. She had admitted killing Allan.

Green pulled his cell phone out of his pocket and dialed a number. He turned away from me and spoke in low tones. I heard him dial again as I drifted into a semi-sleep.

He hung up and turned back to me.

"Okay, here's what we're going to do," he said. "Jeanette thinks you're dead, so we're going to let you be dead. We'll announce your suicide and that the case is solved. If Jeanette is smart, she'll wait to get conformation that we bought her setup, and then, hopefully, she'll make her claim to Allan's money. We don't have to prove motive for Allan's death, but the DA prefers it."

He went up to talk to the driver. He came back as the ambulance made a U-turn.

"Where are we going?" I asked.

"We're taking you to a private nursing home. An ambulance arriving without sirens won't attract attention there, and they have a doctor on staff who can take care of you until we can move you."

I slipped in and out of consciousness over the next hour, during which time the ambulance attendants moved me into the nursing home and the doctor and nurse worked on my wound. I can only assume they were pumping morphine or something like it into my IV. I was feeling only mildly uncomfortable by the time they installed me in a small, light-filled room in the north wing.

The doctor prescribed inhalation therapy, and a nurse's aide came into my room to set up the tabletop machine. He handed me the clear plastic mask that would carry soothing medication and oxygen to my lungs and throat. I asked him to turn on the television set that was mounted on a ceiling bracket as he adjusted the straps on my mask and fitted it over my face.

"Doc say no TV for you," the aide said and looked away. "He say you need complete quiet to rest."

I was sleepy, but I didn't think I could truly rest until I knew Green had found Jeanette and arrested her. My body had different ideas. I fell asleep moments after the man left my room.

It was dark when I woke with a start. I heard a familiar noise, like panty hose rubbing together. I reached up and pulled the plastic mask off my face.

"Who's there?" I said. I could barely make the words come out of my dry throat. I tried to sit up. A hand pushed me back down.

"Why couldn't you just die?" Jeanette asked.

"Sorry to inconvenience you. What are you doing here?"

"Well, I should think that would be obvious," she said. "I can't have you running around telling people what happened between us. This isn't quite how I had planned things, but it should work."

"Why did you have to kill Allan?" I rasped. "Why couldn't you just move on to another boyfriend? If you were his wife you could have divorced him," I said and started to cry.

I knew statistically a person is most likely to be killed by a loved one, but it just never made sense to me. Why was murder a better option than divorce?

"That's classic, Harley. Just move on to another boyfriend." She said it in a high-pitched voice that I supposed was meant as an imitation of me. "You have men falling all over you. Don't think I didn't notice how that police detective looks at you. Girls like me don't have 'another boyfriend' waiting in the wings. Allan was it, my only chance, the only one I ever gave myself to.

"I know he didn't tell his friends about me. That he was embarrassed to be seen in public with a plain, chubby girl like me. But it was okay. It was enough. I knew I was never going to get Prince Charming. When we were together, it was beautiful. He really loved me. He loved my mind, my sense of humor, my cheese omelet. We were happy, and it was our little secret. If Mitsuko hadn't come along and thrown herself at him, we'd still be together.

"He didn't love her. He had a moment of weakness, and she was going to make him pay forever. He would have married her, you know—for the brat. He would have been miserable, but he would have done it. That's the kind of man he was.

"I couldn't have that. I couldn't survive watching her live my life. I would have had to watch them play like they were the happy couple. They'd be at the company Christmas party, the summer picnic, and I'd have to act like the happy maiden aunt. I couldn't bear it."

She pulled a syringe from her pocket. She tilted the capped needle upward, tapped on the side of the barrel and pushed the air bubbles out.

"What's that?" I asked.

"Just a little something to keep your mouth shut. It's beautifully simple. A couple of pills my dad left behind when he died crushed with a little water, and voila! I'm really sorry about this. I did like you, you know. But the news said you haven't named your attacker yet, and I need to make sure it stays that way."

She grabbed my wrist.

The door to the room flew open. Green knocked the syringe from her hand and pulled her arm behind her back in one fluid move. As he snapped the handcuffs into place, he began to recite the Miranda warning. "You have the right to remain silent," he said as he led her out the door. "Anything you say can and will be used against you in a court of law. You have the right to an attorney. If you cannot afford an attorney—" The door shut, cutting off the rest of his recitation.

I started shaking.

The doctor who had stitched my leg came back in and took my pulse. He whispered something to his nurse, who retreated as silently as she had approached.

"I've ordered something to calm your nerves," he said.

"Just let me have a go at Detective Green, and I'll be fine," I told him.

Green came back.

"You knew she'd show up, didn't you?" I accused.

"Well, we weren't sure, but we figured she would have stayed near the house to watch and make sure you were really dead, until someone found your body, just to be positive. When she saw the ambulance, she followed it to the nursing home—I watched her pull in behind when we left your street. I had the driver go slow just to be sure she didn't lose us. We thought she would go home and listen to the news first to see what we knew. We went all over the media this afternoon and evening to say you had been seriously injured in a suicide attempt and that you were unable to tell us what happened. We were pretty sure that, after her success finishing Allan off in the hospital, she would try it again."

"What if she hadn't showed up?"

"But she did," he said. "And you're safe."

"Would it have hurt to let me in on the joke?" I asked.

"We decided you could play your part better if you didn't have all the facts."

"All I had to do was lie here," I pointed out.

"Exactly," Green said. "And we made sure you did just that."

I sighed. "Can I see Noah?"

"If I knew where you had him stashed, I could get him here. I don't suppose you're going to tell me where that is, though, are you."

I turned my head to face the wall.

"I thought so." He got up and turned to the door.

"Wait," I said. Tears filled my eyes.

He came back and sat by my bed. He took my hand in his. "Lady, you stretch my patience to the breaking point."

"I'm sorry," I said through my tears. "I'm not trying to be difficult."

"You were with *him*," he said. It wasn't a question. "When I couldn't find you and Noah." He didn't need to say which "him" he was referring to.

"It's complicated."

"I don't need to hear any more lies, so let's just drop it." I could hear unspoken sadness in his voice.

He wrapped his two hands around mine. His were surprisingly soft, and warm. He propped his elbows on the side of my bed and pressed his lips to my hand, then sighed.

For the first time in days, I felt safe.

CHAPTER 43

NOAH WAS WAITING on the back porch steps when Green pulled into my driveway. The doctor had made me stay another full day in the nursing home and had limited my visitors to Detective Green, who had announced he wasn't leaving in any case. He offered to bring me home, and in spite of my unsettled feelings, I let him.

"Harley, are you okay?" Noah asked as I hobbled across the driveway. He came down and slid under my right arm—my left was in a soft cast—taking some of the weight off my injured leg, which left Green to follow along behind.

Mrs. J opened the back door and herded us to the living room She pulled the ottoman up to the blue chair and helped me prop my bad leg on a pillow. Chris came out of Noah's room.

"Hi, Harley," he said. "Glad to see you home again."

"I'm glad to be seen, believe me. And thanks for your help with the shredded documents."

He blushed.

"I'll fix us all some tea," Mrs. J said. "And I have some warm ginger cake. Come help me carry things, young man." Chris followed her to the kitchen.

We were just settling in with our tea and cake when I looked out the front window and saw Mr. J's Explorer pull up to the curb. Neva Dean got out carrying a covered plate that turned out to be chocolate crinkle cookies. She walked around to the back door and into the kitchen. Mrs. J took the cookie plate and ushered her in to join us.

Chris was the first to speak. "So, why did that woman try to kill you, and what did our shredded papers have to do with anything, anyway?"

"I can tell you about the shredded papers," Neva Dean volunteered. She launched into a lively description of our visit to the Tigard house, complete with my dive out the back window. She carefully left out our true starting point.

"At that point, we knew someone was embezzling money from Sil-Trac, but not who." I picked up the story. "Someone was setting up fake minority vendor accounts and using Sil-Trac's own quantity order price break to supply them. Then they would jack the prices up and sell the supplies back to Sil-Trac. We figured out it was an inside job, and it made sense that it would be someone in purchasing, but we lacked a smoking gun."

"We may never know for sure, what Jeanette's motivation was for killing Allan." Green said. "I don't buy that woman-scorned crap. I'm betting Allan discovered she was cheating the company. She was a convenience for him. The neighbor verified she was a regular overnight guest, but she also pointed out that Jeanette wasn't the only one. And not just the Asian girl, either. I think he confronted her about her scheme, demanded she stop it and ended their relationship. I think the shredded papers Chris and Noah put together were Allan's proof. After she killed him, she came back and found them, probably the day she locked Harley in the basement."

"But why did she attack that young woman at your work?" Mrs. J asked.

"If she was successful in getting rid of me, she said, she was going to come quietly forward and assert her rights as Allan's common-law wife. There was some speculation that Mitsuko Komatsu's baby was Allan's. She needed to eliminate any possible heirs. As it turns out, she shouldn't have been worried."

Green raised his left eyebrow. "Oh, really?" He bit into a chocolate cookie.

"What's happening with the girl?" Neva Dean asked.

"The jury's not in yet," Green said around his mouthful of cookie. "She'll be in the hospital until her healthy baby boy is born, and then she'll probably be moved to one of those rehabilitation clinics. The doctors think she might come out of the coma, but she'll never be the same."

"That's sad," Noah said. "She was just minding her own business and some crazy person ruins her life."

"It is sad," I agreed, "but I think she may have been trying to use Allan for her own purposes."

"So, why did you have to use Harley to catch this woman?" Neva Dean asked. "Hadn't she done enough to help you?" This last bit was directed to Detective Green.

"Ordinarily, I wouldn't have, but this Malone woman was good at concealing evidence. We never found the weapon she hit Allan with."

An image of the fireplace in our cabin flashed into my mind. Jeanette had had a fire going when I got back to the cabin. I'd noticed the scrap of yellow that had probably held whatever she'd used to create her asthma attack, but I hadn't paid attention to the wood that was burning and probably wouldn't have been able to recognize it in any case.

"We didn't find a syringe at the hospital," Green continued, "and there was no weapon found at Komatsu's crime scene. The woman left no prints, and she purposely left fibers from Harley's clothes at each scene. All we had was her attack on Harley. We didn't want to risk losing her. We were hoping she would incriminate herself, and as it turned out, she did. One of the pieces of equipment in Harley's room was a video camera. We got it all on tape."

"What I don't understand," I said, and turned to Mrs. J, "is why did you come to my house when you did? Sonny wasn't due to be fed and put in the house for hours yet. I'm glad you came, don't get me wrong."

"It was Sonny," she said. "I was in my back yard and I heard him. He set up such a fuss howling I could hear him a block away. He only howls when he hears a siren. I didn't hear any sirens, so I came to investigate. When I got here, he kept running into the garage."

"Bless his little black heart," I said.

"So, that's it, then," Mrs. J said. She stood up. "We need to let Harley get some rest."

Neva Dean got up, too, and picked up the cups and plates around her. She looked over the top of her reading glasses at Green. He stood reluctantly.

"I better go, too," he said. "I'll swing back by this evening."

"Will you be okay if I go shoot hoops at Chris's house?" Noah asked.

"Of course," I said. I was tired. I could take a little nap while Mr. and Mrs. J took Neva Dean home.

Mrs. J took the afghan from the back of the sofa and tucked it around my shoulders. Noah put the Sting CD on the stereo.

"We'll be back soon," she said. I was already drifting off. I barely heard the car drive away.

CHAPTER 44

A GENTLE SHAKE AWAKENED me some time later. Sam was sitting on the edge of the ottoman.

"Harley," he said. "Hey." His voice was whispery.

"Sam," I said. Tears came unbidden to my eyes.

He slid into the chair beside me and gently pulled me onto his lap. I laid my head on his shoulder.

"You know you shouldn't have left the safe house," he said. He put his arms around me, being careful not to jostle my injured leg.

"I thought Green said it was okay," I said. A tendril of anger curled in my stomach.

He gently stroked my arm and then cupped my face in his hand.

"Hey," he said again. "You scared me. I went crazy when I got your message. I came here and you were gone, and I checked all the hospitals and you weren't anywhere."

"Green had them take me to a private nursing home."

"Yeah, my source in his office told me about the stunt he pulled, using you as bait to catch that lunatic that tried to kill you."

"He was there the whole time," I could feel my jaw muscle tensing. "I was never in any danger. And I'm glad they have the evidence they need to put Jeanette away for ever," I added defiantly.

"There's always danger when you're facing a killer," he said, and tilted my face up toward his. He brushed his lips gently against mine. When I didn't protest, he deepened the kiss.

"I can't lose you," he whispered when our lips parted.

I looked into his blue eyes searching for answers. If it felt so right being in his arms, why couldn't we make things work? I loved this soft, caring side of Sam, but even now, I knew the hard, paranoid part of him was still there, lurking in the shadows.

The only thing I knew for sure was that I was in no shape to make any decisions about my future. I laid my head back on his shoulder and wrapped my arms around his hard-muscled chest.

"Harley," he said in a soft voice, "I know this isn't the time to make any big decisions, but when you're feeling a little better, we have to talk."

So what else is new? I thought, and fell back to sleep.

END

ABOUT THE AUTHOR

Attempted murder, theft, drug rings, battered women, death threats and more sordid affairs than she could count were the more exciting experiences from ARLENE SACHITANO'S nearly thirty years in the high-tech industry.

Prior to the publication of her first novel, *Chip and Die*, the first Harley Spring mystery, Arlene wrote the story half of the popular Block of the Month quilting patterns "Seams Like Murder," "Seams Like Halloween" and "Nothing's What it Seams" for Storyquilts.com, Inc. From this came her bestselling mysteries featuring Harriet Truman and the Loose Threads quilting group. Arlene also has written a scintillating proprietary tome on electronics assembly.

ABOUT THE ARTIST

APRIL MARTINEZ was born in the Philippines and raised in San Diego, California, daughter to a US Navy chef and a US postal worker, sibling to one younger sister. From as far back as she can remember, she has always doodled and loved art, but her parents never encouraged her to consider it as a career path, suggesting instead that she work for the county. So, she attended the University of California in San Diego, earned a cum laude bachelor's degree in literature/writing and entered the workplace as a regular office worker.

For years, she went from job to job, dissatisfied that she couldn't make use of her creative tendencies, until she started working as an imaging specialist for a big book and magazine publishing house in Irvine and began learning the trade of graphic design. From that point on, she worked as a graphic designer and webmaster at subsequent day jobs while doing freelance art and illustration at night.

In 2003, April discovered the e-publishing industry. She responded to an ad looking for e-book cover artists and was soon in the business of cover art and art direction. Since then, she has created hundreds of book covers, both electronic and print, for several publishing houses, earning awards and recognition in the process. Two years into it, she was able to give up the day job and work from home. April Martinez now lives with her cat in Orange County, California, as a full-time freelance artist/illustrator and graphic designer.

Made in the USA
San Bernardino, CA
02 May 2014